Take Time to Enjoy "Spellbinding Writer"* Shelby Hearon and Her *Five Hundred Scorpions*

"When a reviewer writes, 'I couldn't put it down,' I usually don't believe it. But it happened to me. Shelby Hearon's *Five Hundred Scorpions* is that kind of novel.... For those over 40 this novel does more than Gail Sheehy's *Passages* to explain the ways of man to man."

—Wichita Eagle-Beacon

"Hearon's multilayered, at times mischievous, narrative moves back and forth between Virginia and Mexico as she artfully explores themes of jealousy and revenge, manipulation and deception ... [an] inventive new novel."

—Orlando Sentinel

"Imaginative, perceptive ... Hearon has created a fictional Mexico as mysterious as the real place, a tropical paradise laced with craziness, poisonous water and people who worship with a priest but fear the ancient gods far more."

—People

"With remarkable skill, Hearon takes a contemporary story of a man who leaves his wife to 'find himself,' invests it with specificity and distinctiveness, and slowly segues into the heightened realm of metaphor and myth.... Hearon's prose is as clear, vivid and colorful as representational Mexican art ... an impressive, provocative novel by a talented writer."

—Publishers Weekly

"Hearon writes like a female Larry McMurtry with humor, pain, surprise and resolution in a single entertaining package."

—Los Angeles Times

"Hearon's prose is clear and distinctive, her narrative moves the story forward at a satisfying clip, and her ear for dialogue is unerring."

—*Dallas Morning News

BOOKS BY SHELBY HEARON

SHELBY HEARON

～ FIVE HUNDRED ～
SCORPIONS

WARNER BOOKS

A Time Warner Company

Warner Books Edition
Copyright © 1987 by Shelby Hearon
All rights reserved.

This Warner Books edition is published by arrangement with the author.
Warner Books, Inc., 1271 Avenue of the Americas, New York, NY 10020

A Time Warner Company

Printed in the United States of America

First Warner Books Printing: April 1993

10 9 8 7 6 5 4 3 2 1

Library of Congress Cataloging-in-Publication Data

Hearon, Shelby.
     Five hundred scorpions / Shelby Hearon.—Warner Books ed.
       p.   cm.
     ISBN 0-446-39478-5
     I. Title.
   PS3558.E256F5   1993
   813'.54—dc20   92-30320
                                                      CIP

Cover design by Mario Pulice
Cover illustration by Joanie Schwartz

For *Ross, Juana Maria,*
and Victor

*Of good natural parts and
of a liberal education.*
DON QUIXOTE

FIVE
HUNDRED
SCORPIONS

I A GENTLEMAN'S GAME

WHERE'S Dad?" Charles, eleven, tugged at his mom's sleeve.

Paul could have been two feet away and not visible in the crowd. Peggy had all she could do to see over her younger son's head; they were nearing eye level as he ended his summer's growing spurt.

There were waves of people milling by, most of them spectators, themselves in tennis togs, or sailing gear, or at the least resort linens and imported cottons, eating crab salad and melon, sipping Italian ices, or cappuccino with amaretto. Even Charles had asked for a ham and Brie on hard roll, as if that were old stuff to him. Whatever happened, she wondered, to peanuts and popcorn?

Peggy was there, in the crowd, because Edward, her elder son, was one of the 128 players in the first round of the U.S. Open Tennis Championships.

He wasn't likely to go any further, as he was paired with Aaron Krickstein in the very first match. "Bad news," he'd said. "Stonewalled." Krickstein, just seventeen, two years younger than Edward, had one year ago received the wild-card entry into the main draw of the Open that was regularly given to the Boys 18 and Under Champion. At sixteen, he'd made it to the fourth round, losing to the fourth-seeded player.

(Arias? No, Arias had beaten the boy who beat Krickstein. Peggy's mind went temporarily blank. She had worked very hard to learn them all, those who were up-and-coming, those at the top. People like Teltscher and Scanlon who weren't on your set all the time. Noah. He'd lost to Noah. Not Edward, of course, but Krickstein. From Grosse Pointe, Michigan.)

There was a boy from Virginia who made the starts last year, so that Edward was the second, but he had lost to Vilas, the South American, in the first round. Peggy wondered if they might be listing Edward from North Carolina, because he went to school there, and because his coach was there, but she assumed not, because the list of the top sixty-four players inside her program gave only the birthplace. Which would be Charlottesville for him, of course.

"Dad said he'd meet us here," Charles persisted.

"There may be a dozen food places."

"Two that aren't private. Besides, this is where we ate last year. We had waffles. I had a waffle with whipped cream."

She smiled at her always-hungry son who could recall all meals back to the crib. "He could be running late."

"Not Dad."

"It's hard to park. The nearby lots are full. He'll get here for the match; that's the main thing."

"Edward plays on court twenty-two."

"I know." Each of them, Peggy and her younger son,

had a map of the tennis center, and they each had already checked their present location and when and where their player was going to be.

It bothered Paul that Peggy could do such a quick study of the tennis scene. Not her facility, that wasn't it. But that she wanted to use her time to store a new packet of information about whatever was current. When, he would have said, she could as easily have consulted the program to find what she wanted. Left her mind free for more important things.

They had had a fight, a rather bad fight, of the sort that was becoming more and more frequent. Maybe it was having one boy off at school—it freed the time to deal with undercurrents. Maybe when Charles was gone, too, they would have it out. Maybe then she would ask him, What is it, Paul? What is it you want me to be?

The fight was over a female gorilla, of all things. That might be the reason that Peggy had not seen somebody about this new tension in her marriage. She couldn't see herself going in, sitting down, straightening her skirt, making eye contact and remembering not to fold her arms and therefore indicate a closed attitude, wetting her lips, perhaps, as she told the wise woman with the bun or the receptive man with the mustache: "We had a fight about a gorilla named Koko."

The *National Geographic* (and everyone knew about it now) had carried a wonderful picture story, the way it did, about Koko and the woman who had been teaching her American Sign Language. For her birthday, Koko had signed that she wanted a cat, by drawing whiskers in the air with her hand (paw? what did you say? hand?). Her trainers had got her a toy and she'd sulked and then they got her a real kitty, whom she'd called Ball (it was a male). Love Ball, she'd signed. Naturally, everyone who read it fell in love with Koko, and when the kitty was run over—why on earth had they let it out?—everyone was totally devastated. *People* magazine ran a feature when Koko got her new kitty. It was like a love story.

It wasn't Peggy's getting swept up in the story that had bothered Paul; it was her writing to the woman who taught the gorillas AMESLAN to ask the questions that had immediately come to her. If the gorillas learned what deaf people could learn, and the only problem with the deaf person's ability to learn language was one of hearing, was it possible that the young gorilla's ears didn't form properly? Say that the drum didn't close until past the age when language is acquired? Is it possible they had everything they needed for speech but hearing at birth? That hadn't turned out to be the case, or at least the letter from the psychologist in California had said it wasn't.

Paul had asked her, "All that energy for this?"

"What?"

"About an ape?"

"Koko."

"Do you know how many people in this world—" He had frowned, and she didn't know if he was going to talk about the famine or poverty or apartheid or what, because he didn't finish his sentence. "You know every tennis player on the circuit." It was an accusation.

"I'm interested in what our sons are interested in."

"You encourage Edward to make the sport his whole life."

"He has a B plus average."

"Since when?"

"Since his grades came."

"Is that right?" And he had shaken off his anger as quickly as it had appeared.

Not for the first time, she'd wondered if there was another woman. What else would make you discontent with someone who was the same today as she'd been yesterday? Once she had asked him, when they were having dinner at the Homestead, having the Smithfield ham he so enjoyed and seldom allowed himself, fearing the salt and fat would make him as doddering, through some cause and effect he couldn't spell out, as old Pink—the father whose shadow was always on Paul.

That was last spring, and Edward was already at North Carolina. His grandfather and father for a change united in their disappointment that he hadn't had the grades for Princeton or even U.VA., and hadn't seemed to care, as long as he'd found a first-rate coach.

"I'd feel foolish," she'd said to Paul, "if you were waiting for me to ask. Wives are always the last—" She'd looked away, to give him time.

"What are you saying?"

"Is there someone else?"

"Don't look for a scapegoat. I try not to."

Paul was a shy man—no, that wasn't correct; it was that she thought of him as shy in the sense that a horse shies, jumps back, starts at the sound of a voice, a touch. He shied from her question in just that way.

"Is this where you want to be?" he'd asked later, after their pecan pie. "Where we are?"

She had looked at him. "I think so."

"You don't consider that we lost something, Peg, in these years?"

"What, Paul?"

"Our way."

She'd forgot her train of thought after that and couldn't, now, recall anything more about the evening.

Part of it was that Peggy loved her husband very much, and when you did that, loved someone in that way, then you were happy to see him, happy to imagine him at work; you were always thinking up things to share, looking for ways to please. If you were not in love, the same barrage of daily matters might have an emptiness about it. As it seemed to, for Paul.

He was a very different man from her father. Ned Ruggles had been a charmer, but also a cipher. He'd been a hero in World War II and then afterward had worked out of an office in the Pentagon, so that Peggy had grown up in and out of Washington, which is to say she'd lived everywhere and nowhere. She'd had no idea what her dad did. He left work every day with empty hands, like a shoe salesman, he used to say, coming home promptly at five-thirty and, once there, working on his apple trees, taking amateur photographs, feeding the neighbor's goats. He had a dozen interests or more and never seemed to run out of energy.

It was his garden that got Peggy interested in botany. She used to look—a young girl—at the hard wine red sticks no bigger than a fingernail poking up out of the still, cold ground, ice barely gone, and wonder how they knew when to surface; how they knew when to grow again into mammoth peony bushes, each with three dozen fist-sized deep pink blooms. It was as if every year, say, a baby grew to age five, in shape and sense, and then folded herself back up into an egg the size of your eyeball and snoozed the winter away. Coming up again the next April to grow by astonishing leaps and bounds to five years old again. You'd consider it a miracle.

*   *   *

She and Charles sat in the stands with a clump of other early arrivals. There weren't going to be many fans, on this court at this time of day, with the bleachers facing the afternoon sun. Not for a first round, on a Thursday.

Peggy read about the up-and-coming female players. There were a handful of new stars: a Russian girl, looking about twelve and not at all in the shape of the gymnasts you saw on TV, more like any kid at the drugstore, and, on the same page, a girl from Scarsdale, New York. She squinted at them, imagining how their mothers were feeling right this moment. Larissa Savchenko and Melissa Brown (two Lisas, then). She saw that Savchenko had lost to Hanika in the first round last year but was expected to go further this time. She underlined the two names and put her program away.

Edward had come out.

He had on a yellow shirt, white shorts, his hair cut shorter on the sides than she remembered. It was much the same as seeing someone you didn't know at all, or someone you hadn't seen in ages, and then, after you have passed him on the street, turning back around, thinking, But that must have been . . .

The tennis players were so alone. You got used to watching all the athletes at the Olympics, as soon as their performances were over, rush back to their teammates and coaches for hugs and towels and water. The same way that boxers always had a corner of mop-up men, trainers, supporters. Here the boys came out and stood on opposite sides of the net, each by himself.

The crowd was watching Krickstein, not knowing Edward Sinclair. Ready to root for the favorite, or hope he lost if they were kin to someone he might come up against in the next round. Still, by match standards, it was a small sprinkling of voyeurs, all with sun visors or programs held up against the glare.

After each odd game they changed sides, stopping to take a sip of Gatorade or wipe their faces with a clean white towel, silent. Even in a neighborhood game there would be talk from the people on the sidelines. Here it was not all right to call out or to make a sign, and several times the official cautioned the crowd to be quiet, so that Krickstein would not be disturbed in his service.

Last year a player had doubled over with cramps, and he simply went and shook hands, disqualified himself, and left the field. No one helped him off. In that sense, at least, no matter what they said, it was still a gentleman's game.

Krickstein was in a white shirt with blue collar and cuffs, with *ellesse* stitched on both top and shorts. The brand name seemed out of order, although the program had shots of McEnroe and others in ads for rackets, shoes, and clothes. But if there were not even seconds on the sidelines, then why wasn't it out of line to be wearing trademarks like a walking sandwich board? She noticed, too, that the list of sponsors in the back of the program included Philip Morris, Haig & Haig scotch and Kirin beer. Strange sponsors, one would think, for athletic events.

Charles, beside her, was squirming all over his seat, shifting back and forth the way you did as a kid walking barefoot on hot asphalt. He'd totally forgotten the bystanders, the scouts, kin, coaches, friends of the players about him; his whole focus was on his absent father. He began to make fists of his hands and butt them together, like two rams— punch, punch—oblivious to everyone. He was like Paul: everything other people kept inside was spread all over the outside; every worry, every discontent, every grievance was there. Anybody could look at the boy, now, punching his own knuckles, chewing on his lower lip, not bothering to wipe the sweat off his face, and know exactly where he was. Edward was more like Peggy's dad: everything inside was kept in a well-sealed footlocker, safe from view, while on the outside all was calm and even-tempered. She knew she had been drawn to Paul from the start, in school, because of this very difference. How easy to read he still was, so like this boy beside her—a mass of agitation as the official called for silence.

"Where's Dad?" Charles whispered one last time, casting a frantic look around.

"I don't know." All at once Peggy realized that if her younger son didn't know why Paul wasn't yet there, something had indeed gone wrong.

She turned her attention back to watching Edward gracefully, cheerfully lose his match, 1–6, 2–6, 1–6, to Aaron Krickstein.

"Good show," he'd say, gleefully tossing his new racket in the air. "I got four games off him!"

Crossing the boardwalk from the tennis center back to the parking lot, Peggy looked down on the double chain-link fences, ten feet high and topped with rolls of barbed wire. The space between the fences was a narrow dog run in which guard dogs circled, around and around, trotting as if on drill. Train tracks cut the Flushing Meadow complex on the left, and far behind them tennis buffs went back for another amaretto.

She would drive to the airport hotel and call her husband at once.

2 TERM PAPERS

Paul Sinclair was not on his way to the U.S. Open. Rather, he was packing to leave the country. And everything connected with it—his wife, his law practice, his waning old father, and, most especially, his elder son.

America, love it or leave it, he said to himself, with something of a grimace, as he packed the clothes he had already selected: one extra suit and the rest all rugged outdoor clothes, bought mostly for backpacking the Blue Ridge Mountains, used once or twice in North Carolina. He knew they had that Lands' End air, because they were, but that wouldn't last for long. At least he had sense enough not to be taking an overseas bag of three-piece suits. He had included a down vest; it could get cold if they were near the mountains, the Sierra Madre del Sur.

No teen-ager had ever set out for a summer of hosteling abroad with less preparation or on more impulse than he was in making this journey. On the other hand, you could say that he'd spent at least the last thirty years, since he'd entered Princeton as a brash, idealistic boy intending to give his life away to the very first worthy group that asked, wanting to make this exact quixotic gesture.

He didn't even know where Tepoztlán was. Not that he needed to. They were going to meet him at the airport in Mexico City, delighted he'd relented and joined the project; they needed to show there was a lawyer included, to keep the whole team out of trouble. There was enough money to go around, and, they had suggested, he could perhaps apply for a Rockefeller when this was finished, to continue working for third world rights on his own, if he was of a mind to. If he stayed. If he didn't come back.

Perhaps he should leave Peg a copy of the map of the general area; even though the village was not marked. She'd get all excited, read up on the farming problems in the state of Morelos. Write him a volume about it. For a week or two. Then she'd send him books and be all in a glow about the intricacies of cross-pollinating corn. Then she'd get a job. That would be another project. For six months or so.

He gathered the village was near Cuernavaca, which would mean south of Mexico City, east of the mountains. Some things you knew from having a general education. In my day, he amended, bitterly, in *my* day. He did not think about the term papers in his son's room, or rather, thinking of nothing else, he went about his other concerns the way you read a book in the airport with the planes landing, or the way you listen to the radio at a train crossing.

Peg and the boys would think him tied up with the Wainwright case, if they thought of him at all. His younger son, Charles, would. He was up on the latest details of the family with the messy will. He would tell his mother not to worry, that something had come up. That the out-of-town descendants, a bickering lot, had arrived a week early.

The firm, naturally, Sue Trice, his secretary, in particular, believed him to be taking the 9:40 A.M. flight to Newark, as the two flights a day to La Guardia, the airport closest to the Open, would get him in too late for the match.

By the time his family missed him, having allowed him two hours to rent a car, cross the necessary bridges, and find a parking space, he would be in this nation's capital, on his way to Mexico's. He'd urged Peg to take Charles up the day before, to rent a hotel room and get rested, get the layout of the center. That was in order for him to catch the early flight into National and then make it to Dulles in time to catch the noon plane out. As it was, he'd have about three hours to kill, but no one would be paging him at Dulles Airport.

He should leave them all some explanation. But what? His mind went around and around as he double-checked that he had the essentials: passport; Dr. Guttman's local contact number in Tepoztlán; money; bank transfer information.

It seemed to Paul that he was back in school, working on his senior thesis, constructing an idealization of that moment when the robber barons (had they really used such terms then for the wealthy?) had turned from acquisition to philanthropy. Carnegie. His thesis was essentially on the Carnegie family and their foundation. What it meant for someone to give away ten million dollars eight years before the Sixteenth Amendment put a graduated income tax into effect; to give money away in the same year (1905) that the Supreme Court declared unconstitutional the efforts of a group of baker's helpers who were trying to limit their workweek to sixty hours, saying that the baker was allowed to squeeze all the time from his help and pennies from his business that he could. *Noblesse oblige*, now such a dirty term with liberals, then the bright, new signpost of a more humane world. The Carnegie Foundation for the Advancement of Teaching. He had the paper still, with the distinction noted on it.

That same year a boy in his house at Princeton had been expelled—Todd, Todd Stedman. A scandal that in those days you weren't liable to forget. The boy had been allowed to withdraw, in the end. For cribbing one line from a dusty volume in the back of the library. Unfortunately for him, the book had been written by the professor of the course in question. Still, one line. Today you could lift whole passages from Shakespeare and turn them in.

He would not think about Edward's papers.

He should call his father. Poor old fool. No, poor old scholar who had outlived himself. Still the most distinguished professor on campus, allowed to remain on hand indefinitely as emeritus, working on his monographs, having the history department secretary bring his curriculum vitae up-to-date with each new reprint, each anthologized resuscitation. All focused on that one battle, that one piece of the Crusades, the skirmish between the Germans and Russians at Novgorod; that one moment in history which set the stage for later scenes replayed in two world wars, plus a scattering of movies and novels, plus all those later academics who needed to cite sources, those coming along after WW II, those even younger coming along now, all going back to old Dr. Sinclair's seminal work on the differences between the mind-set of those battling for the Fatherland and those fighting for Mother Russia.

Here in the present, his dad was no longer safe behind the steering wheel of a car, and when not ferried around by his doting lady friend, he took a cab to the campus. To his beloved university with its rotunda copied from Monticello and its arches lifting faculty to dreams of Oxford and Cambridge; to the university that still seated him at every banquet, out of respect and because, with his shock of white hair and deeply weathered face, he looked enough like Robert Frost to delight every returning alumnus.

His dad had been hurt when Paul did not elect to go to U.VA., to follow firmly in the path laid by his father's reputation. Yet he'd been proud to say that his son was at Princeton, taking honors. Paul's choice of the law had also received a mixed response. It was an honorable profession, but who would teach the next generation, and the next and the next, when Pinckney Sinclair was no longer there? Perhaps that's why his father was now well into his ninth decade: he hadn't yet found a replacement.

And wasn't likely to, not in his own family.

Paul tried to recall which of Aesop's fables had to do with pride. He had, after all, brought it on himself, in one sense, this disillusionment. His mind was back on Edward. Rather, he brought the anger to the foreground, closing his overseas bag and briefcase, checking his watch. (He should eat something, toast at least. Though, strangely, he hesitated now to make himself at home in what was going to be Peg's house.)

It had been Paul's ambition that made him pry in the first place—a fact which brought a flush of shame to his face. A shame that covered both his own grandiose dreams and his son's dishonesty.

He and Peg had had a fight—his fault, he being the one who usually started them. It wasn't fair of him, and he knew it when he had a chance to think. Peg was Peg, and if she stayed the same year after year, then that was to her credit, not a matter to be faulted. Yet he did. He could see her as she'd been when they met, not only lovely, with that red-gold hair and special smile, but serious, too, she was then, carrying on about the time clock in plants, about what a marvel it was that trees "knew" when to put out leaves, that crocuses "knew" when to appear from nowhere and bloom their purple hearts out. It was a different concept of life, she'd insisted. People considered plants lesser because they didn't have human motility, yet perhaps their regenerative powers—cut off a branch, another appears, each death followed by a resurrection—were at the forefront of science, a new way to consider sentience.

What had he expected of her? That they would be the Curies working side by side? But he had made that impossible, choosing a fairly clerical field, at least his part of the law was, working long hours, sharing little because there was little to share. (Except with his second son, Charles, who seemed to thrive on even the smallest details of the banking code, the changes in inheritance, the matters of procedure. Charles, at ten, no, eleven now, already thinking like a man of property.)

What would he have had Peg do that she did not? Show some sense of priorities in her concerns, for one thing.

That's what he'd said to her when they'd had the recent fight. She'd argued back: "It doesn't help them over there for us to sit here and bleed, Paul. It just makes a mess, all your bloodletting. I'd rather give my attention to those who, in the long run, are going to make a difference. You're angry at my attitude, but there has to be enthusiasm for those who make the breakthroughs. For instance, did you know that they can actually teach gorillas AMESLAN?"

He had no right to react the way he did, to take his dissatisfaction out on her. Yet he wanted more, both for himself, before it was too late, and with someone else. He knew, or let the fact surface, that in part he was going because of the warm tone of Helena Guttman's correspondence. That he might not have said yes, as he did, on the spur of the moment, if the two letters had come from a Dr. John Guttman instead, telling him that their project required a lawyer, wanted one, and that his time, actually, would be fairly much his own. That they'd got his name from a mutual friend, an old classmate of his—Todd Stedman.

Paul avoided Edward's room, that thinly disguised display case for trophies. His son had won everything locally, everything in the state, had moved on, was now concentrating on seeing how far he could go. The golden boy, Edward: instantly liked, instantly at home wherever he went, whomever he was with. Something stirred in Paul, not envy—he hoped not that—but wonder, every time he saw his elder son in action. He took the world so lightly, his own excellence so easily. He was as blond and dashing as Peg's dad, with the same easy bearing as the colonel, who acted as if it were enough in life to be a pleasant fourth at bridge or golf, to prune the winesaps. All the while managing a chestful of medals, plus, later, working on who knew what. Nerve gas probably.

It had seemed a wonder to him, in 1958, that someone raised around a man like Ned Ruggles would pick Paul Sinclair. Sometimes he asked himself if he loved Peg only because she'd made that choice. If the bulk of his dissatisfaction was that it was no longer enough for him that she made it again each day. Did it all boil down to the fact that he considered his wife *too* content, proof surely that she couldn't see beyond her nose? Or did he, on some unspoken level, fear that her indulgence of Edward, so like her adoration of her father (twenty years younger than his!), meant that she still favored the war hero, had never really appreciated Paul at all?

He'd mulled for days on her quick remark about Edward's grade point average. Paul was surprised. Had his son been consistently getting good marks, then, at his new school? Good comments? Receiving the tiny, penned corrections and additions of an unknown lesser version of Pinckney Sinclair, some untenured scholar milking a career from the dairy farmland of the Piedmont?

Perhaps, he thought, he'd been too hasty, judging the boy by his own standards, out of his instinct to go back in time; one didn't grow up under the thumb of a historian and bear no scars. Edward's was a looser world. With such a personality, such a natural physical gift, and more than decent grades, he might be Rhodes material. Personable counted for a lot. Had in his day; must still. Rhodes hadn't wanted misfits. Only the golden few. Well rounded. Edward had done other sports, effortlessly, not lank and awkward like his father. Soccer or maybe it was lacrosse. Rugby. Or did they all say football now? Sailing. Would that count? Edward was an expert sailor, saying that it was refreshing, took a different sort of attention from the courts. Paul could be a help to his son, he had thought; could guide him, if that was the path he wanted to take.

The boy was only a sophomore. He could beef up his GPA. Could add those necessary elected posts. All of the latter would be as easy for Edward as falling off a log. In high school his picture in the yearbook always filled a whole page. For something. Most Valuable Player. Class Favorite. Class President. Best All Around. Only his grades hadn't measured up. Had dropped further as he began to

do the tours. That was to be expected. Although Paul, at
the time, was not especially sympathetic, he knew that in
his own day he'd enjoyed intermural trips. Debate had
been his field: debates on the possibility of war with Russia.
(Armed with more unsolicited material from his father than
he could have used in a dozen years.)

Paul had hesitated at Edward's door. Wondering what
the rules were for going through your son's schoolwork. It
wasn't like opening a drawer, certainly not like reading
someone's private mail. Class-assigned papers, after all,
were more or less public property. Had been seen by a professor, and these days more than likely a grader as well.
No, not lower-classmen. Surely they were still getting individual attention. At any rate, to look through the back-
pack that Edward used for his schoolwork, or had in high
school, did not seem undue prying on the part of a parent.
He had asked several times first, well, twice, after Peg had
mentioned the good marks. Had asked if he might read a
sample of Edward's work. Had asked the boy what classes
he'd enjoyed the most. But his son was due on the courts,
was headed for the shower, had to get on the phone to his
coach. There wasn't time. "Later, Dad, for sure, I promise.
Listen, I'm late. Tell Mom, will you, that I left those shorts
on the counter. Dad? I've got to run."

Edward's room was the larger of the two boys' rooms,
with the dormers of the Cape Cod, twin beds to Charles's
bunks, and bookshelves filled with awards and unworn letter sweaters. (Paul liked Charles's room better, and would
have picked his younger son's for his own, a deeper and a
more narrow space, with one unbroken wall for books, an
alcove for his desk, a single window.)

Edward's book bag had hung from a hook on the outside

of his main closet door. His was a corner room, and he had an additional step-up closet over the stairs. There were solid doors in the old house, and the short closet had a series of hooks for spare rackets, which, as opposed to wine bottles, were kept upright and not lying on their sides.

From the book bag, Paul had taken out a spiral, two unused textbooks, and an expandable file folder full of term papers, all expertly typed on good-grade bond. He picked out the top paper, holding the rest of the folder in his other hand, thrilled to see the red-penciled A in the lower left-hand corner of the title page, which read: "STRENGTHS AND WEAKNESSES OF DEMOCRACIES AND AUTHORITARIAN POWERS IN WARTIME." It had been turned in to a government class, freshman level, by Edward R. Sinclair.

Putting the rest of the gear on the floor, in order not to muss the stack of tennis shorts on the bed or the tour packets on the desk, Paul had eagerly read:

In spite of the interest which we, as people, take in the human drama of war, our concern here is more with the tangible factors which one encounters with the state of war. Military factors are one of great importance which must be brought to light in any intelligent discussion of war. The importance of both land and sea power should be illustrated not only as they are important as an entity unto themselves, but also in relation to other factors.

The components and limitations of sovereign power is another extremely relevant consideration in any discussion concerning war. In addition to the aforementioned factors, economic considerations must be taken into account and their importance must be given due stress. . . .

In this paper, I will attempt to elucidate not just the various factors at work during war, but also their relationships. Finally, using all the information presented, I will attempt to bring light to the problem of the strengths and deficiencies of authoritarian and democratic systems during the state of war, thereby attempting to bring a special poignancy to the impersonal components of war.

Perhaps the best point of departure for a discussion of the nature and limitations of sovereign power lies in the writings of Niccolo Machiavelli. The ambience in which Machiavelli lived in Italy went far toward shaping his political writings and his general *Weltanschauung....*

Paul didn't read the whole paper; it was twenty pages. The professor hadn't made many comments, a query here and there, the correction of usage. A request for more specific detail. He could imagine the man, delighted to find a serious student—but dismayed at the stilted style, the amount of padding, the downright b.s. Still, the boy had been a freshman and (Paul had felt a flush of pride) had absorbed apparently something of his grandfather's interest in battles. Both grandfathers, to be fair.

Interested now, excited, he had picked up the second paper, which had a big blue B plus on the front, with a note saying *"Good work, needs tightening."* Starting to read, Paul felt the floor fall out from under his feet. Quickly, he sat down, suffused with the first sick rush of shame.

His son, a cheat?

In spite of the interest which we, as people, take in the human drama of psychology, our concern here is more with the tangible factors which one encounters in the works of Sigmund Freud. Libido factors are one of great importance which must be brought to light in any intelligent discussion of Freud. The importance of both id and ego should be illustrated not only as they are important as an entity unto themselves, but also in relation to other factors.

The components and limitations of the superego is another extremely relevant consideration in any discussion concerning Freud. In addition to the aforementioned factors, individual considerations must be taken into account and their importance must be given due stress. . . .

I will attempt to bring light to the problems of the strengths and deficiencies of authoritarian and democratic personalities in the work of Freud, thereby attempting to bring a special poignancy to the impersonal components of Freudian psychology.

Perhaps the best point for departure for a discussion of the nature and limitations of the superego lies in the writings of Freud himself. The ambience in which Sigmund Freud lived in Vienna went far toward shaping his psychological writing and his general *Weltanschauung*. . . .

Paul had closed his eyes. He didn't want to look at the third paper, turned in for history, but curiosity got the better of him. It was akin to looking at the embezzling bookkeeper's last ledger. To be certain.

In spite of the interest which we, as people, take in the human drama of the scope of history, our concern here is more with the tangible factors which one encounters in the state of Athens. . . . Perhaps the best point of departure for a discussion of the nature and limitations of the state of Athens lies in the writings of Thucydides. The ambience in which Thucydides lived in Athens went far toward. . . .

Perhaps the history professor had had a little trouble with *Weltanschauung* in Athens, and that accounted for the B minus. Or perhaps he had read Thucydides.

Paul needed to leave his family some message. He had posted a letter to the firm, to Trice, stating that he was taking a leave of absence, that he had accepted the month's junket in Tepoztlán after all. Count it a sort of sabbatical, long overdue. The Wainwright case could go to the new associate, who needed to try his wings. (If he had any questions, he could ask Charles!) As an afterthought, Paul had penned a personal note to Trice, about the fee.

But to Peg? His hand stayed idle on the paper. Finally, he wrote, crossing out as he went.

Peg,
This is a coward's leave-taking. Technically, I'm in Mexico for the month of September. Will send an address.
That's all I can say at this point. Everything is joint, so you should have no trouble. My car ~~is~~ will be at the airport; you can let Edward ~~have~~ drive it.
I think I have to get this out of my system, saving the world.
~~There is a moment when~~ —Never mind. No point in belaboring it. Don't judge me too harshly.

Paul

* * *

Unable to resist, needing to savor in his mind's eye his son picking up the single sheet of paper off his pillow, reading it, and saying, "Holy shit," Paul left a final note to Edward.

Dear Son,
In spite of the interest which we, as people, take in the human drama of parenting, our concern here is more with the tangible factors which one encounters in the larger social context.

Your dad

3 INTRODUCTION TO THE TROPICS

L ANDING in Mexico, Paul couldn't see the ground until the plane dropped toward the runway. Craning from an aisle seat across a pair of travelers working assiduously on their laps, he had seen only haze, and then, as they dived through the inversion, there it was—a vast, sprawling city. A city of twenty-one million people, the size of six Chicagos.

He sat back in his seat as the plane taxied in; he had really done it. He felt as if he'd been following the leader for as long as he could recall. First it had been his father, pointing out what should be observed, discarded, embraced. Then it had been Peg, on the surface so different from Pinckney Sinclair, but marshaling Paul as effectively, through the byways of her short-lived enthusiasms.

Below his excitement, rising through it, was an enormous feeling of relief, which escaped his lips in a long sigh. He was here. He had got away.

Even the interminable customs line, choked with those carrying sworn affidavits instead of passports, or bulky packages that had to be loquaciously discussed, did not disturb him. No one was at his side, pointing out the amusing and interesting vignettes. Paul Sinclair, at forty-eight, was loose at long last in the world without a guide at his side.

Dr. Guttman's instructions were to go to the coffee shop tucked behind the art gallery, because the airport was so vast, customs so cumbersome, and planes always so late that she would be sure to miss him in the crowded labyrinth. He had not understood how finding a stranger in a restaurant could be simpler than waiting at a gate, but by the time he had cleared the inspectors, sorted out the long halls fanning out in all directions (each designated by signs in four languages), and finally entered an immense, three-story, glass-walled arcade—lined with shops selling liquor, perfume, garments, and souvenirs—into any one corner of which National Airport, say, could be tucked and not even noticed, he was glad for a designated rendezvous. At least, in a café, he could hear his name being paged.

He located an area hung with canvases about a third of the way down the huge corridor which ran the length of the airport. So great was his anticipation that he could not have said, even in the moment of looking at them, the subject of the paintings. He set his suitcase down, to catch his breath. He felt light-headed. Straightening his shoulders, he pulled himself together. It would not do to appear hesitant, not on first impression.

He saw her before she rose and waved to him, a beautiful, clearly American woman: fair skin, loose blond hair, bright lips and yellow dress. He actually wasn't sure it was she, admitting to himself that it might only be that he hoped it was.

"Paul Sinclair?" she asked, rising to welcome him.

"Dr. Guttman?"

"Helena." She extended her hand. "Would you like something to eat, or shall we go?"

"The sooner the better." He offered her a grateful smile.

"Do you know Mexico?" she asked him in the car as they turned into a sea of traffic, honking and almost bumper to bumper. In his desire to get there as soon as possible, he had arrived during rush hour, and for long stretches of time, as they headed around the south edge of the sprawling city, they scarcely moved at all.

"I've been only once, to Mexico City, with my—family." He did not want to bring Peg into the conversation.

"When was that?"

He calculated. "Twelve years ago." That was before Charles was born, although they liked to say that their younger son had been conceived in that small hotel with its stucco walls, blue tile floors, and flowering vines climbing outside deep-set windows.

"The population has doubled in that time. Both the official figure and the true count."

"It must be a very different city."

"It is. Although you won't be seeing it; we've enough to keep you busy in our village."

"I hope I can be of service." He felt himself chafing at this holding pattern of packed cars, eager to be at their destination.

"Did you notice the wonderful pictures as you came through the gallery?" Helena asked, cutting into a lane that had begun to move.

"Not really."

"Beltrán. He was a great influence on our local painter, Jaramillo."

"How did you happen to select Tepoztlán? I would have thought a less well-known locale—"

"We selected it precisely because of the fact it had been the basis of half a dozen studies. There was Redfield in the twenties, with his *Tepoztlán—A Mexican Village*, Oscar

Lewis in the thirties and forties with his *Life in a Mexican Village: Tepoztlán Restudied*, and Fromm and Maccoby in the sixties with *Social Character in a Mexican Village*, complete with Rorschach data."

Paul nodded, seeing that Helena had glanced over at him to be sure he was following her. But, of course, he knew of those works—as any educated person did.

"You see, that's the point for us, that Tepoztlán has been overstudied. But always by *men*. By men who saw the villagers in the way that Mexican men wished themselves and their women to be seen. Social scientists who took their informants' word for the structure of society; believing it, because they also wished to, to be a patriarchy. It is similar to the situation of Malinowski and the Trobriand Islanders. When Weiner went back sixty years later to investigate the same culture, she found that the women controlled most of the wealth, in that it was the husband's task to take the yams from his wife's family and convert them into gifts for her to give back to her relatives. The key transaction between men and women, completely overlooked by the earlier investigators.

"We're calling our study *Tepoztlán: Bypassed*, which is something of a joke, actually, considering how often this village of ours has been pillaged for grant material." She laughed. "But you see we couldn't get funding on our original proposal, so we slanted this one toward the fact that most of the young people of this still partially Aztec community are now flocking to the capital and Cuernavaca. Money came a lot faster in response to a request to record the loss of quaint customs than to prove that the men are essentially being led around by the nose. Literally, as you will see, sometimes by the neck."

Paul listened to her, and heard all she said, but a part of

him was not attending. He did not want to have been summoned down here for the wrong reasons, did not want to be part of some overall plan of which he had not been aware when he accepted the seemingly offhand, almost accidental invitation. "Bypassed," he said, repeating the gist of her last remarks. (It was an automatic habit he had acquired in his practice. "Intestate," he would echo, "previous marriage," "outstanding debt," to show the client that he was listening, to jog the speaker further without betraying any opinion— for which he got paid—on the subject. It was a habit that irritated Peg. "I know what I just said, you don't have to tell me again," she would say, hurt, when he forgot himself, his mind elsewhere, and repeated the last word of her paragraph.)

"You may be too tired to want to hear all this today." Helena had picked up on his lack of response. "I'm obsessed with it, of course, having finally got situated, our nets in place. Unlike Jean, I try to take it easy, go at it slow, but that's difficult, even for someone of my temperament."

"I have a question." Paul formulated what it was that troubled him.

"You must have dozens. Sorry. I've been talking your arm off."

"Why a man? If your purpose is to eliminate male blind spots?"

"Actually there are two of you, did I tell you?"

"Two of us—?"

"Yes. The other man is Japanese. Nakae Takamori." She repeated the name slowly so he could get it. "He's an economist. A colleague of Jean's from Stanford. We're using him primarily to deal with the chicken farmers. Besides corn, chickens are the main—" She stopped herself. "Here

I go again. About to start with charcoal and paper, before the Spanish—"

"But two men?"

"Right. Well, to be frank, we decided to bring you in because the plain truth is, we had no informants locally we could trust in all-male situations. There are simply places Jean and I can't go; events we can't attend. Not just the obvious things, like drinking at the cantinas, but, oh, certain clusters of men around the square, outside certain shops. A silence falls when we walk up. And, of course, for the climb."

"The climb—"

"Later, when you've got your second wind." She had to watch the road, which, as the grade increased, had narrowed to two lanes and was crowded with trucks and cars, all at least fifteen years old.

Paul was glad she couldn't read his face. He felt foolish. Had he actually thought this breathtaking woman with the gold hair had picked him blindly out of all the attorneys in North America? Because of certain reasons, sensing that he was such a person as could be particularly helpful to her, a theoretical man who could grasp the abstractions of her work and, merely by his presence, further them? He was no better than a high school boy who thinks the teacher has a crush on him. He was no more than a chance referral, from a less than savory source, to fill a research slot labeled in its entirety "male."

"This Takamori?" he asked.

"You and he will be sharing quarters on *veintidós de febrero.*"

Paul heard it first as *beintidós,* then quickly realized it was the word for *twenty-two,* must be. He felt a passing fear that his Spanish might not be good enough but calmed himself. He had the language; he was the firm's Spanish-speaking lawyer.

"My office, our cover, is on *cinco de mayo*. The Fifth of May," Helena said. "The principal streets are all named for famous dates. In fact—and this reveals a lot about the local mind-set—they all commemorate battles Mexico won in wars it lost."

The military was an unpleasant echo for Paul. It brought back a difficult time. "You got my name from Todd Stedman?"

"We worked together on a project in Washington. You know he's an architect? It was, oh, an urban development experiment, with a twist."

"He got into trouble at Princeton. I don't know if you knew. He was asked to withdraw."

Helena looked amused. "He said you would remember him because of that."

"It was something of a—"

"It's a funny tale, to hear him tell it."

"I'm sure." Paul tried to remember what Stedman had looked like. Always with a girl. Once, with Paul's girl of the moment. That's all he could recall. Not all that prepossessing. Not wellborn, is what he wanted to say, but discarded the words as springing from the thinking of his university days. Most of them had been more surprised Stedman was there than that he was asked to withdraw. Leave it at that.

Helena shifted the six-cylinder Datsun and, when he tried to read the speedometer, reminded him that every ten kilometers was six miles an hour. So, when it read seventy, that would be forty-two miles an hour. Slower now, on the narrow road.

Looking around him, Paul was amazed at the incredible beauty of the country, the multiplicities of greens, bright, dark, almost shiny in the glow of the late-afternoon sun. He had just left the rolling green farms of Charlottesville, but, by comparison, the Virginia landscape seemed pale and empty. As they began to climb rapidly, he saw, far to the left and behind them, a ring of volcanoes with their scooped-out tops and, pushing through the ground, outcroppings of what looked to be basalt.

"Volcanic ash." Helena said, "Once it covered the villages here, for miles in all directions. The year Christ was born, to give you a sense of the time frame."

"I had no idea there were so many volcanoes."

"Three hundred extinct ones in this range; thirty-five active ones."

"Where is Popocatépetl?"

She pointed over her left shoulder.

"I never saw it in Mexico City."

"You never do. Unless the haze happens to part. Which is once or twice a year."

"How active is active? None of this looks recent."

"In 1982 there was an eruption so bad that twenty percent of the sun's rays couldn't get through the ash in the air. It killed a lot of vegetation. It also caused a mass panic. The local archbishop had to go on the radio and tell the people that the volcano was not God, angry with them."

"Not here, surely. Everything is so green."

"Things grow fast. This is the tropics, don't forget. And the tropics can be deadly. That's why you never drink the water; when it rains, which it does every day at this time of year, the amoeba slide off the leaves into the streams."

Paul looked about. It appeared, in the soft twilight, not

at all a dangerous place. Feeling pressure on his ears, he asked, "How high are we now?"

"Eleven thousand."

"It looks like sea level. I'd expect timber line at this altitude."

"This is the tropics," she repeated. "It never freezes here. That's why you have palms as well as fir. Timber line is at thirteen thousand, if at all."

"It's very beautiful." They appeared to be on a pass, at least it was a high, suddenly flat stretch, with the land falling away on all sides.

"Guerrilla country. This has been a pivotal area for all the revolutions in Mexico. The mountains are the gateway to the capital, as you can see. Look behind you. Troops can threaten without being caught. Zapata, who headquartered his men in Tepoztlán, attacked from here."

"The pines are lovely."

"You can smell them now; we are just after the rain."

Paul rolled down the window, shut against the fumes in the city. The fragrance was overwhelming.

They drove past a small village called Tres Marías. Stands along the road were selling tamales and atole, which Helena told him was a popular sweet drink made from corn and milk. "They also have delicious mushrooms, which grow wild in fields of blue corn. You'll find the food here a delight. A compensation, at least, for the problem of the water."

"There is no danger from crops grown in this soil?"

"Not really. Not the basics. The four of us will eat out tonight, to celebrate your coming. Tepoztlán, not bypassed at all as you'll see, is a resort for rich Mexicans from the capital and Cuernavaca. Picture Taos, New Mexico, fifty years ago. There is a fine inn, part of an eighteenth-century hacienda, which looks down on the village. We'll eat there."

They began to descend as rapidly as they had climbed, dropping quickly to nine thousand feet. Then, heading west in the reddening early evening, they turned sharply onto a narrow paved road, its waysides thick with ruby bougain-villea, and there below, visible past buttes rising like Stone-henge out of the surrounding ground, was a mountain-valley village, old, green and hidden: a tropical Shangri-la.

Paul caught his breath. "How spectacular."

Helena nodded, pleased at his response. "It hits me the same way, every time I come back to it."

Only when she pulled the Datsun off the steep, winding street into a parking lot paved with small, smooth stones, did he realize how tired he was. It seemed days since he had left his notes, which now seemed overdramatic—to Peg—and melodramatic—to Edward—and locked the red-brick house behind him, perhaps for the last time. He could do with a shower, something hot to eat, a change of clothes.

"No, leave your bag here. This is the inn. La Posada del Tepozteco. We'll meet them here. I thought you could use a good meal and some company before you settled into the realities of life on *calle veintidós de febrero*."

He shook himself and locked his door. His ears popped slightly.

"First, while there is still light." Helena pulled him past a small, enclosed garden with a fountain and pool to a low wall decorated with hand-carved stone animals. "Look." She pointed to the village proper far below. "There is the church, the main church. It is surrounded by seven smaller barrio chapels, like planets around a sun."

He saw a medieval-looking church in a courtyard and, nearby, a town square, which also looked medieval. Helena turned and pointed toward the rising rock promontories on top of the mountain. "There, to the north, is the way we came in. Can you see, among the trees, the old pyramid? That's El Tepozteco's shrine. They're in a holy battle, not to make a joke of it, those two." She gestured back to the church below and then to the almost hidden dot perched two thousand feet up the mountainside.

"I expected something more rural." That wasn't what he meant. Certainly nothing could be less urban than the cobblestone streets, the tile and thatch-roofed houses, the central market. But it was ancient; it looked European, what one would expect abroad, on trips to famous places where history had taken place. He had expected, not having put it into words, something like a farming village on untillable ground. Had expected, he might as well admit it to himself, to feel as the educated man does in the presence of the peasant. Instead, he felt like a traveler to the Acropolis who had lost his guidebook. He could see, literally see, four centuries revealed before him, and glimpse, high on the mountainside, twice that many more standing silently amid madroña and pine.

The sense of the sequence of events overwhelmed him.

"If bypassed, then only by McDonald's," he said lamely.

Helena didn't seem to hear. "The church," she continued, "lies only on the surface here, floating like a leaf on a pond. The wits say the Spanish brought language, Catholicism, and syphilis, but that the villagers have found cures for all three." She made a dismissing motion with her hand. "The Indians were happy to be converted. They embraced the Man with a Mother in the Church, adding him to their old gods. They dress their little girls and boys in white tunics and let them wear little crowns of thorns and carry little thorn crosses on their backs, but when they burn a candle

to the Christian god, they also light one for good measure
to El Pingo, their devil, who comes in the form of a man in
black, riding on a horse."

" 'The horse and his rider hath He thrown into the sea.' "
An old line came to him while part of his mind tried to recall
one of his schoolday stories about Cortez. Hadn't he brought
the first horses to Mexico?

"Paul, how nice. You still remember your Scripture."

"That part of the brain holds on to its information
longer." He was embarrassed at himself.

"You can think of Tepoztlán that way: as a very old
brain, with the early grooves much deeper than the later
ones; the later ones more apt to be forgotten now that the
village has passed its prime."

"Has it?"

"That's rampant egocentricity, isn't it?" Helena
laughed. "Why do I think that because we're studying it
now, it must have little future left? Maybe this is just a nap
it's taking, this town, in its babyhood. Its great hours are a
century away, and our generous grant to write four hundred printed pages is less than a scraping from the bark of
the amaquapite tree."

"Amaquapite?"

"Its bark was used for paper. Tepoztlán was the center
of paper-making for the Aztecs. Then the Spaniards' cattle
killed the trees."

"You aren't fond of the Spaniards."

"It's foolish, like hating one parent when you are what
you are because of the two of them. Indians, wholly un-
mixed, no longer exist. The Mexicans I have come to care
for are both. Yet, irrationally, I do hate the Spaniards.
Much as one frequently singles out a parent." She turned

from the view. The last rays of the sun, slipping swiftly behind the cliffs, lit her face and hair. "Listen, the church bells. It's time to go in. Jean and Nakae will be waiting."

Paul cleaned up as best he could in a bathroom off the lobby. Its walls had plumed serpents made of many tiny hand-laid tiles, and there was a drain in the center of the brilliant tile floor.

Helena motioned to him when he peered into the candle-lit dining room. She and her two companions sat at a table next to a window, which he guessed must face the low wall with its stone animals. Because there were no streetlights, and the moon had not yet risen over the mountains, it seemed pitch-black on the other side of the window.

Paul seated himself between the two women, facing out.

"Welcome," Jean Weaver said to Paul, holding out her hand, retrieving it after a solid shake. "Glad you made it." But she did not seem, actually, either glad or curious about him. She and the Japanese had been talking, and she was obviously ready to be done with the formalities. She was small, with dark, curly hair, and wire-rimmed glasses that slid down the bridge of her nose. Her air of impatience at the social interruption was accentuated by the fact that she wore no make-up, as if she hadn't time for an evening out.

The Japanese held out his hand. "I am Nakae Takamori." He was a small man, in thick spectacles.

Paul introduced himself.

"But of course, we all know who you are." Nakae grinned. "What we don't know is why we are here, you and I."

"Maybe that's for the best." Paul tried a light touch.

"I think we're not to know until our tour is over."

Takamori spoke with a strange accent. It was not like

the voices of the Japanese Paul had met in the States, those clearly foreign-educated and -trained.

"Where are you from?" he asked.

"What makes you think I am not Mexican?" Nakae laughed, as if it were a good joke.

Paul flushed. Surely it couldn't be construed as racial prejudice to assume that Takamori was not a Mexican national! He studied the easy way the other man sat, the green Izod shirt, the pleated cotton pants. "California?" He tried to make it a pleasant guess, friendly. Many Japanese were born there after all. He had no desire to get on the wrong side of this man.

"Very good. Although not wholly correct."

Helena told Paul, "Nakae has a fascinating history. His father was brought to this country, along with an entire Japanese house, by Barbara Hutton, the heiress."

"My first eighteen years were lived in Japan," Nakae said. "Soon after I came to this country, I went to the States to school. For many years I was estranged from my father. But you will have time to hear my story later. You have come a long way today. Tonight you must have your dinner."

Helena motioned, and the waiter appeared with a huge chalkboard on which the day's menu was written.

The women ordered wine. Paul was at a loss, unsure what was safe to drink. Nakae helped him out. "I am having Manzanita, which is a carbonated apple drink. Very delicious."

Grateful, Paul said, "Sounds good," although in Virginia he seldom drank the numerous apple ciders and other drinks that were marketed yearly from the apple-rich Shenandoah Valley. Surely Tepzotlán didn't grow apples? Not in the topics. He felt suddenly exhausted.

Helena started to explain the menu to him, but he stopped her. He had eaten at least half a dozen of the dishes listed, and he ordered the quesadillas, not sure what they were, but remembering he had liked them. The other three spoke easily to the waiter in Spanish, discussing what to have, and then, the food ordered, slipped back into English when the four of them were alone. Paul had understood all of what they said—menu Spanish after all—but only a word or two of the waiter's responses. It might take awhile. There was a strong local accent.

"What language did they speak before Spanish?" he asked, as much to make conversation as to gain information.

"Náhuatl. And many still do." Helena told him.

"They do not." Jean Weaver contradicted her without heat, as if this were an old discussion. "Only at festivals, and then badly. It is dying out, has died out; they only believe themselves to speak it."

"How can you say if a people think they are talking something that they are not?"

"Time out," Jean told her, gesturing toward the men.

"Of course, you're right."

"I for one," Nakae interjected, "would prefer it if you did not censor yourselves for us."

"Not censor, just mind our manners," Helena demurred. "We have half a dozen arguments, professional arguments, that we lapse into. We need an evening like this to get our minds on other topics."

"Don't include me in that decision. Eating here is criminal, if you want the truth. Most people in the village don't make enough in a year to buy this meal we're eating." Jean shoved her glasses up her nose.

"Paul is entitled to one decent meal before he starts to work."

"It's your idea, not mine."

"Yes, it is. And a pleasant one."

"It's my grant."

Helena said lightly, "*Your* grant. *Our* project."

"Sorry." Jean looked at Helena and then at Paul. "I can't get out of it the way she can, turn it off. All day I've been standing in line to get my corn ground into tortillas. Trying to gain their confidence. I might as well be one of those yellow dogs that lie in every doorway for all the information I get." She took off her glasses and wiped her face. "It pissed me off that you were probably going to walk into town and get everything we needed in the first fifteen minutes."

Paul felt at a loss. "Information?"

Nakae leaned forward, addressing Paul, "The only word you have to watch here is mother." He used the Spanish, *madre*. "I steer away from using it at all in any context. You are sure to insult someone. Even to say *tu madre*, your mother, is to give insult."

Helena said easily, "But that's because it's shorthand for 'screw your mother.' " She glanced at the nearby tables, filled with expensively dressed Spanish-speaking couples.

"That's a whole vocabulary in itself, Sinclair," Nakae told him. "The uses of that verb, *chingar*."

Jean set her glass down. "I've told you two before that the phrases miss their point if translated only in a crude way." She shook her dark head. "These people feel a sense of psychological rape by the Spaniards; they also remember the literal rape of their women, the original *chingadas*. When they say *chingar*, that's what they connote: the rape of their culture as well as of their land and wives."

Nakae did not seem bothered by the reprimand. "I think Sinclair will miss a lot of what he hears, Jean, if he translates *vete a la chingada* as 'go rape yourself,' and *no chingues* as 'don't rape with me.' " Here the Japanese laughed loudly, as if this time he had won an old argument.

Jean gave in with a reluctant smile.

The waiter set before them steaming plates of exotic peppery food. The quesadillas looked like open-faced green enchiladas, and Paul began to eat at once. He felt hungry, but very relaxed with his new friends. Their emotional investment—even, it was clear, considerable disagreement—didn't bother him. He was part of a team, and he sank into the role with relief. Later he would sort it out; tonight it was enough just to be here. Contentedly, he sipped his bubbly apple juice and looked across the flickering candles at the inky darkness outside, broken only by a few scattered dots of light in the village far below.

He knew he would never go back. Charlottesville seemed unimportant and far away to him now, surrounded here by boon companions and part of an important mission. What had occupied all his time for more than twenty-five years? What had he spent his days doing? He had been only half alive, going through the motions of a life someone else had ordered for him. He felt again the zest he'd had in school. His head was light. "It must be hard," he said, "to keep your mind on your project, surrounded by such beauty."

Helena leaned toward the candles, catching their light. "I hope you won't be sorry we found you, a needle in a statistical haystack, and brought you here to serve our purposes."

"I'm very glad I came."

"We are glad, too."

"To Tepoztlán." Nakae raised his Manzanita in a toast. "And to us."

4 THE BLOND WOMAN

T H E next morning Paul looked up from lacing his boots to see Helena framed in the open doorway. He caught his breath; she looked like a mirage, as if he'd blinked away the Japanese and this woman had appeared.

"Come in," he said, pleased, half rising, then sitting back as he realized he was still holding his bootlaces.

As she came in, he noticed that she, too, had to duck her head to step into the room. Paul had bumped his soundly, coming in last night, then was forced to listen to Nakae explain to him that the low doorways here felt familiar to anyone who had lived in Japan, that it was a form of bowing to enter one's home. Paul, who knew nothing of all that, had been reminded, unpleasantly, of the sheds on the farm at his grandparents' place in Virginia, where, even as a teen-ager, he'd been an awkward beanpole who'd gone about with a perpetual goose egg on his forehead. "Watch yourself, boy," the caretaker would warn too late as they both heard the crack of bone on board.

Her standing there took him back to an image of long ago. Hadn't Olivia stood watching in just that way the first time she came to his rooms at Princeton? Not at all hesitant, even in those days.

He had not thought of her, his first serious girl (woman, rather, because even at twenty she had been that), in twenty-five years. Had, to be exact, willed himself to put her out of his mind when he proposed to Peg. He didn't intend to be the sort of man to carry a dream around, to live with some fantasy tucked in his head. It was a way—he knew this; had seen it too many times—of short-changing your wife. But in the instant of finishing up his boots and sitting upright, meeting Helena's eyes, he could see that other face suddenly, clearly, in his mind's eye. Where Peg was wholesome, outgoing, given to a thousand projects, Olivia had been a committed scholar, passionate about one thing and one thing only: her classics. A dozen times a week in his classes he had wished that she could be there, too. It was the awakening of his realization that women had separate but not equal educations. Bryn Mawr was a fine school; it was not Princeton. He supposed it was no accident that he had started casting about for a way to reawaken his long-dormant desire to save the world the day he'd heard, really by accident from some client, that Olivia, divorced and a professor at American University, had received a Fulbright for study abroad. She and Paul had talked of such trips. "You'll never do it," she said. "You'll never leave home." Breaking up with him, she'd told him, "I'd die in that town, leading that life." What a relief, a balm for his ego, Peg had been. How thrilled she was to settle in one place after moving all around the world with her dad.

Now here again was someone single-minded about her work, someone also barred from certain opportunities, necessary information, because she was female. This time he would be there for her. This time he would not be the coward he had been in school, running home to the security of his father's town, the waiting arms of the law firm.

(Paul, after school, had rationalized his life: he'd do more good in the world if he learned a trade first; if he mastered the law, then he'd have tools to bring to those in need. The law had certainly supplanted the hoe, plow, and tractor in third world countries. Except they had not called them that then. In agrarian societies. Among the techonologically backward. That was, needless to say, before everyone's children had grown up to work farms and throw pots. How circular life became when you were grown; what a straight line it seemed from where you were to where you wanted to be when you were young.)

Helena sat down on Nakae's neatly made bed, as if that were the most natural thing in the world to do. That, too, reminded him of Olivia. "I'm glad you're up," she said. "Did you sleep well?"

"Like a log."

"The tropics can be lulling."

Paul lied to her out of courtesy; he'd hardly slept at all. Part of it was excitement, to be sure, but in the main it was the fact that never in his life, not even in school, had he roomed with anyone. Shared a suite, yes, but not a bedroom. Obviously that wasn't literally true, as he'd been sharing a room with Peg for twenty-odd years, but that was different. After a length of time you grew intimate while at the same time discovering how not to transgress into the space of the other person. If, lately, he had dreaded going up to that bedroom, it was never, after so long, as much of an adjustment as sleeping on adjoining beds in a room with a man he did not know at all. Several times during the short night, exhausted, he had started awake, sat up, heard the sound of someone breathing, then remembered that it was

Nakae Takamori, a stranger, and fallen back on the thin pillow of the narrow cot.

"Tomorrow," Helena was saying, "you must wear a suit." She gestured to his Lands' End shirt and cords.

He tried to pick up on the context but realized that he had been daydreaming. To cover, he rubbed his eyes, as if only half awake. "A suit?"

"During the day at least."

"I brought one other besides what I wore on the plane. I had supposed, in the mountains—"

"You packed vacation clothes?"

"I'm afraid so."

"I assumed all Virginia gentlemen possessed an unlimited supply of Harris tweeds." Helena smiled.

"I should have thought to inquire."

"Todd said you boys had to wear a coat and tie to every class."

"That was U.VA. He transferred." Paul was not going to have his name linked with that of Todd Stedman. The intrusion of the shifty sophomore into their conversation again irritated him.

"Professionals here always wear suits and ties. The locals expect it. You don't wish to appear to be slumming. It's the same as it is at home. You wouldn't want to go into your doctor's office and find him dressed for tennis, even if you had last seen him on the courts."

Paul squinted, trying to recollect what his friend and physician Mew Morris wore. A suit surely. Sometimes even a white jacket, didn't he? Even in the office. Even for a routine examination. Certainly he did, but all the while creating the impression that it had been donned for someone else, shrugging his shoulders with an air of amusement, as if to say, It's the uniform, pay no attention. Yet in fact, he could have left it off for Paul, could have been in his shirt sleeves, even smoking one of his occasional cigars. Would Paul have been bothered? Undoubtedly, he would.

"No matter." Helena didn't look concerned. "You can send for what you need, can't you? A vest. Be sure you have them send you a vest. Every *abogado* from the capital wears a vest. On the weekend, for the Saturday Market, we get tourists from all over, come to buy the local peppers, corn, and cheeses. You have to look the part."

"I'd thought my function was to be unobtrusive."

"Hardly possible, is it? You, here?" She laughed. "No, you'll stand out, but that's what we want."

"What about today?" He suddenly felt foolish in his backpacking clothes, with her in a yellow dress and jacket and heels that he could not imagine negotiating the cobblestone streets.

"Today you can get acclimatized. We'll go to the inn for coffee this morning, so you can get accustomed to the local water, which, even boiled, is tricky. Besides, it's a lovely view in the daylight."

Looking at Helena as she talked, he placed her roughly two college generations behind him. Late thirties, turning forty. One side or the other. With that maturity which a younger woman wouldn't have, that confidence, yet a freedom, an ease, that his peers did not. He wondered about her life, trying to imagine her an entering freshman. How beautiful she must have been. He pictured her at eighteen, carrying books, revealing her figure in a cashmere sweater, wearing the socks of the times, her full lips dark red. What had she meant to do with her life then? What had happened in the intervening years? Had there been a husband? Was there someone now?

Getting up his nerve, he said, "You've got an advantage

over me. You have my complete dossier, and all I know about you is a rough outline of the project."

"What else would you like?" She seemed amused.

He felt embarrassed. She must know what he wanted to find out. "Some frame of reference."

"I come from California, actually come from there. My family is all scattered. My dad sold insurance." She made a face. "Someone's dad has to. My mom did the dishes. Ditto. I married right out of school. And divorced right back into school. I have a sister who did everything right. I used to envy kids who had dogs. Now I have a niece who has two." She looked at him. "Does that help?"

He wondered what he would have said, capsuling in that way (minimal information with a light touch), if the situation had been reversed and some client, say, whose messy private life he had just unearthed, had made the same request. "My dad never—" He shook his head. He'd answered that, he supposed, as he could not imagine a bio that did not begin that way. Or did not end "My wife always—" He tried to look relaxed. "I was wondering what I'd have said."

"Maybe we've hit on the one-minute Rorschach."

He liked her use of *we*; it was generous, inclusive, and made him feel that they were very much on the same wavelength.

"I'd like to take you to dinner tonight. I certainly owe you for that long drive in from the airport."

Helena looked away from him. "Don't misunderstand, Paul, please, but we mustn't single one another out. You understand, don't you? We have to operate as a team, the four of us. Otherwise, it can become divisive. Or, at the least, distracting." She softened it by emphasizing the last word.

That, too, was an echo of Olivia. How quickly he had

made a pass when she came to his rooms, but in those days, when such occasions were rare, it was part of the thinking. For a girl to be there . . . But Olivia had retreated from him, offended at his quick assumption. If this were indeed a second chance, he would have to handle it better.

"You'll have to guide me," he said. "I don't know the parameters. My offer was a gesture of thanks."

"Perhaps I overreacted." She appeared to relax.

"I won't deny that part of my goal was to be alone with you."

She smiled at him. "You may get your fill of that. We'll be together almost every day, you and I." Then, ducking quickly under the doorway, she waited for him outside.

He followed, grateful for her attitude. Later, he hoped, there would come an evening when he was back at the candlelit table with her, talking, just the two of them, with the town far below, with only the faintest light of long-ago stars reflected in the dark pool in front of the low wall. A time when he could touch her, put an arm around her shoulders in the courtyard, take her hand at the table. Later, if they became lovers, the inn would be there for them, ancient, thick-walled, edged in vines, the tile floors uneven with wear, the covered walkways and halls silent as a monastery. No wonder couples came from all over Mexico: what a perfect spot, a private hidden world, high in the mountains.

Out on veintidós de febrero, in the morning sun, Paul saw heads turn as the blond woman, *una güera*, walked by. Taking her arm, he felt his spirits rise and thirty years fall swiftly from him. If he had been again a schoolboy while packing to embark on this venture, he was even more of one now, with Helena Guttman, like some golden-haired legendary goddess, by his side, on the ancient stone streets of Tepoztlán.

5 CHECKS AND BALANCES

WHEN they got home from the Open, Mom had a letter from Dad which made her bite her lip and cry a little and then go outside and get very busy watering the flowers.

Charles went up to her room and read it, and then he searched his room from top to bottom, in case his dad had tucked a letter in there for him, somewhere out of sight so his mom wouldn't see it.

In Edward's room he found the one to Edward. He didn't get it, but he could tell his dad was mad.

Maybe he was so mad at Charles that he couldn't even write.

Over supper, Mom told him, "Your daddy's taken a consulting job in Mexico. It's just for a month."

"How come he didn't tell us before he left?"

"It—came up suddenly, I think." Her cheeks were pink.

"Is he coming back?" He got down to the point, because it seemed to him that what his dad had said to his mom was good-bye.

"I don't know." She pushed her plate away. "I really don't."

"Is he mad?"

"Not at you, Charles."

He wondered if she'd seen the letter to Edward, too.

"Do they know at the office?"

His mom looked at him, then, like he had thought of something she hadn't. "He must have told them. He couldn't just take off—"

"Maybe he's mad at them."

"More likely the shoe's on the other foot. If he's gone off with no more warning than—" She got up and carried away their plates. Cutting him a piece of apple pie, she said, "I wonder if he told your grandfather?"

But Charles didn't care, not then. He was thinking that it didn't make any sense, his dad not telling him.

That night, worn out with jumping up and looking in some other new place he'd thought about, he lay stiff as a board on his back with his face buried in the pillow he held mashed against his face. He wasn't going to let her hear him cry. She'd be in there, and they'd get all mixed up together and make it worse. She was more than likely calling Edward. He could hear her on the phone. Was she going to leave the letter for Edward to find? Sure. She wasn't going to destroy something like that. Edward would, in a minute, but she wasn't going to. Charles thought of hiding Edward's, so that if she hadn't seen it, then she wouldn't find it. Someplace that Edward would look when he got back. In the drawer with his dumb magazines maybe, a letter from Dad. That would give him a shock.

Charles finally fell asleep, although he didn't remember it. It seemed to him that he lay there all night, feeling like he had this big empty hole in the middle of his chest, and then rolled over and the alarm went off. That the alarm had set itself, getting in practice for next week.

He didn't care if school started this year or not. Everybody would be stupid and the same and cheering for the Bobcats like the bunch of stupid creeps that they were. He liked school a lot, but not that part of it, the sports. You were supposed to holler your brains out for these weeds, who you knew didn't care whether they were playing for your school or not, just so they got to slam each other around and see who could smack the ball the hardest. He hated soccer. He could imagine Edward as this stupid kid in the sixth grade who couldn't wait to suit up and beat a bunch of other guys. He must have, because he must have been the same then as he was now, and now he was a big jock. People didn't change. Nobody ever changed. His dad probably wrote notes to Granddad way back in the dark ages, telling him what kind of different cereal he wanted for breakfast or that he was tired of having to wear short pants all the time, whatever they did in his day.

Dear Father,
I regret to have to tell you, but it is no longer my pleasure to partake of Grape-Nuts at our table.
Your son

On the way outside, Charles checked the pockets of his jacket. Thinking all of a sudden that that was where his dad would have put a letter, where Charles's hands would find it first thing in the morning when he went out the door. He never wore anything else, and his dad knew that. It was too hot for it now. Later it would be too cold. His mom would buy him a new one, telling him that the old jacket was a sight and too small and that he needed a new one. She'd been doing that for years. It was okay with him. She could buy him twenty jackets. But when school wasn't going on, he could wear it if he wanted to. Next week he'd have to dress like the rest of the stupid kids at Barclay-Mason, but not today. He dug his hands in, feeling the crumbs and stuff, but there wasn't a letter.

He decided to see what his granddad was up to. Maybe his dad had left a letter for him there. His granddad, whom he liked a lot, lived two houses down from his house on the same street, Park. When he was a little kid, he'd had a lot of trouble getting from his house to his grandfather's and back because all the houses on Park were red brick and looked about as much alike as chocolate chip cookies. His mom would say to people about their house, "It's the old red brick," and not even laugh. To her they each and every one looked different, because everybody in Charlottesville was brick crazy, so that they knew whose house had the oldest brick, whose had brick that used to be part of some other house or, better yet, some public building that got torn to the ground and the brick sold to people so they could say their house was built out of old-building brick. If it was really old, the corners of each brick right at the mortar were worn round and smooth, and the color was a sort of peachy pink, not anything dark and not ever anything near the color they called brick red. What got him was the way new people, just-moved-to-town people, like those on the way to school who built in the wild hollow that used to be shacks, way back, they would build brick houses, too, like they didn't know that brick facing, all one thin wall of composition half brick was a real giveaway, a real eyesore to native brick nuts, who wouldn't like their children to play in the houses of people who didn't know old brick from fake brick.

When he grew up, if he still lived here, he was going to build himself a house out of something else. Black marble or pink granite or even just wood. He bet there wasn't a wood house in town, not his part of town anyway, not even the new part around the school.

It bugged his family, him going to Barclay-Mason, a public school. A public school that just about anybody in any old kind of brick house could get into. "But all your friends go to St. Andrews," his mom said about ten times every year. She meant the children of all her friends. Edward had gone to Barclay-Mason, back in the dim ages. That was the only way Charles got to go. Anything Edward did had to be okay.

In those days, all those people hadn't cut the old lots up into subdivision tracts, and it was okay to say you had a kid at Barclay, playing for the Bobcats. Now his mom told people that it was so Charles could walk. She had become a great believer in people walking to school, or even riding their bikes if the weather was good. There were four bike racks at Barclay, and she had personally raised the money for them. His mom, chairman of the bike rack committee. He'd have to give her that: she did stuff. She was always doing stuff.

Maybe that had made Dad mad. He didn't like it if you did a lot of stuff. You were supposed to stick to one thing. But in that case he ought not to be mad at Edward, who didn't do anything all day every day and probably in his sleep, too, but play tennis.

So how come his dad didn't like that?

Charles couldn't find the sense of it. He knew there was a sense to it, because he knew his dad better than anybody alive, and he knew that his dad had a reason for whatever he did; but you sometimes had to look a long time before you saw what it was. It was like those follow-the-dots puzzles in the paper: you drew your line from number to number, and then suddenly you saw your sheep or something.

Right now the trouble was he couldn't see what this was. Mom got a letter saying Dad wasn't likely coming back. Edward got a letter saying something that meant Dad was fed up with him about something. And he, Charles, his dad's favorite, hadn't got any letter at all.

His granddad was not home. His granddad lived, two houses down the other direction, from a (naturally) red-brick house that had been turned into an old folks' home. He liked to tell Charles, "Two doors down; not much of a move." His granddad was always home except when his friend Mrs. Ebberly, who lived the other way, a block past Charles's house, in a red brick that dated back to the eighteenth century—she was going to live forever so as not to let anybody else have it—came to take him for a drive. Charles liked Mrs. Ebberly, who had been widowed so long she often couldn't remember the name of her husband. He liked for his granddad to get out. They sometimes went to the Boar's Head for dinner, and Granddad got the same thing every time, his baked ham and sweet potatoes and pecan pie, and then came home and took a nap.

But today Charles was disappointed. It must be his granddad didn't know his dad had left, or he wouldn't have gone out with Mrs. Ebberly. At least not without calling Charles first, inviting him along. Granddad would take it personally, his son going off without saying good-bye.

Charles headed home, his hands in his empty pockets, sweating but comfortable in his old down jacket. He had got to the edge of his yard, and was thinking that he didn't want to go home, but there wasn't anyplace else to go, when his mom called out the door. "Charles, can you hear me?"

"I can hear you."

"Your dad's office called. Miss Trice. She said"—he could see his mother in the doorway, she was in a dress, holding her elbows in her hands —"that she had a message for you. From your dad."

The office. Sure. That made sense. Charles felt the relief flood over him. Sure. He should have figured that out for himself. His dad had left a message for him there. His dad had left him a message.

"Come clean up and I'll run you down."

"I can walk."

"It's a long way."

"It isn't even a mile."

"Shouldn't you change?"

"Miss Trice won't mind."

He knew the thing was that his mom wanted to go along, so she could find out what his dad had said. But she hadn't shown him her letter, just left it lying around. He didn't have to let her hog in on this.

She knew he knew how far it was to Dad's office. When he first got permission to walk everywhere, he'd got her to give him a pedometer, and he'd measured how far everything was. It was a mile from Barclay-Mason to Granddad's and a mile from B-M to home, because the side street came out on Park halfway between. Starting at home, it was two-tenths to Granddad's, and six-tenths to the church and Dad's office, which were across the street from each other on High Street. Even in the beginning there was nothing to it: you went down Park to High, then passed Third and Second and First, and then at the next corner there were the offices of Sturdivant, Postewaite, Sinclair, facing Christ Episcopal.

Mom had probably already talked to the rector about it,

he imagined. She had to take every trouble in the world to the Right Reverend Spencer Cox. If his mom was on his case because she was thinking that he wasn't making any friends at school, he always knew it because the rector would come around after church and put his arm across Charles's shoulder and ask him would he like to come on the family picnic, that there was going to be a lot of home-made food and lots of fun games. They were all going to the Sturdivant farm, "You know the farm, Charles," and lots of kids his age would be there.

In church, right before they were all excused for Sunday School, Cox would call them up front, all the little kids, up to age twelve—and Charles couldn't wait until he hit that happy mark next year and could stay in his pew. The rector would call them all, thinking he was like Jesus saying, "Suffer the little children to come unto me," with his big arms out, getting them all to gather around on the steps in front of the altar so he could ask them questions. Charles got it about twice a year. "What do you think, Charles?" "Maybe Charles can answer that." It was something he knew was going to happen, and he'd learned to grit his teeth and then get some words out.

He didn't want his dad's leaving to get mashed up in church. The first thing you knew they'd be praying for Dad in Prayers of Intercession, and that would be the end. If that happened, Charles was never going back. They couldn't make you go to church. It wasn't like school; there wasn't a law. He knew; he'd asked his dad.

"I'd like to think you found something there worth going for," his dad had said.

"But there's no law."

"Compulsory attendance would be antithetical to the teachings of the church."

Charles knew that meant no, loud and clear. But he also knew that it didn't much matter what the law of the land was, or even the law of the church. From day to day what you had to deal with was the law at your house.

He guessed he wished his dad had taken him along. He didn't have a lot of unfinished business the way his dad did. He could have packed his jacket, and his pedometer to see how far things were from each other down there in Mexico, and been ready in five minutes.

He passed the Circuit Court—a big (what else?) red-brick building—where he usually stopped to read all the notices that said "AT THE FRONT DOOR OF THE COURTHOUSE OF THE CIRCUIT COURT OF THE CITY OF CHARLOTTESVILLE ON AUGUST 30, AT 12:00 NOON, THE FOLLOWING DESCRIBED REAL ESTATE." And then there would be the lot and block and number, and when you learned to read the notices, going back through the conveyed stuff, you could tell how old the house was, how come they were selling it, or if it was in a subdivision, in which case you weren't interested.

When he went to his dad's office and walked home with him, they stopped together and read all that, and his dad told him stories about what was really going on. That's how he had learned more or less to read between the lines of all the Deed of Proctor and Adjoining Parcels stuff. From hearing his dad say who owned it and why it was up there and if it was really a public sale or not.

Today he didn't even glance up the stone steps toward the public bulletin board. They could have been selling off Mrs. Ebberly's precious house and he wouldn't have noticed.

Sturdivant, Postewaite, Sinclair was in the last house on

the corner. It was part of what his dad called lawyers' row, a bunch of old bricks that had been put up for sale by all the people retiring to their horse farms, and bought up for offices. He imagined that his mom had called the rector and that Spencer Cox was peering out the door of his study on the side street or maybe even out through a crack between the front doors on High.

Christ Episcopal was a big deal, mostly because it was so old it was actually made out of this dark gray stone which looked like pictures of the Middle Ages, with pointed doorways and pointed windows and these tiny heavy panes that they'd covered in plastic so they wouldn't fall out or be blown into the pews in a high wind. You knew you were in a famous place when you walked in the door. That was the worst thing about church: all the grownups tiptoeing in, dipping their heads, and pulling out the kneelers in this big awe that they were in a famous place. All the pews used to have these brass nameplates, where some bunch of ancestors had sat way back when every pew belonged to somebody. And you could tell that they wished they all still did and that there weren't any people at all at church that they didn't already know. Anybody could come—but you could tell that most of them wished that anybody wouldn't.

Miss Trice was waiting for him, and she seemed totally excited about the whole business. He knew she was in love with his dad, but he figured it would work that way. If you spent all day with somebody, you would get to think that nobody else but you knew what was going on with that person. He imagined Miss Trice was going to cry a whole lot when his dad didn't come back. He imagined Dad writing her a letter of a more personal kind than he wrote to

Charles's mom, laying it out that he was now living in another country, and was maybe going to change his name or something. Miss Trice would be all torn up and forget clients' names and lose their files and generally get everything in a mess. Then she would get a job in Richmond or somewhere, and somebody who didn't even know Charles would come in and say, "Who?" when he showed up. "Sinclair isn't here, sonny. You've got the wrong office."

Miss Trice was different from his mom. She didn't do anything else but the office. She didn't have any other thing in the whole world that she was interested in. Charles knew that. It had used to make him wonder if his dad liked Miss Trice better than Mom because of that; stuff like that happened on TV. Charles liked her because she was a pudge like him. You could tell by looking at her that every night she said, "Good-bye, Mr. Sinclair," and went home and ate three boxes of Hydrox cookies.

"Charles." She called his name, shook his hand, and then got up from her desk and led him into his dad's office, where they both sat down in clients' chairs. His dad's chair looked real empty, with him not there to look out and see the Right Reverend Cox looking back at him. "This letter came to me, but it has to do with you. I thought you might like to read it."

Dear Sue,

Please call Charles for me and tell him that I'd like him to have the fee on the Wainwright case when it comes in. He has done more work on that case than our clerks, and that will give him a reason to stay in touch with the office.

Tell him I'm sorry I left the way I did. That a month will be over before you know it, and I'll be back with things settled in my mind.

Tell him he's to look after his grandfather for me.

Paul

It was on a firm memo pad, written by hand, and underneath his name, his dad had put his initials, PS, out of habit.

"I thought"—Miss Trice took the letter back—"that meant he wasn't coming back, because, you know, it was going to be forever before the Wainwrights settled, but then a check came today. I forgot they like to keep their charges current as they go along, so that none of the settlement will have to go for legal fees." She pulled another envelope out of her jacket pocket. "I don't know how to handle this. But here it is."

Charles looked down at a check for six thousand dollars, made out to Sturdy-Post-Sin. He knew there was going to be a catch. He dad had had this big idea, but Charles wasn't going to get to keep it. Nobody let kids have loose money. Money for kids got whisked away before you ever saw it, and ended up as a column of figures that you were going to get when you were about twenty-five or something. You got to look at the figures once in a while and say, "Thanks," but the whole little book with all its pages wouldn't buy you so much as one Milky Way.

"You see, I've endorsed it."

Charles didn't see. Miss Trice turned it over, and then he saw the firm stamp on it. She must do that with everything that came in. Naturally, nobody else would actually touch checks. She could take it all for herself if she wanted to, probably.

"I can deposit it for you," she said. "I know you have a passbook. But I'll need your social security number, won't I? Maybe your daddy has it here."

Charles remembered how he was supposed to be impressed when his mom told him he had one. But he knew it wasn't going to do him a lot of good. He'd asked his dad did a social security number mean he had to pay income tax on the money that they whisked by him, and his dad said no, so Charles hadn't bothered to learn something that said he existed federally. All that meant was that his folks could write him off some way. He existed federally for *them*; he was maybe not as useful as a rent house, but every little bit helped.

"I don't want it in there."

"But I'm sure your daddy meant—"

"The letter says it's mine."

Trice looked around nervously, at his dad's chair, at the closed door. "It does."

"You're the only one he told."

"Yes, that's true." She seemed pleased.

"Cash it for me."

"Charles! I can't do that." She fidgeted in her chair. "You know I can't do that."

"Dad said it was mine."

"Let me think."

"I knew there was a catch."

"I'm trying to think."

"I bet he's not ever coming back."

"Don't say that."

"Sure. He could write a dumb letter like that, because he knows he's not coming back, and it's no skin off his back that it's impossible. He's probably laughing up a storm right now, down there in Mexico."

"Your daddy isn't like that."

"So, if it's my money, why can't I have it?"

"I'm thinking." She got up and walked around with her hands behind her back. She sort of paced, the way his dad did. She was trying to think like his dad, figure out what she should do. It looked silly, chubby Trice in her suit with the bow and all that puffed-up hair, pacing back and forth and frowning, but he hoped it worked.

In a little bit she said, "He gives the clerks a bonus check every year."

"Lucky for them."

"The junior partners get a special Christmas check, too. Half a month's salary."

"Great." He didn't see what all this had to do with him. "Let me know when you're through thinking," he told her.

In the meantime, Charles was doing some thinking of his own. He knew that by the day after Labor Day Trice would have talked to all three junior partners, and called his mom, and maybe even the widows of Sturdivant and Postewaite, and whichever of the Wainwright heirs was still speaking to his dad. He was never going to see a penny of the money. Besides which, he knew she was right; he couldn't show up with that much cash. People would think he'd robbed a bank or killed his old man and forged the letters to Trice and his mom. He butted his fists together, concentrating.

He wondered what his dad had thought about in here that had made him not want to stay around. It was a swell office. He looked out the window and pretended he saw the front door of Christ Episcopal creep open and Cox look out.

All he wanted was what his dad said he could have: the check. Not the money, just the check. When his dad came back, he could decide what to do with it. Maybe his dad just wanted to know that somebody was taking care of it.

"I mean," Trice said, edging closer, "he doesn't *say* it has to go into your savings right away."

"I already figured that out."

She fidgeted some more, feeling guilty. "It's dangerous, your carrying so much money on you."

But he knew that she knew that nothing was going to happen to Charles Sinclair, walking down High Street to Park. He wished he could stop and show it to his granddad—Mrs. Ebberly would just about faint—but he knew he couldn't. Anyway, all he really wanted was something from his dad, and it looked like this was going to be it.

"Did you mean it?" Trice asked him. "About your daddy?"

"Mean what?"

"That he wasn't coming back."

"Of course not. That was just talk." He tried out his dad's chair, placing the check in front of him on the desk. He took a quick peek out the window.

Trice began to sniffle. She crossed her big knees, leaned forward, and gave him a little smirk.

Then she stood up and went to the file cabinet. "I keep them under H." Giggling and sniffling, she got out two Golden Almond Hersheys. "This one's on me," she said.

And it was just like those great scenes in the movies where the private eye gets out a bottle and two glasses and they slug a couple of doubles, because they've just figured out how to solve the case.

6 SÁBADO MARKET

E AGERLY, Paul dressed and hurried down veintidós de febrero toward the comparatively wide street that bordered the square, cinco de mayo. He and Helena were to have coffee and sweet rolls, *pan dulce*, together and lay out the agenda for his visit. Nakae was off already, dealing with the new chicks at the breeder outside town, and Jean Weaver was gathering her information and grinding her corn.

It was not early by his watch (moved back two hours instead of the one he had thought, because Mexico did not observe daylight saving), but they were in the mountains, and the sun had only now reached their steep east-facing street. The low-lying land past the main church, cornfields and chicken farms, was still in semidarkness. Later today, he would see it bathed in the glaze of the red afternoon sun while their old rocky street fell into early darkness. That was the pleasure of being in the mountains: you never lost your sense of direction.

He felt slightly out of place in a suit and tie; and in the thin-soled shoes he'd worn down on the plane, he felt, quite literally, a tenderfoot in his new surroundings.

In the bright, slanting light it appeared that only the

animals were awake. He saw no one stirring in the adobe houses with their tile roofs, not even in the ones with dirt yards and dirt floors. Perhaps the men had already gone to the fields? But surely not on Saturday. Perhaps he was thinking in North American terms; maybe there was no "work" that had to be done. Early September, Helena had said, was a time when the cornfields were idle, awaiting the harvest at the end of the month. In the old days, he knew from his reading, when the Aztecs' silver production equaled that of all the rest of the world, the men were sent long distances daily to the mines. But now it might be they drank pulque and slept in.

A rooster crowed from the top of a high wall. Three hens ran across the street: a small rust one; a fat white one; an almost iridescent black. Peg would have known the names of all of them. She'd learned the different breeds a few years back, saying it was simple enough to distinguish a Rhode Island Red from a Leghorn; that, after all, any child knew the names of a dozen different kinds of dog. If he thought about it, he would take a few snapshots for her. A decent gesture, when he wrote to ask her to send the additional suits.

A large white hog looked out of an adobe shed in someone's backyard. (Peg had also done pigs and cows, so that, driving the Virginia countryside, she could name what they saw.) It appeared to notice him, and—surely this was accidental, the viewer's tendency to anthropomorphize—leaned its snout on its front hoof and posed for him. Feeling slightly absurd, Paul pretended to shoot its—her (for now he could see the dugs)—picture. "I'll catch you later," he said aloud, somewhat embarrassed to be talking to a hog.

At the bottom of veintidós de febrero he turned left onto cinco de mayo, as he had been told, and was relieved to find himself on a proper sidewalk. Few people were out, even here. He saw a woman in a rebozo, carrying a basket on her head, looking for all the world like a tourist postcard, with the soft blue of the garment, the long rough skirt, thick braid, high cheekbones, sandals. A man on a burro rode by, clay jugs on each side of the saddle. Two small boys, barefoot, in store-bought shorts and T-shirts, lugged a bucket of water past him, their arms straining, and turned the corner to veintidós de febrero. They couldn't have been more than six. Everyone he saw was carrying something. He was set apart from them, then, not only by his clothes but also because he was empty-handed. He wished, fleetingly, that Helena had assigned another role to him; the idea of being in a sport shirt and boots, counting pullets, seemed suddenly appealing.

Cinco de mayo bordered the town square on the west. Walking along the more modern concrete street, he could see stalls on all sides of the square and, in the center, a bandstand. Across the square was the church, only the top of which was bathed in sunlight; the rest lay still in shadows. The storefronts to his left were all closed. Most had brightly painted corrugated aluminum doors which pulled down like garage doors at home; the walls were green, yellow, pink, and orange adobe. He read the signs: HELADOS Y PALETAS, ice cream and Popsicles, PALETAS Y HELADOS, Popsicles and ice cream. AVESTO DE PARAÍSO, a paper-flower shop with a bird of paradise in the window; a drugstore advertising *Nutri Leche*; a wineshop selling *vino tinto* and Pedro Domecq. A man in a three-piece suit, with a grand mustache, was opening one of the corrugated doors to reveal a waiting room with two chairs and a desk. The signs above his office proclaimed: FILOSOFÍA, PSICOLOGÍA, GNÓSTICA, MEDITACIÓN. Next to him, in a waiting room similar to a doctor's, under a swinging wooden sign reading ESTUDIO ANTROPOLOGÍA, Helena sat in a bright yellow tailored dress. A large leather satchel hung by a strap over her chair. "Good morning," she said, looking happy to see Paul. "Let's go have breakfast."

She swung down the aluminum door with a practiced thud, padlocked it, and left a sign propped on the sidewalk which said, in Spanish, back in a little while. "That's to let them know I'm open," she explained, and then, when they had stepped out on the sidewalk, "We won't speak English now. We never do when we are working."

She led him back the way he'd come, except that at the intersection they turned left and crossed the street. She pointed out the cluster of women waiting to grind corn, two more ice cream shops, a candy store, another wineshop, and then, mid-block, a line of medical offices behind the familiar aluminum doors. All offered at least one specialty; many offered general cures. There were signs promising remedies for headaches, backaches, nerves, fever, high blood pressure, indigestion, impotence, and, all of them, emergency maternity treatment, day or night. A few claimed to provide acupuncture. A couple of the doctors, Helena said, were known abortionists, who came from Cuernavaca on certain afternoons.

"You will be watching the doctor in that office." She pointed out the name, Segundo Gómez. "He is named for segundo de septiembre, another famous date. He is important to us."

They stopped at a café which opened out onto the square, ordered coffee and a basket of hard rolls and sugar-glazed brioches.

From their outside table, they could watch a group of

young boys about Charles's age playing a street version of soccer.

"Little Peles," Paul said.

Helena nodded, not looking at the children.

He was content to sit in silence with her as the sun finally hit and warmed the central square of the village, and small clumps of people began to open their stalls for the Sábado Market. An old woman with a single gray braid passed close to them, a bouquet of white lilies in her arms. Two young men carried fresh chickens, holding them by the feet, not yellow-skinned as at home, but the flesh white, and, at the extremities, pink, like skinned rabbits. Half a dozen little girls carried cardboard egg cartons tied with string, thirty eggs to a package.

"I'll show you around," Helena said, leaving bills on the table and getting up.

Out on the square, they watched as men, carrying large baskets on their backs, the weight borne by straps across their foreheads, unloaded what looked like blocks of marble in various shades of white and cream. "Cheese," Helena told him. "You'll not find any better in the world. They bring it from all over Mexico: queso Chihuahua, queso Oaxaca. My favorite is queso Mennonita. The Mennonites support their work high in the mountains by selling it."

"I didn't know they were here."

"Yes. A number of small sects work among the Indians, pockets of the remnants of the old culture served by pockets of the remnants of early fundamentalists. Mining an old shaft, you could say."

On calle dieciséis de septiembre, which ran east of the square in front of the church, they passed little clothing shops selling white socks, earrings, crosses, communion

69

scrolls, paper flowers. Helena explained that each girl at fifteen had a coming-out party, much like a debut, at which she wore a long white gown like a wedding dress, similar to a first communion dress, but fancier. They saw one such quinceañera gown displayed in a doorway.

"You're enjoying your work here?" Paul asked her.

"Very much. Jean says that's because I am still a tourist. I buy my hand-ground wheat bread, my special cheeses, a whole flan to take home for us, and she fumes and refuses to eat. She reminds me that most families here are subsidized by the state. That cooking oil and beans are sold to them for half what it costs the government. You will see them, standing in line for their oil and beans, on which a lot of them live, that and the corn they grow in their plots or even, sometimes, their yards." Helena did not look bothered. "Jean's gone native, I tell her. That happens, you know. Every time you get a group in the field, someone goes native. Nakae will likely do the same; I can feel it in my bones. He moves around in his cheerful way, doing his informant's assignments, pretending to tend the chicken production, but inside he's turning. I can sense it. His father—did I tell you?—converted. A number of them who came with Barbara Hutton did that. Raised bonzais and converted. I'm sure it is just a matter of time—" She laughed, as if she were not quite serious.

"Do you think so?"

"Not really. But the two of them get on my nerves with their local habits. Saying 'us' when they should be saying 'them.' At least," she said gently, "I won't have to worry about that with you."

"Am I so out of place?" He didn't know whether he should be bothered by this or accept it, as her tone implied, as a compliment.

"Yes, you are clearly not of this place, and I'm glad for it. To tell the truth, it was a relief to see you fresh from the plane, and feel I had an ally at last." She said this with such sincerity, looking at him as if she had awaited him so eagerly, that he almost tripped stepping down from the curb.

How beautiful she was! He could see that all eyes followed them as they walked down the street, and he wondered if Helena was aware of the attention and if she enjoyed it.

"Should we be getting back to your office?" he asked, wanting her to know that he was ready to begin work at once.

"There's no rush. No one will expect me back at any certain time. They can see from the sign that I am in today. The morning will be busy with setting up the market, keeping track of the children. In the afternoon, when everyone has eaten, before the rain, they will come by, a few, to see what I am offering, a woman. Many think I must be a midwife, and when I am not, they are curious. They have encountered social workers who come to their homes when the children are in school, or should be, but never a woman in an office on cinco de mayo."

"What is it exactly that you want me to do?"

"Let's walk around a bit more. We can talk as we walk." She strolled on for half a block, then said, "Here is my favorite place: La Salchichería. A woman runs it, North American. She makes delicious sausage, of course, plus her own pastas, half a dozen kinds, wonderful noodles with sesame and sunflower seeds. And her own breads, meaty black and coarse-ground wheat. And an orange cake, thin and iced and soaked in something rich, that is too good to be true. I come here often." She waved through the open doorway to a young woman behind the counter. "The heaviness of the corn and the smell of it get to me after a while."

Paul gestured toward two girls, maybe eleven, who shared the handles on a large basket which contained a yellow fruit he had never seen before. "What are those?"

"Plums. You'll get to know the trees, called ciruelos, they are big and old and heavy and look as if they belonged in Biblical times. You'll see children, with baskets on long poles like butterfly nets, knocking them to the ground. They are sour and take a lot of sugar, but they are a big crop here."

Next to the sausage shop was a store that sold candies and atole, and children were already handing over coins and getting back cups of the thick, sweet drink and running off to enjoy it on the square.

"Here," Helena said, "we can lean against the wall and watch. No one will mind."

They stood side by side, studying the faces.

"I will tell you what we want from you. You and Nakae. Don't think that we got you here on a false pretext, but the real information we need was hard to explain out of context. In Redfield's account, and Oscar Lewis's as well—in fact, it doesn't matter whether the model is anthropology, psychology, sociology, pop culture, the scenario is the same—they trace the young man, growing up, the weak father, the strong mother, the awkward courtship, the virgin wife, the early marriage, the wife replacing the mother, the inevitable mistress. Then, always in another chapter, another section, they trace the young girl, her strict upbringing, her harder physical labor, her tie to the mother, the lack of sexual experience, the immediate children, the passive hostility as her husband takes a mistress, her control of her children. Do you follow me? Does this have a familiar ring?"

"Very much so. I think that's a fair summary of all the social studies courses I ever took."

"What they never tell you is, Who are the mistresses?"

"I don't understand."

"We ask the women, they say, yes, their men wander. We ask the men, they say they have many women: widows, women from the cities. We ask the widows, they laugh and tell us, 'Nothing changed when he died.' In fact, most of the widows are old, poor, and live with their sons or, if the sons have moved, their daughters. They are not carrying on with anyone. No man hunts down a women who is poor and old and sleeps with her, not because she is no longer satisfying but because she arouses too much guilt. He shuts his eyes and sees his mother."

"I suppose here you do not have offices—" He stopped himself. Knowing that to any woman that would be offensive and that, besides, it was something of a cultural fiction. It was not Sue Trice he dreamed of, and never had been.

"A population of single workingwomen, no." She filled out his thought, but her tone was mild enough. "Nor do they have the large surplus of females as is true in the States. Here it is almost an equal number. Women die in childbirth still, move away in the same proportion as the men. No woman stays here without a husband unless she is established as the mother of a grown family who keeps her."

Paul sifted the information. "You are saying the mistresses are other men's wives."

"That is what we want from you exactly: the problem stated as a man would phrase it. 'Other men's wives.' You did not say, 'Women take other women's husbands.' "

"Isn't it the same thing?"

"Not at all. Your concept implies that it is a matter of

dishonor among men. That's what we can't get within a hundred yards of. 'Not wives,' the men insist to us. 'It is never wives.' They fear the horns constantly, yet take great pleasure in inflicting them. That is doubtless the reason for taking a second woman scarcely different from the first."

The conversation made Paul nervous. It was the farthest thing from what he'd seen himself coming down here to do. The whole topic raised his anxiety. He found Helena even more attractive today, with the sun lighting her face and her shoulder sometimes brushing his. He could not believe his good fortune in happening upon this project, this village, and such a woman. He had resolved to let her see that he could be all business when the occasion demanded. In her unsettling presence, it was hard to be matter-of-fact about infidelity.

"What does this translate into?" he asked, in what he hoped was a disinterested tone.

"We want you to watch Segundo Gómez, the doctor from Cuernavaca. Nakae we have assigned to Avelino Álvarez, the chicken farmer. Both men are well known in their circles; both brag a lot about their women. We will provide the introduction for you."

"You mentioned a climb?"

"Yes. Next weekend is the one remaining Aztec festival that the people celebrate. The old god returns; Náhuatl is spoken, although as you heard last night, Jean does not think anyone actually still knows the language. There is a great nighttime ceremony on the mountainside, at the shrine. The story is, reported by everyone, that the men take their other women there. That there is singing and dancing and drinking and love-making. If we are correct, that cannot be so. We know that wives do not go. We need someone to tell us what actually occurs."

"That's more to my liking than the other, informing on a specific person." The idea had an unsettling echo.

"If you'd rather not?" She touched his arm. "Let's move about. Doesn't the sun feel good? You can walk me back to my office. We can talk as we go. Everyone needs to see us together if you are to be trusted."

They crossed through the center of the square, bypassing the soccer players and a cluster of children, scarcely more than toddlers, sitting together eating candy. A few young women were hanging out shirts for sale from the railings of the bandstand, and the bright garments flapped like so many flags from the white, octagonal structure.

Back on cinco de mayo, Helena stopped to introduce him to the man in the three-piece suit who was peddling his *filosofía* and *psicología*.

"This is my colleague from North America," Helena said. "He has just arrived."

The men shook hands with the customary effusion, and then the man went back into his office.

"If that is what you want from me," Paul told her, "I'll be glad to do what I can." He sat in one of Helena's clients' chairs, facing the street. It was a curious relief not to be the one behind the desk. This was her project, not his. Relaxing, he said, "Tell me about Gómez."

"He is rich. He has a wife who collects art. He is an important person locally."

"And you think he has a mistress here?"

"Possibly. Probably. That's our guess. The women are careful. They know we are watching them. You will be able to ask questions we cannot. You will appear to be here for another purpose. You are from the States, thinking of settling here, things at home. . . . You will suggest, perhaps, that there is someone back there besides your wife. I don't know. You'll know what to do. However men convey these matters to one another."

Paul crossed a leg over his knee and thought about that. He had no idea how to proceed. He had never in his life talked with another man about any woman other than his wife. Did other men do that? Share affairs or the desire for one? It seemed wholly out of his frame of reference. Even men he knew to have been in wretched marriages for a score of years always more or less gave the same report on their wives and asked about his, a formality, before getting down to business. Alone with Peg, he might conjecture about someone's troubles. But only at home, never with anyone else. "Will he find that convincing, this Dr. Gómez?"

"That's your job."

"Is Nakae already on assignment?"

"Yes. He took to the idea like a duck to water. He has more skill than the rest of us in probing for the private life." She seemed, ever so slightly, to be making fun of the Japanese.

Paul was silent, not sure where his loyalty should lie.

"However," she teased, "surely a Virginia lawyer has some small experience in gaining confidences."

"Let's hope so."

"Here. I brought us a thermos. Let's have one last cup of coffee before you get acquainted with our village."

He accepted gratefully, hoping she was as reluctant as he to end their time together.

"Jean is going to take you back up veintidós de febrero and introduce you around. The chicken farmer's wife, Esperanza Álvarez, will be with her. She has some standing on the street; hers is the large Spanish house on the right as you go up the hill. She will help you get your bearings."

"Jean?"

"Yes." Helena looked at the line the sun streaked on the back wall of her open office. "I think she'll be ready for you now."

Paul rose, seeing that was in order, but he couldn't bring himself to leave. "Shall I eat lunch on the square?" He felt foolish, as if he were unable to figure out the simplest matters on his own. He should have asked outright when he was to see her again.

"You can see. Avelino and Nakae will be bringing chickens to the market. Perhaps Esperanza will feed you. Or Jean may have other ideas. She is our entrée into the women's lives."

"But I am to watch the men, am I not?"

Helena smiled. "Today you are to look and listen. And enjoy yourself."

He handed her his cup, letting his fingers touch hers.

As if taking pity on him, she added, "Come back in the late afternoon. Everyone gathers after the rain. Cars from the capital start to arrive. Mariachis wander about. You'll see Tepoztlán at its liveliest."

"I'd enjoy that."

"Paul, I'm very glad you're here."

He confessed, grateful, "I guess that's what I wanted to hear."

Paul walked, as directed, back to the southeast corner of veintidós de febrero and cinco de mayo. He could have found the corn mill as easily by following his nose: the heavy smell of just-ground corn reached him from across the street. He found the aroma incredibly enticing, much headier, richer, than anything he was familiar with. It bore about the same resemblance to the corn products of his experience as Braun-ground, deep-roasted coffee beans did to a tablespoon of freeze-dried.

He spotted Jean Weaver wearing a cotton blouse and long skirt and, like the now dozens of women waiting in line, carrying a basket under her arm, in which lay a pressed, embroidered napkin, ready to fold over the hot tortillas.

He watched the mill's process in fascination, just as he had, a small boy, watched his first milking machine on a farm in Virginia. Each woman in turn handed over her sack of corn to be fed into a chute. The coarse resulting grain, mixed with water into a very thick paste, was fed into another chute which dropped paper-thin disks of corn dough onto a conveyer belt; it, moving slowly and continually, turned them over onto a metal strip which ran them past a flame and slid them out as hot tortillas. These each woman then quickly stacked, wrapped in the clean linen, and tucked in her deep basket to keep warm. Most of the corn going in was yellow, but some women brought blue corn, some red, which—when made into the thin, outsized communion wafers—appeared slightly darker than the yellow.

"Be with you in a minute," Jean said to him, not moving from her place in line.

Paul was the only man about, but he did not feel uncomfortable. The women glancing at him did not appear interested; there were no covert second looks, no giggles. Doubtless they all knew who he was and, more than likely, what he was doing there. Surely after having had their village studied in their grandmothers' time and their mothers' as well, they had learned to ignore such North American visitors, much in the way families carry on with opening their Christmas presents while some uncle's movie projector hums away.

He understood now about his suit. Dressed in this way, he had an authority which made it permissible for him to wait two feet from the line of women with their baskets and braids, whereas one of their husbands, dressed for the market in a loose white shirt and gaucho pants, wearing his hat, holding a son by the hand, could not. He would have been intruding, whereas Paul was more like a schoolmaster stopping by to watch a class.

After a few minutes Jean and a local woman joined him on the sidewalk.

"This is Esperanza Álvarez."

"Good morning."

"This is Paul Sinclair."

He held out his hand.

"Mrs. Álvarez is a neighbor. Mr. Sinclair is a friend of

79

the doctor Guttman." Jean, all business, had adopted a fieldworker manner toward him. Her Spanish was better than Helena's, with a perfect local accent. Except for her striking blue eyes, which she could not alter, she had done all she could to blend into her environment.

"You are staying with Nakae Takamori, I believe," the woman said to him. "In the painter's house?"

"Yes." He studied the chicken farmer's wife. She was quite slender, her hair pulled back in a bun, and, in contrast to Jean, wore a tailored, even severe black suit. She looked to him more Spanish than the rest of the women, who were, to his eyes, quite Indian. They looked like the women one saw in paintings, broader across the cheekbones, flatter foreheads, with eyes set deeper. And something else, less tangible, which he could not identify. He hoped he was not staring, or that there was not some prohibition against meeting her eyes. Her hair was dark, as was Jean's, and Jean, bronzed from the sun, was as brown. Yet anyone from either side of the border, glancing at them, would know in an instant that Jean was North American. It interested him that this was so and that he had no idea why. Peg had at least a half dozen books on what she called "body language" and was always telling him how much you could "read" about a total stranger. Trying to see a difference in the way the two women held themselves, Paul could remember none of Peg's rules.

"Esperanza will give us coffee," Jean said. "She is my key informant; I don't proceed without her."

"It is nothing," the woman responded, but she did not seem the least uncomfortable with her role. "You will like the painter, Jaramillo," she said to Paul, in a friendly manner, as the three of them fell into step at the foot of the steep cobbled street. "He will one day be as famous as Zúñiga. His wife cannot see the long view, however."

Jean said, "Rosa is scarcely eighteen."

"I was a mother at her age."

"She wants to leave the village."

"She did not want to come back. She ran off with him to Guadalajara, thinking herself having an adventure. Then he decided to come back home."

"To paint chickens."

"Yes, to paint chickens." Both women laughed.

"And rent out half his house to foreigners," Jean added.

"He must eat."

Paul had not thought of the boy with the thick black hair and scowling face, whom he had glimpsed last night and again this morning, slipping in next door, as being his landlord. He didn't look much older than Edward (although of course, you couldn't tell with people you didn't know). If it was his house, Jaramillo's, then Paul and Nakae had him to thank for the fine flush toilet and the almost luxurious tile shower.

Esperanza Álvarez stopped every few steps to nod to someone, touch cheeks, or speak in low, affectionate tones—a woman going downhill with two baskets of yellow plums, another with the small green tomatoes called tomatillos, an old man with a cane, a rider with clay jugs strapped to his saddlebags.

"What is he carrying?" Paul asked, watching the man on the burro, recalling he had seen a similar one earlier.

"That's the milkman," Jean answered.

At a public well that looked like a wide, deep fountain filled to the top and slightly spilling onto the stones, two young girls, about six and eight, dipped water into buckets.

"Did you notice the scorpions?" Esperanza asked Paul.

Startled, he looked around, then saw that she was pointing to a pair of gateposts to their right: decorative metal lights shaped like scorpions, perhaps two feet high, their brass and copper tails fitted with light globes.

"The real ones are everywhere here. We have five hundred varieties. You must watch your shoes; always shake them before you put your feet in. Always look on your sheets before you go to bed—they sometimes fall from the ceiling."

"It's all the stone," Jean said. "They live in rocks."

"It is much worse in the dry season."

They passed a cluster of houses on the left, close together, including the one where Paul had seen the huge hog looking out the doorway of the shed. He told them about that.

"We can introduce you," Esperanza said.

"That's all right." He was embarrassed.

"She will be pleased to meet you."

Reluctantly, Paul, in his pin stripes and Church shoes, followed the women over a high sill, into a dirt yard. When Esperanza called out, a woman appeared in the low doorway of the orange adobe house, with three small children peeking out from behind her skirts. In the yard a rooster, with one leg tied to a lime tree, hopped up and down, and two yellow dogs roused themselves from a patch of sun to sniff at the visitors and bare a little teeth at Paul. As if on cue, the white pig poked her head out of the window of her pen and waved a hoof at Paul. Having got his attention, she lowered her eyes.

Behind the tree where the rooster was tied, a young girl hung clothes on a short line, and behind her, Paul could see a patch of cornstalks and a tangle of squash vines. He also saw a small adobe building with a curtain for a door, which he surmised to be an outhouse.

While the women talked, he watched a turkey flap up onto the wall by the street, stretch its neck to see both directions, and then flap down again.

Back in the street, Esperanza said of the woman with the pig, "She has a very hard time. Her husband drinks. He runs around." She made a spitting gesture.

"You understand?" Jean asked Paul.

"I think so." *El chingaquedito.* The husband screws around, in a petty way.

"Did you see the bull horns over the door?" Jean asked him. "A prize trophy here."

"They are not the only horns at that house." Esperanza held two fingers up to her forehead.

In all the yards Paul could see more roosters and hens, at least a dozen varieties and colors. He wondered whether each was selected for a different reason or they took them potluck.

The Álvarez house, called Quinta María, was behind a high stucco wall. As Esperanza opened the iron gate, a tabby cat jumped from its perch in a recessed alcove that contained a replica of the Virgin of Guadalupe. Paul noticed that here, also, there were scorpion lamps on either side of the entrance, their raised claws looking like those of giant lobsters. These, more intricately crafted, their scaled tails carefully beaten and welded, were of museum quality. He wondered why they had not been stolen. Whether there were too many eyes here for theft or whether the concept of property was different from that in the States, he did not know. Perhaps a thief here, trying to steal these finely tooled objects from the chicken farmer's wife, would be regarded with horror.

Inside the large, cool house, what struck him first was the absence of wood. It seemed strange to him, coming from

Virginia, where everything that wasn't brick was wood: the floors; the cabinets; the furniture; the paneled walls and bookcases in older homes. He thought of the Blue Ridge, covered in forests, then tried to bring back into his mind's eye the volcanic cones, the rising hummocks of rock, the spills of ash. Certainly there were trees here, but no doubt it was cheaper and easier to burn them into charcoal than to let them grow and use them for lumber.

For an instant, only for an instant, he was homesick for—of all things—the hallway of Sturdivant, Postewaite, Sinclair, with its hatrack, its polished wide-plank pegged floor, its smooth, worn banister rails, the oak stairs, the caned, hand-rubbed walnut straight chairs. He shook the image away. It was only the unfamiliarity of the ever-present stucco, tile, and stone.

He accepted yet another cup of coffee, as strong, dark, and thick as what he had had for breakfast (Greek coffee, or what, in the States, was served as Greek coffee)—and already sweetened, which made it worse. How did any of them grow up with any teeth at all?

Esperanza led them outside, where they sat in wrought-iron chairs on a vine-covered patio. The lot was quite deep, and had, in addition to a stone walkway, numerous blooming hedges and, on the wall facing them, more vines trailing brilliant red flowers. There was no grass but, instead, as he had noticed at the inn, a sort of formal design in the ground made with swept pathways, gravel ovals, and flagstones. The sun cast deep shadows near the far back wall, and gradually, as his eyes adjusted to the sharp sunlight, he saw several children playing under a huge tree. The girls had baskets on the ends of poles and were swinging at the branches. Harvesting plums, he remembered. What a beautiful old tree. Why was it not used for furniture, as cherry was, say, at home? But that would be killing the goose that laid the eggs, he supposed. (Still, on houses such as Esperanza's, the outside doors were made of some kind of heavy wooden boards, held by cross planks, much like those on pioneer log cabins. Only the poorer houses had woven rush doors or curtains or, apparently, none at all.)

Jean brought him back to the conversation. "Esperanza has a story for you, about the corn mill."

"The corn mill?"

The woman in black seemed amused. "You want him to hear it while he drinks his coffee?"

"It's as good a time as any."

Esperanza set her cup down and leaned toward Paul, her voice low. "In 1926," she began, "the women of our village were liberated by the corn mill. Until that time grinding the corn for tortillas took many hours a day. A woman had few free hours. Then someone brought a mill to the mountains, and it was a revolution in women's lives. Later the other villages got them, too, but we were the first.

"The men did not like it. They said the corn no longer tasted so good. They said the women were becoming lazy. They grumbled, gathered together, and finally, one night, burned down the mill. The women were very angry. They talked among themselves until they came up with a plan. They drew lots, and the woman who was chosen poisoned her husband's coffee with toloache, which turns men into the dumbest sheep. She led him through the streets by a rope around his neck. After that, the men allowed the mill to remain.

"Now every woman has her corn ground, and those who can afford to use the mill-made tortillas as well. No woman any longer grinds the corn by hand on her metate six hours a day."

The calm, very Spanish-looking woman seemed delighted with her story. Shocked, Paul felt a rush of sympathy for the chicken farmer, whom he had not yet met. After all, he was not responsible for the damage other men had done sixty years before.

"Toloache is still used," Esperanza added, "when abuse becomes too bad. It sobers a man to know he is not safe in his own house."

The women laughed companionably together, watching Paul Sinclair sip his bitter coffee.

8 THE PAINTER

He dragged back to his quarters, feeling somewhat like a rooster whose leg had been tied to a lime tree.

This was not what he had left his practice and his family for, these mocking games. He tried to talk himself into a more favorable frame of mind. Perhaps that was part of the anthropologists' tactics, the better to mislead the subject. Perhaps Esperanza was supposed to think the point was to ridicule the husbands, the better to get from her information about straying wives.

He ducked under the low doorway, took off his rumpled suit, and stretched out on his cot in his shorts and undershirt. In a little bit he would take a shower. For now he was going to lie still and get himself under control.

But, uneasy, he could not relax. He looked around the small room, which reminded him of how the inside of an igloo might look, white everywhere, with only a crack of light, in this case from a small window set high in the plastered wall—recessed, as they all were. It had too much of the feel of a cell. Restless, he got up, put back on his clothes, and went into the yard. It, like Esperanza's, had clumps of blooming plants and thick vines on the inside of the wall.

There were no animals, save for a cat sleeping in the shade, but the fact that the house accommodated four people meant that it was large, although Paul supposed that once it had held three generations of a single family.

It seemed a cool interior world, the duplex and the yard, abutting a hot communal public world only a few feet away.

As he stepped from under a shady tree into a patch of sun by an old stone well—as these large round troughs of slowly bubbling water were called—the young artist's wife passed him, going in. At least, he supposed it was Rosa. She looked about thirteen in the face but had the full figure of the native girls in a Gauguin painting. She wore a Guadalajara T-shirt with no bra, and cutoff shorts, very North American in her style, but with a flower stuck behind her ear, as if aware that her looks, her long black hair, called for one.

"Good morning," Paul said to her.

"Have you seen Tomás?"

"Early this morning."

"He said he was painting the chickens."

"Perhaps he is."

"No, he is not there. Avelino and the foreigner are there. What a mess. Have you been to see?" She stood very close to him, but her eyes watched the house.

"No."

"Disgusting. They peck each other horribly."

"He might be inside now."

"He's gone off." She went into the painter's half of the house, angry.

Paul decided he should have a telephone number to send to Peg, in case anything happened to his dad. It was one thing simply to take off, but another to be out of touch completely. The old man could go any day, at his age. Possibly

Helena and Jean had a phone, but he could not imagine the
houses on veintidós de febrero with lines outside, and looking around, he did not see poles. Around the square, surely;
even in Helena's office. But he did not want to show up again
and indicate to her that he was someone who had to be hand-
carried hour by hour. Instead, he headed up the hill and
turned right at a street which angled more sharply still. In
a block he was at the inn, La Posada del Tepozteco, and,
grateful for its familiarity and hospitality, went inside,
thinking only to pick up a brochure with a phone number on
it, perhaps to give the people at the desk his name and house
number, so they could send for him in an emergency. But
once inside the lobby he was overcome by a longing to go
back to that first night, when the new land seemed magical
and he had felt at home.

Taking a table for one in the dining room, he looked out
the large window, past the fountains and wall with its open-
mouthed carved beasts, at the blue sky. Somewhere on the
face of the hill to his distant left was the Aztec pyramid. He
scanned the area below the jagged rocks; but in the full midday sun the green seemed to shimmer and move like a river,
and he could see nothing but mountainside.

Not wanting again the sweet apple drink, he ordered the
local mineral water, Peñafiel, specifying no ice, in order not
to fall into the trap of drinking the water after all, as so
many tourists did in cocktails.

He told himself he would not do this again—escape into
the luxury and comfort of the inn for his meals. He did not
want to be one of those men of the type who eat at the Com-
monwealth Club and consider they have visited Virginia.
Starting tomorrow, he would take his meals with the rest of
them, wherever they ate. Again, he realized, he was making
a wrong assumption; he continued to think he was to stick

with them. Hadn't Helena told him where she shopped, the sausage store, with its homemade pastas, its orange cake? And that Jean, going native, cooked local corn-based dishes? The message was clear: he was to fend for himself. If he sought company, he had Nakae. (He needed to be sure about his roommate's name. He knew that North American newspapers reversed Japanese names often, as in Japan the surname came first. He must be sure that the women, calling him Nakae, were intending it as his given name.)

He looked at the menu prices, ashamed at the cheapness, calculating that he could keep a family of four in the inn for a year on a month's income at home.

Guilt inhibits effectiveness, he reminded himself, and shook away such thoughts. He would have a fine, safe meal; he would get used to the local food gradually, work out a schedule, select a café on the square, perhaps. He was, so far, having no trouble with digestion or with the altitude. After all, if not accustomed to eleven thousand feet, or even the seven of Tepoztlán, he at least took frequent hikes in the Blue Ridge.

He had brought his camera along and, back on the street, would snap a couple of shots of the chickens and the white pig, label them "My neighbors" for Peg. Back in his quarters, he would get a letter off to her—he'd seen a basket for outgoing mail here in the lobby—and then take a nap. By late afternoon he'd be ready to tackle his initial assignment.

Starting back down veintidós de febrero, Paul saw chickens everywhere he looked. As if they, like the hog, knew they had an audience. It got out of hand, but he couldn't stop, feeling somehow obliged to snap each in turn as they strutted on stoops, hopped out of doorways, preened on the tops of walls: a rust-red rooster; a solid black rooster;

an iridescent hen; a gray hen with orange markings; a white rooster with a red comb; a scrawny yellow hen. "Go away," he finally said, "that's all." He felt like a talent scout, sending the rest of the kids at the audition home.

Then, from nearby yards and side alleys, children ran out, carrying baskets and buckets, some grabbed in haste and empty. They posed for him in pairs, grinning for the camera, each holding a handle. He recognized the two girls he'd seen earlier when he was walking with Jean and Esperanza.

"Be off!" said a low voice behind him, and the little girls all giggled and the small barefoot boys in shorts stuck out their tongues.

It was Jaramillo, the painter. "Gnats," he said in English. "Mosquitoes." He also wore a Guadalajara T-shirt and worn Levi's jeans. Paul found himself thinking that the boy could not have much artistic talent, at his age. Wasn't it musicians and mathematicians whose gift was apparent from the start? Boys of ten already headed for the concert stage? Of eight already working formulas in their heads that staggered their parents? And athletes. They made it young or not at all. (His mind veered unwillingly to Edward.) But artists took time to develop. Where had he heard that? Why was music something one was a prodigy at and not art? Peg would have a theory—had probably offered one to which he'd only half listened—but he could recall none.

"What's happening?" The painter greeted Paul.

He held out his hand. "Paul Sinclair."

"I am the artist," Jaramillo said. Then, "You are staying in my house," in Spanish. He had thick dark hair that kept falling in his face, and his eyes were almost black.

"For which I'm grateful."

"Have you seen Rosa?"

"She was looking for you."

"Your mother," the boy cursed. "She only wants to be in bed. If I go off to paint, she sulks. I told her I would not be here."

"She may be inside."

"No, she has gone."

Paul decided they must spend a lot of time missing one another. "She'll be back."

"Who knows?"

Paul started downhill, headed for the house with the white pig.

"Forget this, taking snapshots," Jaramillo called. "Come inside. I'll show you my paintings."

"In a minute." Paul took a step away.

"I am very good. One day I will be famous."

"So they tell me."

"It is true."

Paul looked at the cocky boy, deciding that was why he went by a single name in a country where everyone had both father's name and mother's to carry.

Just then Helena came up the street toward him. "Paul, where have you been?"

He wanted very much to take her picture, waving in that way, the sunlight falling on her hair.

"Jean said she lost you. That one minute the three of you were talking, and the next you had vanished. She is making lunch for us. I bought some Oaxaca cheese. She will make us some fine chili con queso." She took his arm and gave it a squeeze, as if she had been looking for him and was glad to have found him.

"Am I invited?" Jaramillo asked, not serious.

"No, Tomás. You had better find your Rosa, before someone else finds her first." She made the sign of horns with two
fingers held up to her forehead.

"Shove your mother," he grumbled, turning away.

"Watch your tongue," Helena scolded. "Go back to your
hens."

The painter took off toward the square, loping in flopping
tennis shoes, not bothered in the least by the stones.

"What are you doing with your camera?" Helena looked
amused.

"Nothing, really. I promised my younger son—" Paul
let the Polaroid dangle from the strap around his wrist, glad
that he had not been caught taking half a dozen shots of
chickens. He felt that he had behaved foolishly, somewhat in
the manner of a boy off at camp. The first minute the coun-
selors let him out of their sight he'd run to eat (how like
Charles he was at heart) and then headed back to his cabin
to write a letter home.

"Did everyone pose for you?" Helena asked.

He nodded, slightly embarrassed.

Laughing, she said, "They love the limelight. The lame
will hobble out in their serapes and the bedridden wrapped
in their blankets at the first click of a shutter a block away.
That's part of the problem of studying a *bypassed* village."

9 A LETTER HOME

DEAR PEG,

I thought you should have an address and phone number. Not that Dad won't outlive us all, and I certainly don't foresee any trouble, but here they are, for good measure. I am staying, with an economist from California, in the house of a local artist. Our address, and apparently nothing further is needed, is

19 Calle 22 Febrero, Tepoztlán, Mexico.

There is no phone here. This is a small mountain village. Imagine Taos fifty years ago. The number I am providing you is at an old inn, quite elegant, used almost entirely by tourists from Mexico City and Cuernavaca. I have alerted them that I am here and given them my address. That number is:

011-52731-5-06-40.

I am having no trouble with the food, although I am playing it safe and drinking bottled water, or with the altitude. I have been told to watch out for scorpions, although I associate them more with drier climates, and have not seen insects or bugs of any sort since my arrival.

* * *

I was briefed on my assignment by Dr. Guttman this morning. My legal advice seems, I infer, fairly pro forma, with no real problems or the anticipation of them. I suspect my presence and that of Nakae Takamori, my fellow addition to the project, are more to satisfy the paper work requirements of tax-free grants than to contribute actual content.

Primarily, Dr. Guttman and Dr. Weaver are, as near as I can learn, duplicating Oscar Lewis's studies, but with the goal of reevaluating them from a female perspective, something, I'm sure, which is being done in many field-work studies.

The streets here are named for the dates of famous Mexican victories, most of them minor skirmishes in wars they later lost. Ours commemorates the death of a leader. The economist says that the Mexicans are like the Japanese: they prefer their heroes defeated. I'm enclosing a few snapshots of some of our "neighbors" on the street.

I hope this has not been too difficult for you. Has even, perhaps, been something of a relief.

Paul

Tepoztlán
August 31

P.S. I sent a message to Charles at the office, not wanting him to take my leaving too hard. If he has not heard from Trice, would you please follow up on that? And, also, could you send me a couple of suits, middleweight, at least one with a vest, as I have been asked to wear street clothes here?

I DON'T KNOW, Fan. I don't. You can read his letter. Here, I brought it. Maybe you can read between the lines. I can't."

Peggy was having supper with Fan Fowler, her best friend. Mew was there, too, for support. Fan, a grass widow (whose ex had died and made her a true widow), and Mew Morris, their doctor and friend, who had lost his wife some years back, kept steady company. They were a couple and always invited together. Peggy knew that they both enjoyed being a twosome for dinners and parties but were glad enough to let it go at that.

She supposed if you had had a bad time with someone, for whatever reasons—alcohol, as in Fan's case, or ill health, as in Mew's, and that must be worse if you were a doctor and felt totally responsible—there must be relief in being able to go home and close the door and sink into a hot tub or light up a big cigar, respectively, and think your own thoughts.

She wondered if that was how Paul felt: that he had reached a point when he needed to get off by himself. But then, a team of social scientists in a Mexican village was hardly off or alone either for that matter. Although maybe it was, in a personal sense. The same way Mew had his practice, which kept him with people from morning to night, and Fan had her craft shop, which, with Christmas only three months away, was massed already with shoppers not wanting to miss out on the fine embroidered coverlets, or stuffed hen doorstops or china pig canisters, all handmade by Virginia artisans and beloved as gifts. All wrapped in Fan's special hen paper, which she designed herself and changed four times a year. So that the little yellow hens would be wearing new Easter hats or football mums or New Year's Eve party hats, or, her biggest season and her special wrap, in Santa suits or (last year) dragging tiny green fir trees behind them, tucked under one wing.

Peggy had not seen this year's wrap, but it should be ready soon. Here it was the first weekend after Labor Day, and everyone in Albemarle County would be flocking to Fowler's Fancies, lists in hand, starting on the old aunties and kissing cousins, wanting to get the Sunday School teachers and Sewing Club friends and such as that checked off before starting on the immediate family. Those could wait, and had to, since children especially were full of last-minute wants.

She watched Fan read Paul's letter and pass it on to Mew, shaking her head. She had already shown them both the awful announcement letter, left on her pillow ten days before, such a dreadful thing to come back to from the Open. Thinking all the way home that something had happened to Paul. The boys had taken it hard. Edward said he had got a "bummer of a note," but he did not share it with her, and now he was gone again, trying to get a circuit lined up for next year, get his tennis in order before he went back to North Carolina. Charles, distraught at first, had been almost chipper since Trice called him in. She would get the secretary something nice, a little gift, for the way she handled the situation. What she did for Charles no amount of money could buy, and Peggy only wished that someone would come along who could do the same for Edward. Fan and Mew would, she knew, if they could, but she had shared none of that with them, respecting her elder son's silence.

What on earth could have possessed Paul to run off the way he had? It was an act of cowardice, as he himself admitted in that first note. But Paul, of all people, ought to know that admitting something didn't make it all right. Wasn't he the lawyer? A client couldn't confess embezzlement and have that absolve him of his actions, now could he?

"I don't know," Peggy said, in answer to Fan's asking what did she think. "It doesn't sound like Paul at all. And he enclosed six pictures of"—she was afraid she might tune up and cry with the frustration of it, the frustration of having no idea what was going on—"these chickens!" She passed the bright Polaroid shots along to Fan.

"If it were a spy story, I'd think that he had hidden a clue for you. Enlarge them and there would be a map of the safe house. Or a coded message about the plans for the bird colonel's bathroom in the Pentagon."

"I'm afraid they're just chickens."

"I think you're right. Maybe he's having a mid-life crisis?"

Mew, who was older than Paul, tsked at her. "Why can't you girls take him at his word? He's gone down to help the third world, good old liberal that he is, and get it out of his system. When he sees they don't want his help, he'll be back soon enough. You can hardly expect him to join the Peace Corps; that wouldn't be his style. Or quite get up his nerve— Peg, honey, I'm not picking on your man, you know that, just trying to get you to see it in perspective—to go over there to Africa where it's hopeless and ghastly and you know full well that nothing is growing in the ground, and until it does this next Good-Samaritan planeload of Purina is just a drop in the pot. Paul isn't very good, and I don't mean that personally, none of us are, we're all ostriches, everyone is if he can be, about facing something hopeless. Mark my words, when he gets back he'll be happy as a hound let in by the fire to be here. There's nothing like a sniff of the cold wind of the outside world to change a man's politics."

"A family isn't like a job," Peggy argued. "You can take a junior year abroad, if you're in college, or go clerk for a year, if you're just out of law school, or, later, take a turn on the bench, and then go back to the firm, and everyone is delighted. They get the benefit of your experience. But you can't do that with a family, Mew. Can you?"

Fan clucked sympathetically. "Tell her what she's asking: has he left her?"

Mew turned the letter over, then handed it back to Peggy. "Man to man?"

"Man to man."

"Straight from the shoulder?"

"Straight from the shoulder."

"That is the letter of a man who is stalling. He's keeping matters noncommittal until something. Until they serve you the papers. Until he gets over his little affair. Until he figures out what to do with the corpse he's left in Trice's garage."

Mew was kind. He had answered her, but the way he put it, Peggy couldn't do much but laugh. Having it out in the open that his hunch was the same as hers relaxed her. "Maybe I'll have another sherry," she said to Fan. "It's warming me all the way down, and I admit I got a chill reading that. 'The number I'm providing you is at an old inn.' 'Could you

send a couple of suits?' The nerve." She tucked her feet up
under her on Fan's deep white sofa. Just saying the words
aloud cheered her.

She had worn a long-sleeved, shirred taffeta dress, much
too fancy for Saturday night with just the three of them.
Brand-new, deep green, with the new shoulders that made
her feel like a halfback. She'd worn a faux emerald choker
and done her hair high in the front. She knew they wouldn't
care, old friends, if she came in a ballgown or nightgown or
garden clothes, whatever made her feel better. But she'd
come in the mood to be festive and drink a little and tell
funny stories about their not-too-close friends.

"You can have all you want," Fan said, refilling the heavy
wineglass which had been her grandmother's. "It's just us
chickens." She laughed at her joke.

"Paul wouldn't mind if he were here. He doesn't mind if
I drink."

"Certainly not." Fan made a small face. "He never
creases his high brow when you ask for a second. Or gets
up and takes a stroll when anyone pours a double on the
rocks. Not your man."

But Peggy didn't want to dump on him, like a jilted wife.
Paul was Paul, and she loved him dearly. She liked his
serious manner, his abstinence from any and everything that
he found self-destructive. She knew from living with him
all these years that it contained, at its most hidden depth, a
fear that he would do himself harm, defeat himself, and she
respected that. Besides, it was no longer strange for him not
to drink; after all, a good number of their friends had gone
through it and come out dried up and a good bit more self-
righteous than Paul.

"Ummm, that smells wonderful." Peggy leaned back into
the deep upholstery, letting the anticipation of one of Fan's

famous meals soothe her. She was in the mood for a feast.
She would have some of everything, the corn pudding, but-
tery rolls, some of those vegetables that Fan did with the
special spicy purées, a big hunk of the pork loin that was
roasting, and all, every bite, of whatever gooey dessert was
in store.

Then she would go home, alone, and face up to what she
must do. Sometimes at two in the morning, while Paul slept,
she got up and wandered the house, settling something that
was troubling her. It was a habit she had got from her dad.
Ned Ruggles was a night owl and could frequently be found
in his study, having a glass of milk, computing something on
a yellow pad—not a problem in the usual sense, but a personal problem, a career problem. She had acquired the habit
at home. And, like him, wore an old velour bathrobe, a
man's, ruby red, and, like him, woke the next morning as
fresh as if she hadn't taken a big bite out of her night.

At home she would have her bath and then get out her pen
and pad and see what she could come up with. What clues
Paul had dropped that she had missed. But for now, she was
going to have a relaxed, wholly pampered evening.

"The pork"—Fan came in from checking on her meal—
"will melt in your mouth. I cooked it with plums and pars-
nips and wine and garlic and cumin, and have been boiling
down the stock. It's sublime. The smell, anyway. The perfume is the thing. That's the secret of cooking, you know."

Peggy's longtime friend scooted her chair close to Mew's
and held out her hand to him. They were both such elegant
people, tall and big-boned, with the big jaws and deep-set
eyes of horse people. They didn't raise horses, either of
them, but they looked as if they did. Both had had such
lousy marriages, to such weak people, and borne up under
them with such resilience, even growing sturdier for it, the

way carrying something uphill builds your muscles. Peggy liked them both a lot. Mew had grown children, off somewhere in the West, making money, he liked to say, but Fan had none. That part was sad.

Peggy sipped her sherry and let out a contented sigh. Charles was with his grandfather for the night; she did not have to watch the clock. "Tell me some gossip," she begged. "Something juicy. Something so scandalous that I won't believe a word of it."

"Do you worry that this business with Paul is making the rounds?"

"How could it not? I don't care especially. Buzz, buzz, buzz. It's what to do about it myself."

"Have you talked to Spence?"

"Yes. I went by the rectory yesterday. He had a minute, and I told him what there was to tell, which isn't much. He said he would pray for me. I said, 'Pray for Paul.' Spence is a good man, but how can he really help if his goal is that of official soother? I see him endlessly calming us when sometimes he should be alarming us."

"That's his function, to be the shepherd."

"Oh, come, Fan. Sometimes the shepherd has to shout, 'Look out for the wolf.'" Although Peggy liked Spencer Cox, she didn't consider she had to feel reverence toward him. But there wasn't any point in going on about it. Fan never liked to hear a bad word about Spence, and Mew preferred his own brand of irreverence. Besides, Peggy didn't want an earnest analysis of the role of the clergy. What she had wanted from Spence, she got: a proper conversation, so that when he heard about her and Paul from someone else, as he surely would, he'd have prepared words on the matter. The Right Reverend Spencer Cox would provide a very firm party line, and for that she was, truly, grateful.

"Something juicy," she said again, to Mew.

"Let me see." He began a tale. "I shouldn't talk out of school, but this is too good to keep under my hat. Girls, if you promise."

"Cross my heart."

"Sealed lips?"

"Sealed lips."

"It concerns someone we all know *well*—" Mew took a slow sip and gazed out the window. He was about to enjoy himself, being one of the greatest and most ruthless gossips that Tidewater Virginia had ever produced. He often didn't have much of a story, but he could embellish it, give it a wicked twist. Peggy was sure that was half of what Fan found irresistible about him, because Fan, by contrast, was unable to see the most obvious situation right beneath her nose. "If it was a bear, it would have bitten you" was invented for Fan. An attitude that made her a perfect foil for Mew, and the two of them a constant pleasure to be with.

As Peggy listened to his story, she admitted that she never had quite such a good time when Paul was with her. Although he tried to be a good sport, the seams of his effort frequently showed, putting a damper on the evening the four of them spent together. More than once Peggy had explained to him that Mew was not being either spiteful or, in Paul's eyes worse, trivial. That both he and Fan, because of their early bad times, found it fun to be out and not have to worry about possible public scenes or later recriminations. Besides, she argued, Mew was a doctor at the med school; he dealt with the worst of the worst all day long. It was enough for him to be around people who weren't sick. He liked well people; he liked them a lot. They didn't have to be deep or have the right politics or even, as Mew liked to say, good sense. All they had to be was doing fine.

But Peggy knew there was more to it than that. It wasn't just Paul who would have changed the evening; Mew would have been different, competitive, if any other man were here.

Men were different from women. She couldn't imagine living the way men did. Women had a lot of friends; that was how they operated. They needed a lot from and gave a lot to each other. Men had the other men they learned from. Paul had had Sturdivant and Postewaite. Edward had his coaches. Charles had his grandfather. Even her dad had his generals. Having it handed on to you, then handing it on. Just being friends, with no hierarchy, didn't seem to happen with men.

Mew refreshed her drink, and his, and began another story. "There's a tidbit of scandal I shouldn't be mentioning, but likely it will cheer you up. It concerns none other than our most upright, uptight—" He stopped midsentence when the phone rang, turning to Fan. "I'm not here. No matter who it is, I'm not here."

"They like to catch you on an empty stomach," Fan told him, getting up to answer it in the kitchen.

"Will it be for you? I thought you weren't on call."

"I devoutly hope not."

"Me, too." Peggy smiled at him.

"You're looking mighty pretty."

"Thank you, Mew."

"You going to be all right?"

"I seem to be mostly angry."

"Small wonder."

"If it were just me—"

"How's my godson?"

"With his grandfather. Pink thinks Paul is away on business. But he's glad for any excuse to have Charles. And the feeling is mutual. I told him he could stay all weekend. They need one another at this time in their lives."

Fan stuck her head in the door. "It's Edward."

"Is anything wrong?"

"No, no, it's fine. I told him if it was going to be bad news, you weren't here."

"Thanks." Peggy got up. She was glad to hear from Edward. Her heart had been aching for him. She knew that although he went around seeming totally unfazed, he was keeping a lot of hurt inside. That was the difference between the two boys: everyone who passed Charles was going to know he needed a hug, but Edward did not let that show.

"I asked him"—Fan followed her to the phone—"how did he know you were here. He said, 'Where else would she be?' "

"Edward?"

"Hi, Mom."

"Where are you?"

"Home."

"Here? How nice. Are you by yourself?"

"As a matter of fact, I've got this friend of mine from school, Baxter. He's on the tennis team. His dad's with him. I ran into them, and they said they were coming to Charlottesville. His dad went here or something. I said I'd come with them."

"Can they stay with us?"

"I already asked them. They're here."

"There are clean sheets in the guest room, I'm sure." Peggy looked at Fan, raising her eyes in a question.

"The thing is," Edward was saying, "Baxter's dad wanted to take us out to eat—"

Peggy said, "Oh?" and then, "Hold on a minute."

"How many?" Fan asked.

Peggy held up three fingers.

"Tell him I'll do the loaves and fishes."

"Fan says she has plenty. Why don't you all come here?"

"You sure?"

"When you smell this roast, you'll see why I don't want to leave."

"You want us just to walk down?"

"Tell me their names, a little something about them, can you?"

"I told you: Baxter and his dad. Their name's Stedman. His dad said to tell you—"

Peggy listened and then hung up the phone. "Thanks," she said to Fan.

"Six is as easy as three when one's my godson. I thought he was off somewhere?"

"He was in Washington, playing a match and trying to set up a tour. This boy who's with him is apparently a friend from school."

"What's the frown? It's a treat for me. Edward hasn't been in this house for a meal since last Easter, I do believe. Can that be right?"

Peggy went back over what Edward had said. "The strangest thing . . ."

"What?"

"Edward said that the boy's father told him, 'Maybe your mother could use a little company.' "

"Edward must have mentioned that Paul was gone."

"No. He said Mr. Stedman already knew about the Mexico trip." Peggy stared at her friend, then flung her arms around her neck. "Oh, Fan, what if he's come to tell me something?"

II A LETTER TO TEPOZTLÁN

Charlottesville
September 7

D EAR PAUL,

How interesting to get the photos of the chickens. I assume you wanted me to identify them for you. I've made small numbers on the lower left corners—ink tends to slide off the Polaroids—and here is the key. I imagine that the breeds are somewhat different, but this will give you a rough identification.

1. NEW HAMPSHIRE ROOSTER.
2. DARK CORNISH ROOSTER *(the iridescent are Cornish, although he looks larger than we find here.)*
3. WYANDOTTE HEN *(I think).*
4. SUSSEX ROOSTER *(I think).*
5. *I don't know this. It looks a little like the Buff Orpington mixed with a Rhode Island Red. Maybe a local hybrid?*
6. *This is a hybrid, too, primarily a layer, and probably highly inbred.*

Would you like me to send you some books? I'm sure the local poultry and produce shop will have a catalogue.

Yesterday Edward and I had dinner at Fan and Mew's with an old Princeton classmate of yours, a man named Todd Stedman, and his son, Baxter. A nice boy. It was a marvel to get so much news about your project from such an unexpected source! Todd said that in fact—small world, amazing coincidence—he had given your name to Dr. Guttman when she and her colleague were searching for two men to bring in for their controlled study. He said they must have screened over a thousand names before they found who they were looking for.

I was very interested in the whole project, especially the idea that women, gay women, would perceive and be informed of a lot of material which standard men in the field had not, and that they could go over the same information and interpret it in a different way.

Todd is coming back next weekend, and we are planning to have dinner out and go to church, then see the boys off to school. To tell the truth, I'm excited to be seeing someone, even in this capacity, and to have the chance to learn more about your anthropologists.

I don't mean to fuss by mail, but the suddenness of all this wasn't the easiest thing in the world. Charles did all right, once your Sue Trice called him in and they had their talk, which I didn't pry into. But Edward has really had a dreadful week. He's like my dad—it doesn't show on the outside, but it's eating him up on the inside. I hope that whatever you said to him—he only mentioned that you'd left him a "bummer of a note"—you'll patch it up before long.

In order not to have things too awkward here, I talked to Spence, and we agreed that he would simply tell people when they asked, which, of course, they will, that you and I were separated, with no immediate plans to make it legal. If that is not true, if you intend this to be more final than you've indicated, please tell me, Paul. I know it's your way to let things happen, and that works out fine for you in your office, where most problems solve themselves by default, but I hope very much that I am not going to hear second-hand that you are planning to stay or are living with some-one else.

I have to say it was *quite* painful to get your letter, which sounded as if it had been written by someone on the square in Mexico City. (Remember them? The men with type-writers at outside tables who would write your business or personal letter for you for a quarter?) I had hoped to get at least a snapshot of where you were living, to see if it looked like that little hotel where we stayed, with all the bougain-villea and the shutters that kept out the midday sun. (How beautiful that was!)

I can only think you are staying somewhere that I am not supposed to know about and that there is something you're keeping from me.

I know it sounds stupid to say to someone who has left you, that he's keeping something from you, but that's how it feels.

It hurt a lot to find out so much from a total stranger—not that Todd is really a stranger, since Baxter is a friend of Edward's, and he knew you when, and knows the couple who hired you, but still, I kept saying to him, "Oh, I didn't know that," "I didn't know that," and that made me feel at first shut out and then very angry.

Todd said that you were like that in school, acting out of something in your own head, and again I felt that here was someone who hadn't seen you in over twenty-five years who knew you better than I did.

I think it would be easier if we didn't write anymore. I guess it's pretty obvious that I'm upset, and this is only making it worse. It's the contrast, in part. We had such a wonderful time last evening, the six of us. I haven't seen Edward so relaxed in years. He reminded me very much of my dad, young pictures of him at least. Mew told all his unsavory stories, and Todd, who is an architect, told funny tales about people fussing over zoning. He's a big man, who looks like a former football player—perhaps he was?—you know the way they get heavy in their chests and around their jaws, and Mew, of course, is big. It was something of a sparring match. I think the boys had a good time, listening to grown men compete, with them not having anything to do but sit back and get a little flattery and a lot of Fan's good food. You know Fan. She had some sort of sponge cake with a custard layer and a chocolate cream layer and then chocolate-laced whipped cream on top. And I needed every calorie of the meal and every minute of the laughing.

How could I not have known how bad things were? Paul, how could you not have told me?

I thought we were so happy, our fights good for us both. Isn't that what wives are supposed to say? And it's true; I had no idea. I've heard women say that and thought, But of course you would know, if it happened to you.

I think it would be good if the boys spent Christmas with you, but I won't send Charles unless Edward is also invited. Unless you patch things up with him. Christmas in Mexico is supposed to be splendid—no, it's Epiphany, isn't it?—really marvelous in the little villages. (Remember, when we were there, everyone said we should have come later, after the rainy season?)

If you write again, I'll give the letter to Trice to answer. Right now I'm going to get out my pad (I'm in my robe) and sort this out.

Peggy

P.S. I'm sure you can find a tailor in one of the nearby cities, surely Cuernavaca?, who can take care of your need for additional clothes.

12 THE JAPANESE

It is a matter of shame, Sinclair."

Nakae was dressed and ready to go, waiting for Paul, who was shaving at their tile sink and trying to come awake. The Japanese wore the wide pants, sandals, and collarless loose shirt of the locals. Paul assumed that his dressing in this way was part of the anthropologists' assignment, just as Paul was confined to his out-of-place business suit.

"Matter of shame?" Paul toweled his face dry and finished the thick black coffee that Rosa left for him outside the door in the mornings. (The third day here, Nakae, seizing upon the North American's groggy state, had said, "I will find out how Tomás has coffee in the morning. I have seen him drinking on the patio. Perhaps Rosa will bring it to you. The painter is a lucky man.")

Nakae, who always seemed to have an excess of energy and bustled about in half a dozen different directions with a dozen projects, had begun their morning with a continuation of last night's conversation. In the ten days since his arrival, Paul had received at least an hour a night's disquisition on some matter pertaining to the village or its people. Nakae had taken his friend's education upon himself and was doing a thorough job. At first Paul had felt awkward, talking from their adjoining cots in the dark of their whitewashed bedroom. He'd had no experience with it. He and Peg had said little more than good-night in their bedroom. If they sat talking, it was usually in the study, with the door closed so the boys couldn't hear, or else it was in the driveway, with the motor idling, finishing up some subject after an evening out. In the bedroom, if they were not going to make love, there was a slight constraint, a hesitation, almost a formality, as if even a casual word might have implications.

But Paul had got used to Takamori's stream of words, the bits of history, catalogues of facts, and, as now, sweeping generalizations that he was pressing on his new acquaintance.

"Here they do not share the passion of your country or mine for order and detail. They have no interest in our economic planning or our legal expertise. You will see for yourself that your trip to save the Mexican is unnecessary; you have come to free a pardoned man."

Paul slipped his tie over his head and pulled the knot tight against his collar. He put on his slightly rumpled suit jacket.

His roommate nudged him. "Sinclair?"

"You were talking of national character."

"Let me tell you a story."

Paul ducked under the doorway. "I'm listening."

They crossed the yard and stepped out into veintidós de febrero. Nakae was, if anything, less sure-footed on the rough cobblestones than Paul. The Japanese seemed to hesitate before each step, then thrust his body forward, do or die.

The street was already crowded, with everyone carrying something for the Sábado Market. Women had fresh flowers or fruit in big baskets on their heads. Children with buckets from the well stopped to pose in case Paul had his camera.

"My ancestors," Nakae continued, "on the island of Kyushu in the sixteenth century, received the European missionaries with distrust and cruelty. They tortured them because they feared them. My father, growing up, fed on the legends of the brave Jesuits who died—scalded, burned, flung chained into the sea—was shamed for his nation. When he came to Mexico, he was already a man of forty-three, expert in the bonzai art and love. He worked for the North American heiress. But after two years he fell under another spell, more potent than hers: that of the Catholic Church. He converted because he had found a religion that took his shame and carried it for him. That is the reason they make it a most serious sin to take your own life; if you were permitted or, as in my country, even expected to do so, there would be no need for the church. Where you cannot end your shame in an honorable fashion, someone must take it from you. That is the church's hold on its people—beside which our offers of self-improvement are of little interest."

Nakae stumbled along, trying to keep up with Paul on the rough street that looked like a dry stream bed.

Paul nodded to show that he was paying attention.

"When I was young, Sinclair, I desired to understand my father. Now I am his age, I wish instead to understand this country. That is because Mexico is a glass which shows me another view of the past. The Mexicans and the Japanese have much in common. In their origins they are both Eastern peoples. Their memories and their history go back a very long way. Here, as in my country, the man struts about claiming that he is the master, but everyone knows that in

the home it is the woman who rules. We revere our mothers
and do not know our fathers. I believe that if Japan had not
banished the Portuguese priests and closed its doors for
three hundred years, it would be the Mexico of today. In the
same way, if Mexico had not allowed the Spanish church-
men to impose their language and their cross, it might now
be the world's Japan. There are many similarities between
our two countries. It is something to consider."

"I will do so," Paul promised his talkative friend.

At the corner of cinco de mayo, he glanced toward
Helena's office. If he was not to be with her this Saturday,
at least, he thought, he was not being handed over again to
Jean Weaver, with her grim tales of husbands duped and
drugged.

"How are you progressing?" Nakae asked, as they
crossed to the little café south of the square, where Paul had
first had breakfast with Helena only a week ago.

"All I have done so far is to get the four of us invited to
Dr. Gómez's house for Sunday dinner."

"Tomorrow?"

"Next week."

They continued their conversation over rolls and coffee.

"He has a very beautiful wife, Segundo Gómez," Nakae
said. "Her father was a German so that she has the looks
of two countries."

Paul shook his head. "You know them all." He pulled his
chair around to face the square.

"I enjoy the conversation of pretty women, don't you? In
Japan we have bars with many hostesses who like to talk
with the patrons, as they do here in the cantinas. It's too bad
you and I are stuck with the chicken patrol."

Young men and boys poured out into the square, dressed
in elaborate feather headdresses, leather loincloths, and

necklaces with dangling metal moons. They were dragging a huge replica of a pyramid, made, it appeared, from papier-mâché, on which was painted a giant Aztec serpent. Several of the boys knelt and pressed their foreheads against the snake while others shook rattles and stamped their feet to jangle the bells around their ankles.

"They will dance tomorrow," Nakae told him. "This is the celebration of the old god's return. Originally, Tepoztlán was famous for the cult of Ometochtli—two rabbits—the god who invented pulque. It was considered a great privilege to participate in the festival, the orgies, in his name. Later the god was called El Tepozteco, for the village, and when the church came in, the villagers pretended he converted, to appease the Spanish. But one of the first acts of the Dominican friars was to destroy the great image of Ometochtli which sat at the top of the mountain, there—" He pointed in front of them, to the north. "He could be seen by all eight villages in this area. The priests thought that when the idol crumbled, the people would see that he was false. But when they pushed if off and it tumbled down the cliffs, making a great noise, darkening the sky, and sending the birds shrieking through the forest, Ometochtli's image did not crack. It did not even chip. The priests had to break it apart with hammers. Now, each year, when he returns in the form of El Tepozteco, the people think that this year he will take his revenge. Tonight we will see for ourselves when we climb the stairway of the pyramid."

Paul watched the dancers with interest. He saw that Tomás was among them, brilliantly dressed and exaggerating his movements, completely into his role. Perhaps he was already painting the ceremony in his mind, starring himself as the god, with the serpent come to life and clutched in the claws of the feathered bird: Mexico's symbol. "I am looking forward to the climb," Paul said truthfully, tired of being on the sidelines.

He finished his coffee, which he had learned to drink slowly and with milk. (He had worried that the milk, unpasteurized he was sure, was as bad as the water, but Helena said no, a little in the coffee would not hurt.) His impression, which he suspected was bad science, was that any bacteria that fell into the mug of barely strained caffeine were not going to make it out alive anyway. The taste of it was a daily disappointment, because the fragrance of the fresh beans poured—as did the smell of hot, sweet bread—from the doorway of every café around the square. That, and the ever-present odor of corn, which he had come both to like and to abhor, meant the olfactory had taken over the visual as his first impression on reaching the intersection of veintidós de febrero and cinco de mayo each day.

Nakae finished his hard roll. "We must go," he said, rising. "Avelino is waiting for us."

Paul left coins and two folded bills—paper money, Monopoly money—on the table. Although he had learned to divide by five hundred to get the North American dollar equivalent, after ten days he was getting a feel for the currency on its own terms. His memory, which he would like to have checked with Peg, was that on their trip to the capital twelve years before, they had divided only by ten. Could that be true, such a rate of inflation?

"Have you thought, Sinclair," Nakae asked as they walked out into the sun's glare, "that perhaps we have not been told the real purpose we are here?"

"Other than to inform on the two men assigned us?"

"Yes."

"Tell me what you think."

"How easy is it to put the horns on? That is what the female doctors wish to know. Perhaps we are to find out for ourselves." He looked at Paul slyly.

Paul shook his head. "I hardly think so." He rejected out of hand the idea that he and Nakae were themselves being watched. He put it down to Takamori's voyeurism; it was coloring his thinking. "You are daydreaming. Wishing yourself alone with Rosa."

"Perhaps. But my suspicion is that in such projects it is not easy to determine who is the true subject."

Back out on the street, Paul looked around in the hope that Helena might beckon him to her office. He had not yet found a pattern as to when he was to report to her. The professional parameters were as unclear as the social. He never knew if he was to have supper with her and Jean Weaver or, if so, whether they would eat out or cook in, whether they would also include Nakae or, sometimes, Esperanza, although never the chicken farmer. Two nights he had found himself completely alone, the town dark, very dark as there were no streetlights, without the sight or sound of anyone, and had walked back to the inn—wishing, each time, that just once Helena could be at his side.

He and Nakae passed Segundo Gómez's office, in the part of the block crowded with practitioners and apothecaries, all with signs that proclaimed an instant end to miseries of all sorts. Besides the standard cures for insomnia, nerves, vomiting, diarrhea, here were found those promising to help you out in bed: *polvo matrimonial*, so that "it won't dip on you," *polvo agotamiento*, "to get it up again and again." Other signs offered salves and ointments for the women, many with the suggestion that stronger potions could be purchased. (The dread toloache no doubt.)

Paul felt disgust as he watched men gathering in the doorways, waving in greeting, shouting insults, all holding up the perpetual two fingers to the brow. Is that all they ever thought about here, cuckoldry?

And sweets?

Every child he saw not carrying a bucket, basket, or brace of hens was licking a Popsicle, sucking a hard candy, slurping an atole, tonguing a dripping gelato, fingering a fresh sugary crumb.

The whole crowd, blatant and willful hedonists all, closed in on him. Nakae was right: they did not want his North American notion of progress. And, he flushed and quickened his step, why should they? It was a sunny Saturday, the day of a fine, favorite festival, and no one seemed aware of hardship or hunger, no one seemed in any way conscious that the lot of them were going nowhere. A happy crowd, eating, drinking, jostling one another, winking and making gestures. Who was Paul to pull a Puritan face?

He suspected Peg would suggest that he was thinking of himself, worried that there was no place for him here. What had he come to do? Feed the hungry? The state was taking care of them, giving oil and corn to everyone. Bind their wounds? But surely the church was doing that. Nakae was right; he was wasting his time.

Trying to cheer himself, he thought of Peg getting his letter, possibly today, laughing over the chickens, selecting a couple of suits with vests to send him, adding, thoughtfully, a tie or two, a few shirts. A note with news of his dad. A show of interest in his adventures. If nothing had come from her by midweek, he would check at the inn, in case she had sent his things there.

Turning on calle dieciséis de septiembre, the street where Helena's sausage shop was, they walked to avenida revolución 1910, which bordered the square on the north. They passed the old convent yard, already filling with crowds, families from the seven barrios, dressed up for the festival, standing, old and young, in the shelter of the great, gnarled ciruelo trees, which looked as old as the church.

Around the corner, they stepped through an open doorway into a noisy room filled with half a dozen chicken cages.

"So soon?" Avelino Álvarez said. "I am selling." But he went in the back and came out with a sign much like the one Helena had put out that first morning, saying back soon—although Paul knew from Nakae that it was a half hour's ride each way to the breeding coops, and certainly at least another hour would be spent there.

Appearing with him from the back was Rosa, in a much-embroidered blouse and full skirt. She looked less angry than she usually did in the house on veintidós de febrero, but when she saw that it was only Paul and Nakae, her face fell back into its customary sulk.

"When will you be back?" she asked Avelino.

"Who knows?" he said.

"Bring Tomás with you."

"If he is there."

"If he is not there, it is because it stinks."

"My chickens do not stink." Avelino had a big stomach that hung over his rope-tied pants. His loud manner offended Paul, who had met him two days earlier. He could not imagine him with Esperanza. With distaste, he registered the evident pleasure with which the merchant watched Rosa slowly exit out the darkened doorway, into the crowd.

Avelino, catching his glance, leered at Paul. "The blond woman likes you, I hear. But I have my own hands full."

Son of a whore, Paul thought, longing to break his fat neck.

"My friend Álvarez," Nakae murmured, "was having a siesta in good company?"

"She was looking for her husband."

"In your storeroom?"

Paul told him, "We saw Tomás with the dancers."

"It is possible." Avelino shrugged.

Nakae bustled the other men out into the street and guided Avelino in locking the shop.

Paul gathered himself together as they climbed into Avelino's truck, parked at the curb. The official story was that he was thinking of setting up a law practice in Tepoztlán—another version of the story he had given Gómez—and might want to invest in chickens on the side. The idea being that, annoyed but greedy at the North American's interest, Avelino might confide in Nakae.

"In Virginia, where I live in the States," Paul made an effort to get started with his instructions, "fryers are big business. I own part interest in a fertile egg distributorship."

"What do you mean, fertile eggs?" Avelino shook his head and looked questioningly at Nakae. It was evident the phrase meant nothing to him. Perhaps all eggs in Mexico were fertile. (Dropping small red half chicks, as sometimes happened on the farm, in your skillet?)

"We raise eggs." Paul tried again. It was absurd. He did not have the words in either language to make even a pretense of being knowledgeable about hatching chickens. "Layers?" That was right. He could recall signs out in Albemarle County, advertising layers.

"We do not buy eggs," Avelino told him. The fat man took up half the cab of the truck. "We do not want them."

Paul had the urge to smash the greasy man in the face

but held himself in check. What had he expected? That Álvarez was going to say, "Gracious señor, please invest your North American money in my hens?"

"We buy chicks from Acapulco and Tabasco. They are sold before they lay. That way we do not have to worry with the eggs, which are great trouble and expense." He wheeled out of town along a packed dirt road. On the mountain side the fields were covered in corn; on the valley side, with dairy cattle.

"I see," Paul said. Not understanding at all how it was possible to be in the poultry business and have no eggs.

"Bees are also a business here." Nakae, ever the guide, pointed to the clusters of hives that dotted the cow fields like bales of hay.

After a good half hour, Avelino pulled across the road and stopped at an immense metal gate, electrically wired, which looked as if it could be the entrance to Sing Sing. He pushed a button which rang a loud buzzer off across a muddy field, somewhere in a series of vast, low sheds.

Here, far outside the village, Paul could see the line of afternoon clouds building up over the monolithic rocks that crowned the mountains. In town each day he had been unprepared for the rain. Out in the sun, breathing the air with its special high-altitude dryness, he'd felt each time, when the rain suddenly began to fall in a steady mist from the still-blue sky, as if some god on the pyramid had overturned a sprinkler can on the village below. But the local people knew almost to the minute when the cooling showers would come, and right on schedule mothers gathered up children, men called to old fathers, those checking on the cornfields came in, and before Paul felt the first drop, everyone stood in the doorways, looking up.

Avelino rang the buzzer again. Finally, after a time, a

small man wandered over. "What's happening?" he said.

"Let us in." Avelino gestured.

The man opened the gate for them, waited while Avelino pulled his truck in and parked it as near the fence as possible, away from the ant beds, and then locked the gate behind them.

They sloshed through muddy ground to the door of the first shed, a large hangar-type building with wire on the sides, a tin roof, and half a dozen feeders and water tanks that looked like giant, overturned canisters, funneling their contents into long troughs. They operated, in a sense, exactly as did wild-bird feeders at home, turned upside down, the amount controlled; like the red sugar water in a hummingbird bubble or the chutes of mixed seeds for sparrows. But the similarity stopped there; here were more chickens than Paul could have imagined.

"How many?" he asked.

"Twenty-seven thousand here," Avelino answered, leading them into the passageway between the two halves of the shed, first being sure no chicken had strayed through the inside doors, where the caretaker's scratching yellow dog, nosing his way in, could find it and create pandemonium. "Twenty-two there." He pointed to the next shed. "Twenty in the old one." He gestured to the third. "More in here. This is a better coop. It has a lower roof, the lamps are lower, so it gets warmer. Not so many die."

"How many can you sell?" Paul tried to continue in his role, but the sight and smell of the thousands of chicks shoving, squawking, and pecking each other made him nauseated. What did they do with the ones that didn't live? Leave them in the cages until they swept out and hosed down after the last batch were sold?

"Maybe two-thirds. Who knows? We buy seventy thousand; we sell maybe fifty. Maybe forty-five. When they are all gone, we get some more. At the last, we sell them cheap, before they lay the eggs."

"No eggs." Paul shut his eyes as if calculating, so as not to see the sea of feathers and gristly, yellow clawed feet. "I'm more familiar with brood-hen layouts," he lied.

He was struggling to recall something about the chickens from his past. At his grandfather's farm, in the rolling farm-land east of Charlottesville toward Richmond, he had been to the henhouse. The caretaker and his wife kept a little brood, as they called it, and young Paul would go with Mr. Binder into the henhouse early in the morning when the sun was just up and his father still asleep. Mr. Binder would gently lift one by one the laying hens off their nests until he had a breakfast's worth of eggs.

The small house had no windows, only lamps, and the hens nested on graduated boards like spectators on bleachers at a ball game. Each plank was covered with a thick layer of fresh hay, and each hen's spot was her own, shaped by the weighted curve of her nestling bottom. "Upsy-daisy," Mr. Binder always said. "Come on now, Ada," or Bessie, or Lucy—they all had names—"here we go." And he would put one warm egg in each of Paul's small hands: fragile, still, amazing, smooth, brown and white, and mysteriously alive.

Out in the yard Paul sometimes spotted one lying on the ground and ran to get it, but Mr. Binder never took the outside eggs. "Roosters out here," he said. "No good eating them."

No eggs. Seventy thousand chickens and not one egg. It was pornographic, not to mention being incredibly short-sighted.

He made himself look at the chickens. They were all in that gangly stage right after they stop being round, yellow "Easter" chicks, when they've begun to lose the baby fuzz and get their first real feathers, and their necks stretch out and their beaks and feet poke out in adolescent clumsiness. It was as if you had devised an internment camp for children from the ages of five to twelve, so that you didn't have to mess with the unpleasant stages of either infancy or puberty. Get them when they're old enough to feed themselves; sell them before they're sexually mature. Lose a third, but what did that matter? It was cheaper than starting out with incubators, cheaper than separating the roosters from the laying hens.

He tried to get control of his panic. It was impotence, that was it. All the talk of horns, for over a week, and then the sight of thousands of birds and none of the hens going to lay here, none of the roosters going to crow.

"Excuse me," he said, and let himself out into the yard, finding it suddenly unbearable to be so long without a woman. The caretaker's weary yellow dog followed, having, like Paul, no better place to go.

13 PREPARATIONS

PAUL LEFT Nakae and the chicken farmer standing on the sidewalk of avenida revolución 1910.

"We must assemble at six," Nakae told him. "The ceremonies start at eight, and it is a two-hour climb. For us. Some of the men say they can run up in half an hour, but we will give ourselves plenty of time. There will be a big group; everyone comes to see the return of the old god. At the top there is a dance and speeches and drums and torches. You will see."

Paul promised to return to the square well before six. It was only four, and he wanted to get off by himself. His excuse was that he had to change his clothes for the climb. Surely, he thought, Helena did not expect him to go two thousand feet straight up the mountainside in a suit and tie.

The relief he felt on entering their cool, whitewashed room alone was overwhelming. He stretched out on the bed, his hands under his head, and shut his eyes. He didn't want to move. Nothing had been accomplished all day. It had been a foolish, frustrating trip, made the more disagreeable by his dislike for Avelino Álvarez. However, if his role as outsider was successful, then even at this moment Avelino was confiding to Nakae his sexual exploits, real or imagined.

Paul felt even more relieved to be spared that.

On the other side of the wall he could hear voices, murmurs. Probably it was Rosa and the painter, taking a siesta, although with the first light drops of rain the heat had passed. He listened, despite himself, as the voices grew louder. Rosa shouted; Tomás shouted back. It was clear they were having a fight. Their voices were accusing and heated. Paul got up. He didn't want to hear. Jealousy seized him. It was not that he coveted his neighbor's young wife, but rather that he coveted the fact that he had a wife with him. That he had a woman in his room and no one to disturb him.

Paul felt overcome with the need for sex. It wasn't only that he was sharing a room with Nakae, or that the painter and his Rosa had obviously begun to make noisy love, but that he felt caught in some awful schoolboy time warp where everyone talked of sex but no one got any.

How stupid, at his age, that he couldn't even give in to himself here on the bed, for fear that at any instant Nakae would barge in, say, "Sinclair, my friend, do you know why the Mexican is temperamentally suited to the raising of chickens? Let me tell you a story." And there Paul would be, feeling the way he had as a young man when his father came unannounced into his room, full of his Battle of Novgorod with all its intricate subplots.

He went into the bathroom, careful to remind himself he should be grateful for the commode that worked, the running water, and stripped and stood under the tepid shower that drained in the center of the tile floor. He and Nakae had been warned to take care; water was precious here in the mountains, drought always a fear. They were not to be fooled because they had come during the rainy season; for seven months of the year not a drop fell, and then even the livestock went thirsty. He did not disbelieve Helena, because he knew that much of the old religion had to do with praying for rain, but he did not understand it in his bones. It was a guidebook fact to him. He had not watched the skies all through the dry months; had not planted corn and wished fertility on every grain of it, seen it wilt and sag in caking ground.

Drought did not seem possible here in such a tropical world, where everything was green and blooming. Still, there was no grass, no sodded hillside and lawns such as he was used to in Virginia. Trees, he knew, drank deep, and vines, cut back, turned dormant. Flowers, after all, bloomed in the driest ground. Tepoztlán, as Helena had suggested, did resemble a Taos of half a century ago: a brilliant profusion of flowering vines and shrubs only minutes from the desert.

He shut off the water and dressed in a flannel shirt and heavy cords. The climb would be an adventure, and he was ready for it.

He was lacing his hiking boots when he felt eyes on him, and looked up to see, as once before, golden Helena standing in the doorway watching.

At that instant, her return on cue seemed no less reasonable or more amazing than the fact that every time he lifted a black box to his eyes a clucking, crowing, grunting, giggling barnyard of animals and playground of children materialized from out of nowhere.

Mexico rearranged your notion of cause and effect.

He knew it was foolish, but his first thought was that he should have put his boots back on yesterday or the day before, in order to make her reappear sooner.

Delighted, he half tripped himself getting up. "Come in."

"I hope I'm not intruding?" She sat on Nakae's bed.

"Not at all."

She had tied a yellow scarf around her head to keep the rain off, and he saw that the light cotton sweater thrown over her shoulders was damp. He wished he could drag the slatted door closed behind them and take her in his arms. He knotted his laces.

"I feel so selfish, Paul. I haven't really asked you if you want to do this. I'm so single-minded I've just assumed you would." She studied his face. "You know that you don't have to go. I'm sure Nakae can tell us what we need to know. Although, I'm afraid, he'll be noticing different things from you. Still, if you have any reservations . . . If you have cold feet?" She glanced at his boots and smiled.

"I want to go."

"It is not an easy climb."

"Anything that Avelino and the painter are participating in can't be that difficult. The worst that can happen," he said, trying to exude confidence and credibility, "is that the chicken farmer will never shut up."

"You're sure?"

"I only wish you were going with me." Again he felt it unjust that she, who knew far better than he what she wanted to see and hear, was prohibited from the climb.

"It is frustrating." She looked away. "It's a no-win situation. If I go, when women don't, then I'll see what women don't get to see, except that if I go, then it won't be there to see. It's much the same as a child going into her parents' bedroom: what she wants to see can't take place with her there." She forced a half-hearted laugh.

"It's unfair."

"It makes me want to tear my hair, if you want the truth."

"I'll take careful note of everything."

"I know you will; that means a lot to me." She fished a small paper sack from her shoulder bag. "Here. I've brought you something. You'll get thirsty. These will keep you from being tempted by the streams."

He looked down at a cache of lemon drops. What a thoughtful gift. Small, easy to carry, the yellow hard candies appeared to him an immense treasure. Tucking the sack into his pocket, he felt every bit the knight setting forth on a crusade, with his lady's talisman inside his armor.

"Are you ready then? I'll walk you to the square."

She rose at the same time he did, and they stood facing in the narrow space between the two beds. Then she quickly ducked through the door, waiting for him outside.

On the street, they moved slowly, as if to prolong the time before he had to leave her behind.

"Jean and I are going to church while you're having your climb."

"Church? On Saturday night?"

"Yes, they have scheduled a three-hour mass, from eight to eleven, at the same time as the celebration on the mountain. Rather unfair competition, isn't it?"

"But who will attend?"

"I don't know. Jean says we should see. Whether it is the women only or if some of the men are there. If they are praying for the souls of those brave enough to climb to the old ceremony or if they only pray for themselves, the faithful. We can learn a lot by seeing who is there and who is missing." She looked at him, convincing herself. "We can add what we learn to what you learn. You see, until now there has been only a one-sided account. No one has been present at both."

"But a three-hour mass on Saturday night?" Paul found it wholly outside his frame of reference.

"That's what they say."

In the courtyard, the smell of gunpowder filled the air in little gusts. A large crowd of men, wearing hats against the damp drizzle, were shooting off rockets and firecrackers, trying to hit one another's in the air, making coarse jokes of which Paul caught only snatches. He pulled up the hood of his lightweight windbreaker.

Under an arch to the left of the church, a six-piece band played loudly. He glanced at the carved Virgin of Guadalupe over the door; he could see the crescent moon under her feet and the stars on her cape. Following Helena inside, he saw that already, at five-thirty, the benches were filled with old women—heads bowed, gray braids under rebozos—and small children played about.

Helena showed him a massive wooden cross leaning against the stone wall at the back of the sanctuary. It was constructed, he calculated, from a ten-foot length of four-by-four nailed to a five-foot length and seemed too heavy for anyone actually to lift. The sight of such a weight of wood was overpowering. It conveyed a sacredness more real than anything on the altar. He found his hands reaching out, as if to verify that here, in the tropics, the heart of such a tree really existed.

She told him that every year one man was chosen to carry the cross and then to let himself be suspended on it from Good Friday to Easter. Last year, she said, the man had died, although he had not actually been fastened to the cross but had only lain on it (it being propped against a stone), his feet braced.

"He died from exposure. Or from being motionless too long. Or simply from the shock of reenacting the Crucifixion. I have no idea. Everyone tells a different story. Some of them say it happened last year; some that it was years ago; others that it was not here but in a neighboring village, on another cross." Helena sighed. "Everything I try to learn is like that. It is impossible to get the truth."

"He must have scared himself to death." Paul considered the way in which one's own worst fears were realized.

Stepping out into the mist and popping rockets, he almost had to shout, for not only was the band of six guitars and violins playing away, but now a second band, strolling mariachis, had come into the courtyard and was strumming loudly, walking up the flagstones into the milling mob of people dressed for church. Watching, little girls in white, tiny earrings in their pierced ears, looked up with the provocative glances of women.

"Here's Jean." Helena pointed.

Paul looked in the direction of the square but did not see the anthropologist. A small group of women were moving toward the church, carrying baskets, tucking the little linen napkins over their warm tortillas. The fresh corn smell drifting on the damp air filled the space between them. Then, when one of them lifted her head, he saw the deep-set blue eyes and realized it was Jean Weaver. Her hair, not long enough for a braid, was tied back with a blue scarf, knotted on the back of her neck.

"Here you are," she said, coming up to them. Then, to Paul: "I understand they pick someone out of the crowd up there and, just when the lightning flashes, drive in the knife. Usually a foreigner."

Paul laughed. "Don't kill the messenger."

Jean laughed, too, but with obvious effort. "Sorry. I'm having climb envy."

"You must come for breakfast," Helena told him. "As soon as you wake tomorrow. We will want to hear every word."

Paul nodded. He looked up at the tiny dot he knew to be the pyramid, stuck high on the cliff, surrounded by green. He resolved not to disappoint her.

"Take care." She touched his face, searching it, then hurried after Jean into the church.

At that moment Nakae called to him, and Paul turned to see his roommate crossing the street with Avelino.

Before they had taken two steps, Esperanza came running up to them. "You must be quick," she said. "A storm is coming. I could see it from veintidós de febrero. It happens every year on this day. The people say it rains for the god."

The three men followed her to a stall that sold blouses, scarves, handworked shirts, and table linens. There she asked the man behind the counter to outfit them in large squares of plastic, for which she gave him a handful of bills. Quickly, the shopkeeper cut three lengths from a long bolt, each of which he folded into a square, cut a corner from, and then unfolded into an instant waterproof poncho. "Now for the faces," Esperanza instructed him, and this time he cut shorter lengths for hoods, each with a narrow half-moon slit for the eyes.

No sooner had they put them on than the sky grew dark and the clouds opened.

"I am going now," Esperanza said. "Good luck." She spoke only to Paul and Nakae. She and Avelino hardly glanced at one another.

"How do we know where to go?" Nakae called to her, looking nervously about.

"Avelino will take you to Tomás," she answered, starting up the hill.

And with that the men were on their own.

14 RETURN OF THE GOD

ALL AROUND the square merchants were bringing in their wares, pulling down the flaps on their stalls to keep the water off. In the market proper, sellers huddled together under plastic awnings, more sheets of plastic spread over the blue and yellow corn, beans of all varieties, strips of dried beef, precious coffee beans, black and red chilies. Women who had draped shirts to sell on the bandstand gathered the garments in their arms like flapping birds and ran for cover.

"The gods favor us," Avelino said, but it sounded like an automatic comment, something akin to "bless you" for a sneeze, a ritual thanks for plunging them sock-deep in cold water.

"Hey," Tomás called to them. "We are going to be late. Follow me."

"Where are the others?" Nakae asked. "Perhaps it has been called off?"

"The others have already begun the climb. It will be slower in this rain. We must be at the top at eight, when the mayor comes with the drum, the drum which must be present at the ceremony. He will arrive with the keys to the trap door." Tomás was in a bright yellow slicker much

134

like the one Edward had worn for safety patrol, and Paul wondered how it was that the painter had it whereas the rest of them were all wrapped like vegetables in the super-market.

"A patron gave it to me," Tomás explained. "Someone who bought a picture."

"You are lucky."

"I am an artist."

The three other men set out behind Tomás on a dark street on the mountain side of the church. Paul did not know exactly where they were. The street was low, and water ran between the stones like a swift river. Even his boots, which had been oiled against winters in Virginia, filled with water, and he was more than ready to call it quits.

"Are you sure this is the way? Where is everyone?"

"They have gone already. We are late."

But Paul did not believe Tomás. They hadn't seen any group assembling, although standing in the churchyard had surely been the wrong place to join a throng of worshipers of El Tepozteco. He had been following Helena; she should have foreseen this and sent them along earlier. However, in that case he might have been caught in the deluge in his lightweight windbreaker, and that would have been worse.

"I do not see any others." Nakae appeared to be in grave misery, and Paul knew if he suggested that they give it up and go back, the Japanese would readily have agreed. Paul himself could feel the seductive pull of the heavy crossed timbers in the warm church.

"Here is where we turn," Tomás called back to them. "By the wall."

It was pitch-dark. The storm had dropped night on the village, and without stars or streetlights it was hard to see even two feet in front of them. As they turned right, Paul could sense rather than see that before them was some obstacle, and for the first time, he heard the sound of other voices. His heart lifted in relief. There were others. It was not going to be a snipe hunt, after all.

"What's happening?" voices called. "You'll be late."

Tomás called back to them, "Now we are here, it can start."

The four men slogged along by the wall, which Paul reached out and touched to steady himself. It was wet and slightly mossy, covered here and there with vines, but he used it as a railing when the rough stones that made the pathway became larger and slicker and the grade of the trail grew steeper. He was accustomed, hiking in the Blue Ridge at home, to get his wind gradually, walking thirty minutes at a slow pace, resting five; walking thirty, resting five. Here they were starting at an altitude of seven thousand and climbing rapidly. After a few minutes he'd fallen to last in line.

"Wait up," Tomás called to Avelino, who was now in the lead. "Our friends—"

It was insufferable that the fat chicken plucker was leading—with eyes that could see in the dark and feet whose soles were made of steel.

"A drink will help them," Avelino said, and produced from a paper bag a bottle of what he identified as *aguardiente*, burning water, which, by the light of Tomás's flashlight, looked clear as gin. He poured some into a tin cup and handed it to Tomás, who, tucking his flashlight between his thighs, drank it down. Avelino filled it again and handed it to the Japanese, who shook his head.

"You, Pablo?"

"No, I'll need a clear head."

"Forget your head. Relax your feet," Avelino crowed.

"How far are we from the top?" Nakae asked him.

"Who knows? Two hours, maybe. We have not yet got to the trail," Tomás said. "A drink will warm you." And he got out a bottle of his own from under his slicker and drank straight from the neck, then wiped it and passed it to Avelino, who pronounced it good.

With a signal from Paul that indicated he was ready, the group started up again. Ahead of them, but faintly, they could hear the voices of other men, from time to time someone laughing or calling out a friendly insult.

All at once the path seemed to dead-end at a pile of rocks, and then Tomás told them that the real climb had begun. No longer was there a path or even stone steps, but now they navigated from boulder to boulder. At this point they began to grope single file in the dark, with Tomás occasionally shining his flashlight back to help them pick their way. Several times Paul misjudged, and a foot sank up to the ankle in an eddying pool of water caught for a moment on its rush downhill.

After about an hour of this, another group came up from behind them at the same time that a group of men ahead of them stopped to rest and drink, so that they were now in the middle of about a dozen men. Those at the back carried torches, only two of which were lit. They looked to be bundles of rags, smelled of gasoline and billowed black smoke. Avelino explained that they were for the ceremony on top, so would have to last all night, and that was why not all of them were lit. Their flames seemed a sun in the midst of the men, and Paul could see at last where they were.

Where they were was on a narrow ridge of land. To their right the path dropped off into a deep canyon—seemingly

137

bottomless—on the other side of which a face of stone, moss-covered, rose up out of sight above them.

"On top of that"—Tomás gestured—"is where we are going."

Paul shivered. To their left the water ran like a stream, and an outcropping as high as their heads made a natural wall that their path curved against. Ahead, before the torch-bearers, moving on, passed out of sight and they were once again in the dark save for the weak beam of Tomás's flash-light, Paul could see trees, the same mix of fir, madroña, and pine that he had seen driving over the pass, past the volcanic cones, for his first glimpse of Tepoztlán. The trees promised shelter, and he wiped his face and tried not to look to his right.

Whenever he thought he could not take another step—with his feet slipping and even his hands sliding on the wet rock face, and him forced to make his way almost on his hands and knees, ashamed but glad no one was behind him to see—Tomás would call out to Avelino to wait up, and they would warm themselves with a few drinks. Tomás did this with such grace, and with no air of condescension, letting his flashlight beam back for the North Americans while he and Avelino discussed the evening ahead, that Paul vowed if he ever got off this mountain face alive he would make Jaramillo, the artist, a household word.

This time, when they started up, the rain running steadily off their noses and eyelashes, Avelino called back, "Stay to the right around this bend."

Paul, reaching out his left hand to steady himself when his foot slipped on a sharp rock, found nothing.

"It drops off," Tomás told his friends.

"Look," Nakae whispered to him, stopping and pointing

until Paul's eyes focused and he could see—two feet to their left—a white cross, stuck in the ground.

"It is tricky here," Tomás warned. "Suddenly there is a hole. Many years ago someone fell."

"Last year. It was last year," Avelino argued.

"Every year someone falls."

Nakae pointed again, and Paul, afraid to lean too far over to see, took his word for it that there was a second cross on the edge of the spine of land which suddenly fell away into an abyss on both sides.

"It is tricky here," Avelino told them, not slowing down. "Stay in the middle. In a minute we will be to the trees. It is easier there."

Nakae held back and pushed Paul ahead. "I will watch behind you," he said, and Paul thought he heard the Japanese relieve himself, although with the sound of the voices ahead and the rain he couldn't be sure. It was a sign of the strain on Nakae, who had scarcely said a word since they began the climb.

Behind them now they could hear another party catching up, and Tomás hurried them along, past the narrow, dangerous stretch, around a sharp turn which was something like climbing over a rubble heap in the dark, until they reached a fairly wide stretch of dirt, dry and smooth, with occasional flat stones. They had hit the trees.

It was a wonderful relief. Paul wiped his face, shook himself, and adjusted the hood that he had been holding between his teeth to keep it from slipping off his head. He straightened the poncho, which, twisted to the left, had allowed his right arm to get soaked to the skin.

"Here we can have fresh water," Tomás said, and he and Avelino cupped their hands and bent down to take a long drink from a stream that spilled, now a small waterfall, on their left onto the path and quickly fell away into the ravine on their right. "It is delicious."

Paul was sorely tempted. He had got unbelievably thirsty, although that seemed impossible in such a rain. His mouth was gasping and dry, but he remembered what Helena had said, "Whatever you do, don't drink the water. The amoeba slide off the leaves and into the streams," and he could sense them all around him, so that even licking his lips he felt that he had already tasted the forbidden water without intending to. Then, as if being rescued, he remembered the tiny sack of lemon drops she had given him for just such a moment.

But in the pocket of his drenched cords his hand encountered only a gummy, sticky syrup. Sick with disappointment, he spit and rubbed his arm across his lips.

Nakae caught up with him and then moved ahead. "How much further?" he asked.

"Who knows?" Avelino said. "We have not yet come around the curve of the rock."

"Perhaps they have canceled the ceremony?"

"El Tepozteco always sends rain for his festival," Avelino told them. "To favor us." He laughed and poured himself a drink. "They cannot start without the mayor. He has the keys to the gate and the sacred drum."

Behind them they heard voices approaching, some speaking English; one, German. Then, as they stood in the wide sheltered clearing, reluctant to start on again, a snakelike chain of people came into full view, lit by four huge torches, not homemade fuel-soaked rags this time, but something that looked like permeated wool, slow burning and brilliant. Half of the group carried them; the other half hauled equipment under heavy plastic tarps.

"We are from the TV," the man with the front torch said in Spanish. "What's happening? How much more of this mother-killing climb have we got to do?"

"Who knows?" Tomás answered. "Maybe we are halfway."

There was fresh cursing.

"Maybe more."

"Did you see those crosses?"

"We almost lost our cameras."

"This better be good."

The group—there were eight of them—stopped and set their strobes and power packs gingerly on the ground, making sure they avoided puddles. There were seven men and a *woman*, and all had heavy rain gear and knee-high waders and even, most of them, rubber gloves for carrying their equipment.

"It'd better be worth it."

"When is it going to start?" the woman asked. "At the rate we're going, Tepozteco will have been resurrected and buried again by the time we get there."

"Who knows?" Avelino poured himself a drink. "People are still arriving."

"We know that. We're here."

"It cannot begin without the mayor," Tomás told them.

"Maybe he's home in bed, staying dry."

"He will come."

Paul asked them, "Where are you from?" It had gone through him like an electric shock, seeing a woman on the mountain. If this one could come, then why not Helena? He imagined her near him, brandishing a torch, missing nothing. But then anger took over. What if this woman, uninvited, unwelcome, kept him from bringing back the information for which he'd endured this God-awful climb?

The man with the lead torch answered him. "The capital. This is the first time we've made the trip. This festival has caught on, and lots of people come for it; at least so they say. We got permission, our bad luck, to shoot it."

"Who gave you that?" Tomás asked.

"How do I know? We're just the camera crew. The Aztec himself maybe." They all managed a feeble laugh and shouldered their equipment and started on, taking their blazing flames with them, so that they cast a long snaking shadow behind them under the dripping branches.

"Let's go," Nakae said. "If we stay close to them, we can see." And the foursome started up again, with Avelino all but leaping up the path, his fat legs traveling the uneven ground as effortlessly as a boar, which he resembled in the disappearing light.

After about an hour of easy going, the path narrowed, the ravine on the right ended, and they were at the bottom of what seemed to be the face of a cliff.

"This is where we are going." Tomás pointed straight up, and near the top Paul could see the flickering light of other torches. "We are almost there."

"It is time for a drink," Avelino said, pouring freely into his cup. "Here it becomes difficult."

Ahead of them Paul could see the TV crew, inching up, looking like mountain climbers connected by a rope.

There didn't appear to be a path at all, rather a sheer rock wall, but gradually Paul could make out footholds and see the way the others were stepping. Nakae called back instructions half-heartedly. Paul could see the soles of Nakae's shoes ahead of him and realized that they were of the thinnest leather. At least he had made the climb in decent boots.

Halfway up they stopped. They were on a narrow pas-

sageway which seemed cut out from the rock on both sides.
The trees overhead were gone; but the sky was black as ink,
and the rain had slackened, so that sitting at last, they were
free to shift in their clothes and grow thoroughly chilled.
Ahead of them, scattered on similar rocks, were about two
dozen men, in groups of two and three. Most had bedrolls,
wrapped in plastic, and unlit torches covered in more plastic.
All had bottles and were passing them back and forth. They
did not seem impatient. Now and then someone called down,
"When is the mayor coming?" and someone else answered,
"Who knows?"

Nakae drew Paul aside, away from Tomás and Avelino,
toward the camera crew, who had settled just above them—
not anxious to lug their heavy gear any further until there
was something to shoot.

"Do you know why these men are together?" Nakae
asked in English. "They are watching one another."

Paul was thirsty, and the water running down his face
again was a torment. Surely, he thought, there could be
nothing wrong with rainwater, straight from the skies, and
he licked his lips furtively, with little relief. "Why?" he
asked, in a hoarse whisper, aware that the television people
could understand them.

"They do not trust one another. Avelino thinks his wife
fancies the painter; the painter sees his Rosa flirt with the
chicken farmer. Each fears the other." He made the gesture,
fingers to forehead.

"How do you know that?"

"It is how each will not let the other out of his sight. See,
they try to get each other drunk. A drunk man is not going
to slip away down this mountain to a tryst."

"But the same thing could be accomplished by each
man's staying at home in his bed with his own wife." Paul

143

bit his lip, surprised at the emotion that accompanied the words.

"Not at all. Then he would not know what his wife was up to. This way, if one of them tries to leave, the other will be sure."

"All the men here are the same, then? Watching one another?"

"I think so. I think that is the case." Nakae tried in vain to clean his rain-streaked glasses.

"Us, too?"

"Perhaps. The women have sent us to keep a check on each other, isn't that so?"

They were interrupted by the unmistakable sound of a drum coming up the mountainside.

Shouts went up. "It is the mayor."

"About time. It's past nine o'clock." A crewman shifted a tripod to his other shoulder.

"He will have the key."

"It is the drum."

Everyone had another round, and two new torches were lit, sending the stench of gasoline into the air as the flames shot up through the rain as if it were not there, making gusts of black smoke and billows of steam.

"Hello," the man with the drum called out, and everyone in turn touched him, patted him, offered him a drink, as he passed through them—clearly drunk out of his mind, stumbling blithely from rock to rock. "The mayor will be here soon," he told each cluster of men. "He is on his way. He promises soon. He sent me ahead with the drum." And he played, slap, slap, on the tight stretched hide the size of a dinner plate. "This is very sacred," he informed them. "One time El Tepozteco himself played on this drum."

"How long," one of the TV men asked, "before the key arrives?"

"Soon. Very soon."

A fight broke out among the camera crew.

"*I* am not the cause of this swimming party," the woman said in English.

"You might be."

"Ask them, then."

"I said you shouldn't come."

"*You* said? This is my assignment; you are with *me*."

"You are the cause."

"Oh, Christ, ask them."

One of the men from the capital struggled down the hill to Tomás and Avelino. They conferred in low voices, but everyone could hear the chicken farmer's reply: "No, no. Women come. Women come to the ceremony. From other villages, they come."

As if his words confirmed their opposite meaning, the woman cursed, "Your mother." She signaled the others. "Let's forget it. We'll catch this Tepozteco dancing in the square tomorrow. I've had it."

Agreeing, relieved, all of the crew hoisted their valuable cargo back on their shoulders or under their arms, arranged the tarps, and said to Paul and Nakae, "It's all yours, friends."

Paul watched them go with profound relief. He hoped that the woman's leaving would mean the gate could be opened and the old god return. He found himself feeling some need to cast a spell over the ground where she had stood or wave something in the air to erase her presence; he wiped his face, ashamed to find himself caught up in their superstitions.

When the TV crew was out of sight, Tomás said, "It is not the woman."

"After the mayor comes," Avelino told them, "then the women will come."

"What is the delay, then?" Paul asked.

"Who knows?"

Nakae took Paul's arm and pulled him close. They were both afraid to take a step on the slick ground with the flares now out of sight around the sharp bend at the foot of the cliff. "It is not the woman."

"What then? Maybe there is no key?"

"There is a key."

"Maybe there is no mayor." Paul was having trouble breathing, from weariness, the altitude, and the rain, which had begun again in earnest.

"The mayor will not come during the mass. They know that. They don't say it, but all of them know it." Nakae's mouth was at his ear.

"You mean they knew they would have to wait?"

"I think that is the case. The church sets the mass to last until eleven. By then everyone is tired and drunk. The mayor's wife is not going to let him come up the mountain at that hour. The time has passed. 'Next year,' she will say. 'You can open the gate next year.' She will invite him to bed. The priest has told her what to say. It will be warm and dry in his house. She will pour him a drink and open her clothes. He will hear the rain outside. His bodyguards will have disappeared. He will sigh and send a prayer to El Tepozteco asking him not to send the drought, thanking him for the blessed rain—except tonight, of all nights. Then he will cross himself, as his wife has taught him, and climb into bed, dead drunk, and sleep like a dog."

"If I were Tepozteco—"

"You have a god of wrath. Here, in this country, the god who wins is the god who waits best."

Avelino called to them. "Listen, the other villagers are at the top." They could hear voices from the other side of the crest. "They bring their women, the other villagers." He clucked and said something low to Tomás, who answered back, their voices sharp but joking.

Paul did not believe it for a minute. He pictured the seven other tiny villages of the area, all with their steep trails leading to the locked gates that ringed the remains of the old god's shrine. Each telling stories about the others: that they came by the hundreds to the festival, that all brought their mistresses and fireworks and musical instruments and potions to make them erect all night long. That each other village had a bacchanalia that lasted till the cock crowed and could be heard swelling down the mountainside: the laughter of women being pleased, the singing of men full of spirits, handmade flares and rockets, and maybe even the cries of live animals.

And all of it a pathetic lie. From each village only a handful of soaking men, jealously guarding one another, clinging together in fear, without the keys, with only one drum among them to play upon.

It was a snipe hunt after all. The biggest, stupidest one imaginable. "Sons of whores," he cursed through gritted teeth. He longed to rip open their chests and tear out their collective hearts. He imagined the astonishment of the chicken farmer and his companions as Paul crashed through the gate, grabbed each conniving fool in turn, and piled one on top of the other in a heap on the old shrine, blood flowing like rain. *That* would be a story they could tell the other villagers: the night they pushed the North American too far. Mother rapers, the lot of them.

He felt himself grow warm in his rage. "It's us." He collared Nakae. "It wasn't the woman; it's us. We're cramping their style. How can they lie to themselves with witnesses here? Let's go. Let's go, and tomorrow they can tell us that after we left the mayor opened the gate, hundreds came, they carved the hearts from wild pigs, and ate raw chickens, and El Tepozteco himself appeared to them with an eagle in his hand and live snakes around his ankles and told them he would never die."

"They will take us down." Nakae, babbling, grabbed his arm. "They will take us down. One will not want to let the other go without him. I will tell them you are sick. I will ask the painter to take you home. I will tell Avelino he does not have to leave."

Paul craved satisfaction. He would get even with them, turn them in. He would tell the women the truth; the women would announce the crime to all the village. That would fix them. The wet cold had returned, and he shook off a feeling that he had felt this same fury once before and sought revenge in the same way. But the idea of the downward plunge with its slippery footholds took his attention, and he could not focus on the idea further.

Nakae pulled on him. "If we are lucky, we'll be lying in our beds fast asleep by midnight."

Paul shook loose. Helena should have come. It wouldn't have made any difference. He imagined her turning on her heel, spitting and swearing, like the TV woman, in two languages. She could have seen for herself. He would wake her and tell her when he got back. They could listen together to the pathetic sounds of nothing, of nothing at all happening on the mountain.

In his fury, as he prepared to stumble back down the treacherous trail at risk to life and limb, it seemed to Paul that these were the same foolish, cringing cowards who had caused the idol to throw himself off the cliff in exasperation and, giving up on the lot of them, allow himself to be hammered to shards by the priests below.

15 NEW FRIENDS

"THIS HAS been a wonderful weekend, Todd." Peggy looked at the bear of a man before her and thought, not for the first time, that he reminded her of her father, although she couldn't put her finger on why: Ned Ruggles was a much more compact, dashing man.

"For me, too."

They were still at the table, listening to the sounds of Edward and Baxter upstairs getting ready for church.

Peggy had fixed an old-fashioned breakfast: grits; apple rings; sausage; biscuits. It had been wonderful to have a crowd to feed.

"You were good to come again," she said. "It's been great for Edward to have Baxter around, to have you, too."

"I like coming. I have unfinished business here."

"You remind me of Dad."

"I'm flattered."

"You don't know my father."

"Ned Ruggles was a hero to half the country, including me. I can see those pictures of him when he was not many years older than our boys, his chest full of medals, his hat on the back of his head, with that dazzling grin that said flying

missions was only intermurals after all. He made wartime
the big game we little kids wanted to believe it was."

"His is a sad story."

"Would he say so?"

"Of course not. But all those years at the Pentagon. I
think he's somewhat ashamed."

"You're reading today's attitudes, today's press into it. I
suspect he had a fine time plotting secret weapons."

"Nerve gas, I think."

"Worse, filing forms."

"His home life hasn't been too stable."

"A man his age is entitled to a few flings."

Peggy smiled. "I guess I'm jealous of his girl friends."

"More likely you're jealous that he's free to have them—"

"Am I?"

"Aren't you?" he pressed.

"I don't know. Until this happened, I never thought of
anyone but Paul. He's been a constant in my life for a quarter of a century."

"You built your house on shifting sand."

"That's Spence's job, quoting Scripture."

"Out of turn, besides. My own divorce has made me wish
it upon every attractive woman I meet."

Peggy felt disappointed to be lumped in a class that way.
She hadn't had such a good time, a happy time, in years.
They'd eaten with Fan and Mew again, the pair acting as
both old friends and chaperons. That was Friday. Then
Saturday—the boys were playing tennis somewhere—
they'd had brunch and driven around town. He'd gone to
school at U.VA., apparently, for his last two undergraduate
years, and he'd wanted to see the campus again. He'd even
had a course from Pink, and on impulse, they'd stopped by
his house to say hello, but he was out.

Todd had said she should come spend a weekend with him in Washington, and she thought she would. That was a city she loved. He'd asked, What is your favorite sight? So she had told him she'd love to go to the botanical gardens. There was never a chance when she went with Paul and the boys. She loved to see the tropical and subtropical plants, especially those that trapped insects. That complex evolutionary adaptation—the same that allowed some flowering plants to alter the colors of their blooms to attract certain insects—had been her major interest in school.

"I never knew anyone who studied botany," he said. "To tell the truth, I find it hard to imagine why anyone would. How did you get interested?"

Peggy hardly knew where to begin, there was so much stored in her head about the vegetable kingdom that she never got to share, such enthralling information and conjecture. Finally, she selected one example. "I had a professor who started our course by asking that we think of plants as alive, but in a way wholly alien to our usual way of conceiving life. Almost as mindless monsters who fed to breed and bred to feed. Seen by humans as blind, deaf, and stationary but, in fact, in motion, at such a slow speed that we do not perceive it; forests, after all, do move, take over, regenerate. In other words, *beings*—although with a completely different time frame from ours."

Peggy had been afraid she had said too much, but Todd had been fascinated.

"That view of plants is amazing, if rather frightening. It raises the question, Do they already own the world?"

"Yes, it does."

It was Peggy's idea that they go to church this morning. She didn't want to be hiding Todd's presence; Spence had put out the message that she and Paul were separated, and their sons would be with them, so he would be like a friend of the family after all.

Besides, Charles, who was meeting them there with Pink and Mrs. Ebberly, was a crucifer today, and she wanted to be present to watch him march in. Edward had been an acolyte in his day, but then he had never had any trouble taking his turn in public. Charles was another matter, with his stubborn attitude toward anything Spencer Cox requested him to do. He'd been in a swivet all week, a frame of mind not improved by learning that his older brother and his brother's friend would also be in the congregation.

"Peggy—"

She realized she'd been lost in her own thoughts.

"You know I said that to put you off guard."

"I didn't even think of it."

"I don't want you to suspect how single-minded my interest is. You're likely to bolt and run."

"Fan and Mew are coming back with us for lunch."

"Should we take them out?"

"They'd be insulted. Fan thinks public places are only for out-of-town kin you can't abide; where the slow service and endless piddling, as she calls it, over what to have, fill up the time, and the hefty price salves your conscience."

"They're a fine pair."

"They're a case against marriage, as they like to say."

"Do you believe that?"

She hesitated. "I like my life to have structure. What a mess it would be if we all set out to be special cases of everything, living in any arrangement we pleased, each of us teaching our own kids, praying in our own parlors, burying our dead under the maples." She smiled. "I'm an army brat. Anarchy is not appealing to me."

153

"I'd think a hero's daughter would be drawn to special cases."

"Dad did what he did within the system." Peggy twisted her ring, her mind moving unwittingly to the present. "Paul of all people—I wake up sometimes in the middle of the night, and I'm half out of bed, not sleepwalking but simply rising up as if to call out to him, and I feel as though I'd been shouting at the top of my lungs. How on earth could he have walked out the door without a word to me? I don't mean how could he do it to *me*—heavens, that isn't the point—but how could he, of all people, *do it*?"

Todd let her refill his coffee cup. He looked about to comment but then shrugged. "Mid-life crisis?" He said it lightly, giving her an easy answer if she wanted one.

"That's absurd."

"I agree. No, I don't agree. I agree the term is a catchall, but what's behind it may have a grain of truth. Some men, some people, I suppose, although my sample of women is considerably smaller, get so imbedded in a life where all the rewards are down the road and all the risks are bypassed that one day they look up and feel much as you might if you were standing on an island in rising water: it's sink or swim."

"What were you going to say, Todd?"

"Was I?"

"Something else. That you thought better of. Something about Paul, not about middle-aged men."

Todd fixed her with his eyes, trying to get a reading. His bulky tweed shoulders leaned forward. "He and I go a long way back. I'm talking about the past. I only knew him then."

"I'm beginning to think I did, too."

He paused. "I'll regret this the minute I say it, but here goes. I think Paul Sinclair would travel halfway around the world for the opportunity to inform on someone."

He walked to the breakfast room window and looked out, and Peggy knew why he had reminded her of the young bird colonel of her girlhood. Her dad had been comfortable with hatred; it had been, in fact, the avenue of his glory.

"Do you dislike him that much?"

"More." He walked to the doorway, to be sure the boys were not in earshot.

"Your being here has nothing to do with me at all, does it?"

"Probably not." He sat back down. "I could at least have had the decency to pretend."

"I'm glad you didn't." She had been sure that he was going to lie to her, and he hadn't. It made her far more interested than she had been before.

"It was Edward."

"How so?"

"That kid turned a knife in me. Did you see the snide note he got from Paul?"

"No. He only mentioned it was bad."

"Well, I did."

Peggy was surprised. She would not have thought Edward capable of sharing anything so personal. She looked at Todd, trying to see what sort of man he really was. Someone, obviously, her son trusted.

"Somebody needs to give that boy some decent fathering."

"Uncle." She felt elated. "All boys need an extra uncle." She rose and carried their plates to the kitchen. She checked the oven, which was slowly baking Indian pudding. The rest, cheese-sauced crab and cucumber soup, was covered and ready for lunch. She'd bought half a dozen tiger lilies to mix with the last of the yellow roses for the table.

Todd stood watching her, frowning.

"Call the boys," she said. "If we leave now, we can walk. It's glorious outside."

"I don't want to be his uncle."

She met his eyes. "I imagine not."

Charles and Pink, and Mrs. Ebberly in a large, sweeping black hat and a bosom loaded with pearls, met them in front of Christ Church. Peggy liked Mrs. Ebberly; she knew that somewhere tucked in her silk dress, or perhaps in her bag, or even down her ample front, would be a scented black handkerchief, ready to dry nearby tears. She thought, not for the first time, that it would be nice to have a mother such as that, hugging you fiercely, tangling the ends of your hair in her immense diamond brooch; nice to lose yourself in the safe odors of lavender and Lavoris.

Peggy's own mother had been such a silent, brave person, taking on herself all the pain and worry of Ned Ruggles's risks and secrecies, shutting out the adventures and escapades. She worried, down inside somewhere, that she had some of her mother hidden in her, or else Paul would never have run off the way he did.

She kissed the doddering old gentleman who was a good grandfather to her boys.

"Charles informs me," Pink said, "that he's carrying the cross. Reason enough to get myself out in my Sunday best. I recall the weight of the thing myself, pressing into your lower abdomen. Certainly it wouldn't do to have it a flimsy burden, now would it?" Not waiting for an answer, he took Mrs. Ebberly's arm, saying loudly to Peggy, "Don't let that rector make a fuss over me. Now, here, I've forgotten his name. They come and go and, to my mind, get jollier by the decade. I preferred the aesthetic type who went about with arms crossed behind him, gazing at the floor and contemplating the collection plate." He chuckled.

"Pink—" She could see that he and Mrs. Ebberly were going to be carried in the front door by the crowd, and she would not have made her introductions.

"Have I mentioned that I hope you don't mind that I seem to have appropriated your young son since mine has taken himself rather abruptly to another country?"

"Pink, this is Edward's friend Baxter Stedman, and his father, Todd, who was a classmate of Paul's at Princeton, and, I believe—"

"A student of mine as well. Isn't that so, Mr. Stedman?"

"You were the highpoint of my education, Dr. Sinclair."

"I don't doubt it. I was the highpoint of education, period. Today they run about lip-reading their Cliff Notes, dressed like gardener's assistants. I expect they can't even get themselves into bed with one another without a pony of some kind." He watched the effect of this on Edward and Baxter and was pleased to see them ill at ease. Still addressing Todd, he said, "You went into some field I was opposed to, as I recall."

"Architecture."

"I've mellowed in that regard, haven't I, Charles? We take our constitutional about the campus primarily in order to study the old buildings. Jefferson's best. Then there was Wren. I couldn't see it in those days, but where man domiciles himself has a profound effect. Its history is his history. My apologies, only don't inform me you're doing those plate-glass banks." He peered up at Todd. "You're not, are you?"

"Not at all. Although I have learned that it is possible to use materials other than red brick."

Charles, anxious as a cat in a paper bag that he was going to be late getting dressed for the processional, spluttered with laughter.

"Our boys play tennis together," Todd said, to include Edward and Baxter in the conversation.

"You were an athlete yourself, as I recall."

"You hadn't much to say about that either."

"Should have. Rhodes liked his boys to play all the sports. Well rounded." The old man gave each of the boys a handshake. "My grandson is, I understand, something of a star. Is your boy?"

"He likes the game."

"I hear a reprimand in your tone. Well deserved. Likes the game. Yes, we used to argue such matters. After a time a great number of students are forgettable. But the ones who argue, they stick with you. You got a B in my course, as I recall."

"With some relief."

Edward laughed, and Baxter, shyer, slightly confused by what was going on, slicked down his red hair and joined in. The idea of his dad's being a student seemed to tickle him.

"Come on." Charles gave his grandfather a tug.

"Very well. Go get yourself ready. We'll be in our usual spot."

Peggy led her visitors down the aisle and sat toward the front on the left. There weren't really assigned pews anymore; the little gates that had once enclosed them had been removed, and, with them, the brass plates with surnames etched in script, and the special kneeling pillows stitched by a grandmother. Still, habits picked up as a child lingered on, and most of the congregation sat at least in the same general vicinity each Sunday—chiding themselves for being bothered when they could not occupy their usual seats because some new couple, in attendance for the first time, had marched right down and sat themselves where they didn't belong.

Peggy did not cross herself in the aisle and looked to see whether Todd did. She was not as High Church as Christ Episcopal. Something in her clung to the upright posture and straight-ahead gaze of her grandparents' church, less Anglican in its airs.

She recognized the daintily embroidered altar cloth, green still for Pentecost, as one that Fan had done years ago. Perhaps she had done the one on the lectern also. She spotted Pink and Mrs. Ebberly on the right, in the nave where the church widened out, below the old windows with their dove, cross, and crowns on fields of lilies, fragile leaded glass protected from hail by heavy plastic covers.

Inside the cool building with its vaulted ceiling, a great deal remained of its Revolutionary War origins. The national flag stood to one side of the altar, balancing the church's brilliant red, purple, and gold banner; a carved eagle thrust itself from the front of the lectern like a ship's masthead.

The music began, and they all stood as the processional started. Charles looked solemn and slightly awed, carrying in the heavy brass cross, its base fitted into a strap at his waist. Behind him came the other acolytes, two older boys and two girls (still a strange, new sight), all in the white half robes over their black gowns, and then the smaller kids carrying candles, and then the choir chanting the invocational hymn. Spence followed, in his flowing robes, and stopped to offer a prayer from the center of the aisle.

Peggy was distracted as the choirs were seated, the senior

choir on the left, the junior on the right, and the candles were lit. Her mind on what had gone on out front, she went through the confession, lessons, and praise by rote, standing with the rest of the congregation to sing "America" as the offering was taken.

She watched Charles go up front with the other young people to gather around Spence for the children's homily. She could remember back to the days when Edward was up there, a small blond boy in a blue wool suit. That was when Charles was only a baby, and Edward was Paul's pride and joy. What hopes he had pinned on that small boy; no one could have lived up to such expectations. She smiled as Charles squirmed, now, put on the spot while Spence described the church picnic set for next week, with special emphasis on the food. It was not her imagination that the rector had set his cap for Charles, wishing, no doubt, to take credit for starting him on a life of devotion to the church.

Then Spence gave his little message on caring for others, reminded the parents that with summer over, the Sundays which counted for the perfect attendance record had begun, and then dismissed the children. At this point the little ones, and the bigger ones through high school, and their teachers all went out the door through the nave in front of Pink into the education building behind the church, which had long had an enclosed hallway so that coats and leggings and mufflers didn't have to be produced and time taken out of the service to dress again in the winter months.

Then those of them remaining settled down to the (not always easy) task of following the Right Reverend Cox's sermon.

Peggy strained to attend, hating it when her mind wandered. After all, Spence had spent days preparing his remarks, tying them into the season and building on the previous Sunday's discussion.

Today, as always, each paragraph was delivered as a unit, followed by a generous pause in order to give everyone time to let one idea sink in before receiving the next.

Spence had taken as the point of departure for his text a passage from the Book of Wisdom. "Blinded by their own malevolence," he began, "they did not understand God's hidden plan. They never expected that holiness of life would have its recompense. They thought that innocence had no reward."

"Godless persons," he continued, "are those who malevolently attempt to decide their own fate. Those who by their words and deeds excoriate their enemies as if they held control over their own lives and the lives of others."

But Peggy's mind did wander. Todd a student of Pink's. The implications were slow to sink in. Surely that was the seat of the animosity between the two men. How Paul would have envied such a man: husky, athletic, aggressive. Daring to argue with Pinckney Sinclair, daring to challenge his father in ways he could never have done.

Pink would have spoken of his students, special students, those with spunk or gumption as he called it, at home. Repeating tales that would have flayed Paul's thin skin.

No wonder he had never mentioned this old schoolmate. No wonder, too, that Todd still felt anger toward him. Perhaps Paul had snubbed him, a former classmate at Princeton now moved closer to home.

Men small and large had such jealousies of one another. Such lasting enmities.

Not her father, she thought, but then amended that. What did she know of his relationships with the other colonels? Or those who had stayed in the field and made general? Or the young men with whom he had clashed long before her time?

She looked at Todd and saw that he was watching Pink, and something in his attitude struck her deeply. The old man had given him a long-overdue permission to go his own way and build his buildings. That much was clear. But after how many years?

As she pulled down the kneeler, Peggy prayed that it would not take that long a time for Edward to receive a word of pardon from Paul.

16 OLD ENEMIES

I T WAS LATE afternoon and still light as morning. What beautiful weather, more than an Indian summer, more like spring, the light and the smell of flowers in the air, but, of course, looking at the trees, tinged red and gold already, you knew that it was fall, and soon fires would be blazing and blankets out and windows steaming over from the heat. Peggy felt like taking a long walk through town, all the way out to the campus maybe. She had changed into walking shoes and a tweed skirt, carried away by the feel of the day.

The boys were in jeans, rackets packed in zippered cases, sweaters knotted over their shoulders. Such good-looking boys, Edward the more handsome, but Baxter had a flash, an energy which made him every bit as attractive. She could identify with redheads, not that hers had ever been that color, really brick, but with the way people attributed to you the fiery temperament they supposed to go with it. The way they gathered around to warm themselves as if the very color of your hair guaranteed a certain heat. Dark people, especially, married redheads, and she could easily imagine the quiet, steady brunette who waited somewhere for Baxter Stedman.

"We need to catch the plane, Mom," Edward said, looking at his watch, eager to be gone.

"The airport is fifteen minutes away."

"And," Todd reminded them, "your plane doesn't leave for two hours."

"We can check in—"

"How about some popcorn?" she offered.

"You've been feeding the Great Digester too long," Edward said. "That blimp is nothing but a gut in clothes." He had been slightly hurt, she thought, when Charles declined to come back home with them after church.

"You're lucky," Baxter said. "My sister eats once a week whether she needs to or not. She has a library of books on anorexia, trying to figure out how to get it. She thinks it may be transmitted sexually."

Todd shot him a look.

"Well, she never eats, and that's the truth."

"She's not playing in competitive games."

"Ha-ha, you think."

Todd let himself smile. "I'll have the popcorn. And something to wash it down with."

"Tea?"

"How about Scotch?"

"Of course. I should have asked—"

When she got back, Todd and the boys were standing looking at the yard. They were watching squirrels, but she felt they were all looking out so as to have some excuse for not looking at one another. She recognized the posture; it meant someone had just said something serious. She set down the popcorn and a large kitchen salt shaker shaped like a rooster, and handed Todd his drink.

"He hates your dad, is why," Baxter said.

Todd turned to Peggy. "Edward reasonably inquired

how come, if I was in school with his dad and a student of his granddad's, I'd just now shown my face around here."

Peggy sat on the couch and pulled her feet up under her. This was interesting. Would he be as truthful to the boys as he had been to her?

"We're glad you did," she said mildly, to give him a moment.

"He's right," Todd said. "I don't like your dad. It's ironical, you and Bax hitting it off."

Edward sucked in his breath. He looked as if he didn't know how to react to such directness.

Peggy gestured to a place on the couch beside her, and Todd sat down. "I'm sure your dad has used me as a bad example once a day since you were in diapers."

"No," Edward said. "I never heard of you."

"I'm the guy who got expelled from Princeton for cribbing the line from the textbook."

"Jesus." Edward stared at him as if seeing a legend.

Peggy felt the same. Paul had told that story for as long as she'd known him—twenty-five years. Todd Stedman, Paul's cheat?

"You want to hear my side?" Todd asked.

"Sure."

"Bax?"

"Go ahead. You've told it often enough." But the boy did not seem bothered. He looked at his dad with a lot of affection, as if he intended to stick by him. "They can't expel you again."

"I'm never sure." Todd shifted his bulk and spoke directly to Edward, although his arm rested lightly on the back of Peggy's shoulders. "We had this wager. Five of us. We were all honor roll, racing for the top of the class. We played intermurals together. Roomed in a row on the quad.

Our first initials spelled *Grunt*, so we were the Grunts. I was the *T*. Geoffrey, Randolph, Underwood, Nigel, and Todd." He looked wistful, remembering.

"We were burned out on working our brains out and getting back these papers that proved the professors hadn't read a word of them. 'I bet,' I said, 'you could put a line in from one of their own books, and they'd never know it. Maybe think it had a nice ring to it.' We decided that was a great idea. For three days we pored over the tomes in the library that our professors had made their reputations writing. Finally, I found a sentence so all-purpose, so sweeping, that we decided we would *all* use it in our next paper. Then, if one of us was caught, we could tell what we'd done. They weren't going to kick out the five of us. The Grunts ran the school. Or so we thought."

Peggy listened to the telling of this version of the familiar story. Could this be how it had actually happened? Or was this tale put out in the aftermath of his expulsion? Had he had the idea, maybe, but been the only one to carry it out? She felt a great sympathy for him, because she knew what was coming next.

"Great idea. We had it; we did it; we forgot it. Exams came and went. Maybe we told a few people. Underwood had a tendency to blab. We talked about chiseling the line on a stone and leaving it behind for future classes." Todd finished his drink. "It was a couple of weeks later when I got called in. We had an honor system then. You were to report dishonesty." He looked at Edward directly. "Your dad was the one who turned me in."

Peggy grew cold. She should have guessed.

"Holy shit," Edward moaned. "What about the other guys?"

"Dad didn't get them in trouble." Baxter answered for him.

Todd nodded. "It had been a joke, and then it wasn't a joke anymore."

"But couldn't you—" Peggy twisted her hands together.

"I could own up and drop out or go through the whole procedure and get myself officially expelled. I was, because of my record, allowed to withdraw."

"But surely Paul didn't know how it really happened? I'm sure if you had talked to him."

"I did. He said that if everyone claimed exemption from the consequences of his actions because of intention, we couldn't have a government of any sort."

"What a creep." Edward sat crumpled with his elbows on his knees, staring out the window.

Todd shrugged. "It's time I got over it. It wasn't the end of my life. I only thought it was then."

"What did the other Grunts do?" Edward asked.

"Became the Rungs," Baxter answered, grinning at his dad.

"Disbanded, more than likely. I didn't go back to see."

Peggy said, "It must eat on Paul's conscience, or he wouldn't tell it so often."

"Mom," Edward said, slinging his sweater over a chair. "Dad let me have it, too. In that letter."

Peggy didn't know if her hesitation was to spare her son or herself. "You don't have to tell me."

"I want to. It's been driving me nuts. It's like somebody takes a shot at you and you can't shoot back. I wrote him down there ten times, but every time I tore it up."

Baxter looked at his friend. "You didn't even show it to me at first."

"The Great Digester read it." Edward made a disgusted noise.

"How do you know?"

"It had been moved. You wouldn't do that, Mom, but he noses into all my stuff."

"Charles never said anything."

"Naw, he wouldn't tell. Actually, it helped. I mean, I knew he'd seen it, so somebody saw it, and the world didn't blow up."

Todd reminded him, "I read it , too."

"Yeah."

"Come on, let's get it," Edward said.

Alone, Peggy and Todd didn't say anything for a minute. Then she turned to him. "That's what you meant by informer."

"The crack was uncalled for."

"I still don't think Paul could have intended—"

Todd spoke quickly, watching the door. "I want to come back here, after I take them to the airport."

"That's not a fair thing to ask, not now."

"I'm asking."

"You're out of bounds."

Edward came in with a stack of papers. "You might as well know about the whole mess." He dumped them on the glass-topped coffee table. "Here they are. My big good grades. All of them copied from this essay that was making the rounds at school. You'd think the profs would catch on. They were selling this at Clemson and Emory and Auburn, I heard. It came from Duke, or so they said. I paid top dollar. I thought it was funny, at first, the way you said, to see how many different topics I could write up with the same stupid paragraphs, and then, gee, after the first one got an

A, hell, I said, they can't think this stuff is serious; I mean if you read it you can see it's pure crapola. Any prof should be able to see that."

Edward handed Peggy and Todd the term papers, and they each read a page and then traded. Todd was laughing. He read the first page out loud, and then he took the second and read it aloud, laughing again. "Inspired," he said. "Whoever dreamed this up is a genius. I bet you could sell these, longer versions, I mean, for books. Books on whatever subject was in demand."

Peggy placed the papers on the table. "Edward, how could you? Did your dad see these?"

He handed her Paul's letter.

Peggy read: " '...our concern here is more with the tangible factors which one encounters in the larger social context.' Oh, Edward. How terrible for him. Of all the things you could have done to hurt him—"

"I knew you'd say that. You always take his part. That's why I didn't show you."

"It was wrong of him not to say it to you face-to-face."

"He couldn't. Because he knew what he'd hear. That school is his idea. This big scholar thing, that's his plan. I'm just there to make him feel good. What does he care what I'm taking or how I'm doing as long as I get the grades?"

"But he does. He does care. It simply doesn't occur to him that you might not want to be in school. How could it? He's Pink's son."

"See, I told you she wasn't going to understand." Edward appealed to Todd, who stood by the boy, lending support.

"What do you want to do, Edward?" Peggy asked her son.

"You and Dad would kill me if I dropped out."

Todd made a suggestion. "Is it possible for him to take a year off to do the circuit? Look up next September and see where he is?"

"Mom?"

"The semester has hardly begun; I'm sure you can withdraw." She felt angry at Paul, not for his letter to his son—that she would think about tonight, when everyone was gone and she was alone—but for leaving her with the aftermath of his own hurt pride. She would have to think about that, too. Why had he been unable to talk to her about this?

Men fought each other constantly, she thought, tooth and claw. All of them, all the time, as if they were back in the era of clubs and stones. Comparing, competing, you could see it in the smallest boys. It left women on the outside.

She looked at Todd Stedman, so attractive, so at ease, the two young men—their sons—aligned with him, gaining solidarity from him. A prank gone sour, twenty-five years ago. Another, more serious perhaps, but still, something of a lark, fingered and judged by the same man who had blown the whistle the first time.

Later, with the boys packed onto the plane, relieved and full of plans, Todd intended to come back here, to take the last measure of his revenge by bedding Paul's wife. Peggy wished for her dad. Ned Ruggles knew all there was to know about besting other men.

She took stock. She hadn't the luxury, she saw, of thinking it out later at night, the way she liked to do. Of taking her time, fitting the pieces together in different ways, as her grandmother, tilting forward in her straight chair, used to do over those thousands of almost identical pieces of the schooner on the rolling blue ocean. Jigsaws that all but put Peggy's eyes out even as a girl.

Something was wrong here. If Paul—leave his personality out of it, the implications of unfairness; start again. If Paul had felt that the *deed* was what should be dealt with and not the *intent*, then he would have called in all the Grunts. Not just the one. If he called in just the one, then it was because that one, Todd, was the one he was after.

"There is something else you can do, you know, Edward, besides drop out of school. I mean if you want to show your dad that his ambition is not yours and that grades and a degree are not important to you right now."

"What?" He drew away from Baxter and Todd, but it was clear he felt that she was interrupting.

"You could do your own work and make Cs and Ds. All and nothing are really two sides of the same standard, aren't they?"

Edward frowned, not sure of an answer.

His hesitation was enough; it was a break in the mood that Peggy was after. "You've left one thing out of your story, Todd."

He raised his brows and smiled at her but kept his shoulders turned toward their sons, holding them by his stance. "What's that?"

"Why Paul didn't turn in anyone but you."

"My bad luck or greater visibility." He waved his hand.

"No. You had taken something from him, something he wanted very much. He was getting even."

Todd dropped his arms and stepped away. "He saw his chance to make an example of someone, that was it, pure and simple."

"Of you. For what?" Peggy stared him down. Knowing she was right gave her a strength that the difference in their positions could not diminish.

Todd looked at his watch.

She persisted. "You started this story; you have to finish it."

He met her eyes, calculating. "It must be a guess on your part. I know wild horses couldn't drag it from Paul."

The boys, anxious now to leave before they heard too much, gathered their rackets and sweaters. "We got to catch the plane, Mom," Edward said.

Todd spoke with some satisfaction, still. "I married the girl he was engaged to."

Baxter looked funny. "Mom? Not Mom?"

"Actually, yes."

"Dad? Engaged?" Edward looked amazed. He couldn't imagine his dad before this family.

"Meet you at the car," Todd told the boys.

Peggy wanted to be by herself, but she let him say what was on his mind.

"I won't try to come back today."

"Maybe you've done what you came here to do."

"No, I haven't. Seeing Old Pink. Getting this story out of my system. Sure." He took a step toward her, but stopped. "I'd better get the boys on that flight."

"Yes."

They stood a minute more. He rattled his car keys. Then he asked her, "How did you know?"

Peggy flashed what she hoped was the famous Ruggles smile. "Instinct. You spent twenty-five years hating Paul, but I have spent twenty-five years loving him."

17 CONSOLATION PRIZES

Todd sent her three rubro lilies the next day. Sending flowers was obvious. But the choice pleased her. It wasn't a dozen roses. Only three lilies, Japanese, and favorites. She set them in an old bottle-green vase in her bedroom. Their deep crimson rims looked lovely on the polished table by the windows.

It was one o'clock in the morning when he called.

"Did I wake you?"

He hadn't, actually. Peggy had been in her robe, trying to sort out her thoughts. "No, I'm something of a night owl. At least these days."

"I wanted to thank you."

"You did. The flowers came at lunchtime."

"I wanted to thank you when I could hear your voice. That session yesterday, or the day before, to be technical, didn't quite turn out the way I intended, but on balance, I'm glad of it. It's a relief to me. I should have told Baxter the part about his mother long ago. He's certainly heard the rest of it often enough. I think he liked the idea of her as a college girl being fought over. She's rather anti-male these days. I should have told him before. I think, perhaps, with all the unpleasantness, I'd blocked a good bit I shouldn't have."

"It was a guess on my part."

"On the mark."

"What is her name, your former wife?"

"Olivia."

Olivia. Had Paul ever mentioned her? Peggy could not recall either of them ever talking about old flames. She had told him all the exploits of Ned Ruggles, had shown him scrapbook after scrapbook of clippings about her dad. Paul had introduced her to Charlottesville. If her dad was the old beau in her life, the town was certainly the first love of Paul's. Or so she had thought. She would, in fact, have bet her best wager that he could have left her, the boys, even the firm, before he could have left the town. That he had done so gave her pause. She had missed something she ought not to have missed.

"I'm uncomfortable with it," she said. "Both of you in love with her. I feel somewhat like a consolation prize. First Paul's, then yours."

"It isn't that way. Not at all."

"But of course it is."

"No. It is more that we were a lot alike. Looking for some of the same things, if not going about it in the same way. How else do you account for Bax and Edward hitting it off? They didn't know the history of their fathers. Besides, they're good kids. They aren't wrapped up in old grudges."

"That's true." She paused. "Perhaps Olivia and I would get along."

"I'd prefer you didn't."

She laughed. Todd was doing all right. She warmed again to the sharp edge in their conversation. It excited her, as it had when he was in town. She had grown rusty through the years, complacent.

"Where are you?" she asked.

"You mean physically? Baxter and I live in a brownstone. I have the top floor. I'm looking out a window at the branches of some trees and a bit of street corner. The phone is near a drafting table."

"That sounds pleasant."

"It is. Come see for yourself."

"I thought you'd finished your business with us."

"I told you I hadn't."

"I like Washington."

"We can have dinner, see the botanical gardens."

"I'd like to see your work, although I'm not sure I'll know what to say. 'My, that is a building.' "

"How about: How good it must be to work there. Or live there—I've done some low-income complexes."

Something stirred in Peggy's mind. She had a clipping about a high-rise in the District. She'd locate it. It would give them a place to begin, a way to start talking about concepts of interior space.

"I can do better than that," she told him.

"I'm sure you can."

"I thought all architects lived in their own homes."

"I don't do houses. I never did. I like urban solutions; private solutions are beyond me."

"Let me think it over."

"I can't imagine the war hero's daughter having trouble making up her mind."

"Let's say I'm having a little trouble with the decision I've made."

"That's better." He didn't keep the pleasure from his voice.

"Give me time to get used to it."

"I'll call tomorrow night."

"No, I'll call you. Tell you how the lilies look in the window. On my nickel, find out something more about where you're coming from."

"How do they look in the window?"

"At home."

"I envy them."

She didn't answer; there was no need to.

"I want to know you're also glad to get that old story out in the open." He was pushing her.

"About Paul?"

"Yes, what really happened."

"You're still wanting to get even with him."

"Not through you."

"It seems to me he was the one who settled the score; it should be over and done with now."

"It isn't, not as long as you let it get between you and me."

Peggy said, "Fair enough." She liked that; he had shifted the blame, the acting out of old enmities, from himself to her, and done it neatly. She tucked up her feet, eager to see where this was going to take her. "Very well," she told him. "I'll come this weekend, over Saturday night."

"I'm glad." He sounded elated.

"Good night, Todd."

"I'll talk to you tomorrow."

Replacing the receiver, she sat a long time, sorting it out. It must be, she concluded, that it had been she, not Paul, who had kept them where they began.

She'd loved Charlottesville from the start, every brick house and tree-lined street of it. She knew that part of the reason she'd married Paul was to share the seamless stability of his world. Imagine living all your life in the town where you grew up! Plus he had the continuity that his dad's

long teaching career offered. For much as Paul got angry
with his father—for being overbearing, meddling, and, now,
somewhat dotty—still, there was no questioning the fact
that Pink had made a place for Paul in Charlottesville. He
had made a very visible structure of his life, which Paul, as
a small boy, a student, and even a grown man, could inhabit
or reject as he chose.

A very different life, indeed, from Peggy's.

By comparison, her own growing up had been on shifting
sand. Army brats were supposed to land on their feet; certainly she had learned to. First and second grades were in
Richmond while her dad was overseas, wrapping up his
war. Third and fourth at Camp Chaffey, fifth at Fort Ord,
sixth—split because her dad was moving up—divided between her grandparents and Fort Bennington, down in
Georgia's red clay. Then back to her mother's family while
Ned Ruggles went overseas again. A year in Germany, then
all of high school at Fort Sam, and then, as she went off to
college and he finished up the Korean War (like a sandbox
exercise, to hear him tell it, only it wasn't called a war, except by him), her mother gave up on living with him and
later gave up altogether.

Once Peggy had counted, what with temporary moves
and shuttling back and forth to grandparents, that she'd
appeared in brand-new classrooms ten times before she got
out of high school. It taught you several things, whether
you wanted to learn them or not. To look good, because nobody took up with an ugly kid. To read the signals: what
was going on; who was who; what they were looking for.
You learned you could skip certain things, like multiplica-
tion tables, and pick them up on your own. You learned you
could do the same things you'd already done, like diagram-
ing sentences, without saying that you'd done them a dif-

ferent way before. Mostly you learned—which they all still teased her about—how to learn.

In those years she'd been eraser duster, class census taker, homeroom helper, student aide, safety patrol, sergeant at arms, National Honor Society, Key Club, cheerleader, and class president.

When she married Paul, she'd been so relieved to be through with all that, through with having to keep up her guard, stay on her toes, always look for the smallest signal indicating how she was doing, that she'd relaxed and let herself go anywhere that her wide reading took her. (She suspected sometimes that Edward's single-mindedness was a reaction against her voracious amateurism.)

But she had not seen in time that what pleased her most, most irritated Paul.

Nor had she suspected that the Peggy of those days, eyes and ears honed to the slightest inflection, social senses tuned to the smallest cue, brain working overtime to fit the classroom pieces together, was eager for a comeback.

The bedside clock said 2:00 A.M., but she did not feel the need for sleep. She was alert and wide-awake. It was like old times: the first day of class at a new school. She felt the adrenaline stirring; she would have to be on her toes with Todd. Wrapping her robe around her, she felt an excitement she hadn't known since she'd settled down here into the arms of Paul and his town.

She felt a kinship with the new peony shoots in her dad's garden, suddenly poking through the earth, ready to come back to life and bloom ruby red again after a long, dormant winter.

18 A LETTER IN REPLY

Dᴇᴀʀ ᴘᴇɢ,

You're upset to learn about my project from someone else?
You're upset? How do you think I like hearing that the
women with whom I am working and from whom I take my
instructions are gay? And hearing it via someone I wouldn't
trust to tell me whether it's night or day? Thanks very much,
but I'll reach my own conclusions about the sex lives of my
co-workers.

A lot has become clear after your letter. Todd Stedman apparently got me invited on this team in order to get me out
of the country so that he could make time with my wife.

I tried to get you by phone today, from the inn that I mentioned, but there were no lines out. It's just as well. I was in
no mood to learn where you were at the crack of dawn Sunday morning.

Separated. I come home after another awful day with the
greasiest womanizer in the village, wet from the pouring
rain and stinking of chicken feathers, to find that you and
the rector have decided to tell the entire congregation of
Christ Episcopal that we are separated. That Fan and Mew,

our oldest friends, had a cozy dinner for four for you and Todd Stedman the first weekend I was gone.

Let me tell you, Peg, that man is not to be trusted. He's a liar and a cheat. He cheated his way into and out of school. He's the last man on the face of the earth I'd wish to see around our son. Edward is already an expulsion waiting to happen. If he hasn't told you what he's up to, you'd better ask. I'm through protecting that boy. I've given up on him.

Peg, Peg. I needed a chance to get away, and you've made a fool of me the moment I leave town. Everyone here is preoccupied with horns. Horns. That's all they think about. I read your letter and stood in front of this piece of tin they call a mirror in my bathroom and stuck my fingers to my forehead and cried. You don't have to believe that. My roommate, Takamori, who handles all this better than I do, caught me at it. He thought it was a great joke and wanted to know who I was after. He thinks we've been selected to romance the wives of certain men down here, and that we're really under observation. I think he's like a grade school boy having fantasies. We are here for something, I'm sure of that. The two of us were not chosen at random. But I can't fathom for what.

I've been up since before daylight, which occurs late because we are in the mountains. I can hear the roosters crow now; this means soon the sun will hit the top of our street.

I didn't want the chickens identified, for Christ's sake. The villagers don't care what kind they are. They take whatever breed the chicken grows into, it's all the same, like kids taking the gum balls from a machine. The concept that you could select eggs for a certain breed of hen is higher-tech than our chicken farmer can conceive. I took them for you, thinking you'd get a kick out of them.

"Send the boys down Christmas if I write Edward?" Christmas? Do you realize that it is only the middle of September? I only signed on for a month. I told you so; I know I did. A month. Send the boys for Christmas? Is this an announcement that I've no home to come back to?

I know that snake Stedman got dumped by his wife. That's been years. I don't know why she stayed with him that long. (She was someone I knew in school.) Did you happen to know that he took classes from my dad? I told Dad he'd better check every paper twice. But he's an old fox. He didn't give the kind of assignments you could cheat on. I remember he said, "That boy's lazy." Those were his words.

Peg, listen, I should have talked this over with you. I saw red when I found out what Edward was up to. Wanted to pull the plug on everything.

I don't understand about Charles. You say (I've read your letter until that flimsy blue paper is in tatters) that he was cheered up by his meeting with Trice but that you "didn't pry." I gave him the check that was due for the Wainwright case, for God's sake, thinking he'd shown more interest in it than our good-for-nothing clerks. Naturally, I assumed that Trice would convey it to you, and you would put it in his savings. An eleven-year-old can't do anything with a check. Will you find out where the thing is? We're talking about SIX THOUSAND DOLLARS, Peg. I tried to call the office when I got your letter yesterday—the inn sent a man around; but it was late, and I forgot that the office was closed on Saturday. Besides, I couldn't get a line out. We're talking about

SIX THOUSAND DOLLARS. Surely Trice called you? Charles told you? She must have misunderstood, deposited it in my firm account. You take your eyes off things for two weeks, and all hell breaks loose.

Damn it, Peg, I miss you. I wish I were home to straighten things out. Sometimes I hate this place. Most of all, I hate being helpless to get through to anybody.

Will you tell that bastard to stay off my turf? Peg?

I'm living next door to this painter and his wife, and they are at it like rabbits or else they're at it like hounds after a fox, twenty-four hours a day.

(Do you know the thing about the Japanese? This is confidential. They laugh at any and everything. Some days I want to say to him: if you don't stop, I'm going to lock you in the chicken coops. And then I feel like a fool; if I didn't have him, I'd go nuts.)

I was going to write you about the climb last week. What an adventure. But I had a cold for days, from getting soaked to the bone. And then when I got your letter yesterday, I don't mind saying it knocked the wind out of my sails.

Paul

Tepoztlán
September 15

P.S. It shouldn't be too much of an effort for you to box up two suits (with vests, please).

19 DINNER FOR EIGHT

PAUL KNEW he could have got the letter back. The mail doubtless fell into a box and stayed there until someone at the inn had an errand in the capital. He checked the dates again: Peg's had arrived in eight days, or it was eight days before the man had walked around the corner and down veintidós de febrero to Jaramillo's place. Still, sometimes it could take that long to get a letter out of Charlottesville—if it got lost in the tons of mail processed by Washington—to a client in Roanoke. Awake, assisted by the pungent coffee he now drank gratefully, his stomach having obligingly put on its own version of an aluminum liner, he decided his letter had sounded disgruntled, self-pitying, angry.

Fairly accurate, in other words.

(He should never have allowed himself the indulgence of the comment about Nakae. Probably all mail was opened and read by every pair of hands it passed through.)

He had been, he had to admit, not in the best of spirits. After the mindless three-hour trek back down the mountain last week, a grueling descent even more treacherous than the climb up, he'd fallen into bed in total exhaustion, leaving his wet clothes where they fell on the floor. His single thought, even as Nakae, shivering in his nearby cot, began to rehash the whole ordeal, had been that at least he would get revenge. His first act upon arising was going to be to tell the anthropologists every humiliating detail.

Their reaction was totally crushing. Jean Weaver, the dark-haired corn grinder, had made notes, acting, it appeared, as Helena's secretary. But Helena herself, whom he'd counted on to respond with disbelief and then outrage, to pronounce sentence on the vicious, flabby chicken farmer and his colleagues in perfidy, to expel them from the village, at the least to expose them for the frauds they were, had only looked amused and, from time to time, nodded her head.

"Perfect," she'd said at one point. "That's exactly what we surmised." She had stretched in the warm, dry living room and beamed at the men as if at good students. "You did well. Now let's eat. Jean has fixed us a wonderful breakfast."

The letter from Peg, which arrived late yesterday, was very nearly the final straw. If anyone but Todd Stedman had said the women were gay, he would have thought it an attempt to reassure Peg. You have nothing to fear, Mrs. Sinclair, even though your husband is seeing this beautiful woman, yellow as sunlight, every morning and many nights. But it *was* Stedman, and the farthest thing from his small mind was to reassure.

Paul groaned and kicked the smooth stones under his feet.

Tepoztlán was lovely to behold in the morning. He could stand here in the middle of their steep street and see the sun hit the luxurious green rise of the mountains. The sun was waking El Tepozteco, whose altar was set at an angle on the north ridge so that it faced east. Surely his eyes must be the first to see the sun.

Ever since the climb up that accursed slippery slope, Paul had grown protective of the old god. Sometimes he imagined a giant likeness of him with his feathered headdress and entwined serpents: the Winged Messenger carved out of stone, twenty feet high. Imagined him tumbling down the bluff, falling intact, his huge face gazing beneficently out, to rise again from his own ruins.

Other times he conceived the god as an undulating snake sunning itself in the morning light, lying in wait in the afternoon shadows, bedecking itself at night with feathers and soaring over the village to shine down on the Stonehenge-like pillars that crowned the mountain.

He didn't know why he'd told Peg he was leaving when his month was up; her letter had infuriated him, implying that the choice of whether to return or not had been taken from him. He had not yet done what he'd come to Mexico to do. To put it tangibly, the sum total of his accomplishment to date was today's invitation to Dr. Gómez's house, but intangibly, he had done a lot. The people knew him, women that he had met through Esperanza, men who had grown used to his face around the square with Nakae.

More and more, Helena was turning to him for help with her work, expressing in a dozen ways her appreciation of his perspective, his approach, his clear-eyed way of interpreting conflicting facts. If he'd been hurt by her response to the climb, it was on personal, not at all on professional, grounds.

He didn't want to leave this village. He had just begun to fit himself into its slow pace, to make a start toward sorting out the eddying undercurrents of its life. The surface was so beautiful to the eye, enticing to the mind; it was, in that way, the true tropics. Yet underneath the apparent sloth, or at least ease, of the people was an enormous collective will. He didn't wish to call it spirit, because he didn't like that word. More the idea of the collective unconscious; only here, perhaps, it was a collective conscious.

Living in a place such as Tepoztlán, you could believe in a being composed of many parts, and the villagers were the parts. The whole, the being, was formidable as five hundred scorpions. Words you learned for it in school—mass psychology—fell far short of the mark. Were terms that could only be used by those reared in very individualistic societies. Here you said "the village" or "Tepoztlán" or "us," and all the rest was implied.

The car was crowded, with him and Helena in the front seat, Esperanza and Jean on either side of Nakae in the back. Paul did not ask why the chicken farmer had been excluded from the outing but noted it with a relief he imagined Esperanza to share. They bumped along the rudimentary cement tire strips out of the inn parking lot, then curved around to the left, south, rather than the way he'd first come, north toward the pass. Behind them, as they left the village, the church bells rang for noon mass.

"Thanks again for setting this up, Paul." Helena turned to smile at him, as if they were alone in the car.

In the back, Jean and Esperanza were talking across Nakae, who—happy man—had an arm lightly around each woman.

"The invitation was Gómez's."

"It was you who got it for us." She had gone out of her way to be appreciative ever since his rain-soaked fiasco.

Peg's letter still gnawed at him, although he fervently wished to put it out of his mind. "How is it," he finally asked, in what he hoped was a casual tone, "you know Todd Stedman? If you told me, I forgot."

"We worked together on a project. He's an architect—

I imagine you know that; this was urban renewal. The idea being to claim a part of the inner city before gentrification took it away from the families living there. He built a high rise, but with a revolutionary feature. The apartments formed the core of the building, and around these, in an outside, glassed-in corridor, was a hallway onto which each opened. Each had a doorway, much like the entrance to a row house, a little window complete with a window box, a bench, an actual flat stoop set in the floor, and a working lamppost. Each tenant was free to decorate or embellish in any way she saw fit that particular twelve feet of right-of-way. You could walk down the hall as if down a street and see geraniums, daisies, plastic birds, toy dogs, cushions, awnings. It was a marvel, and no one vandalized. There was absolutely no property damage. I got in on it because they wanted an anthropologist's authentication, and I needed the credentials on my piece of paper. In fact, all any of us did was walk around amazed that such a simple idea had worked so well."

"I recall that was written up." Paul felt a ball of anger shift in his stomach. He hadn't seen the article; Peg had read about it, all agog, in the *Post*. Not getting a response from him, she'd tucked it away in one of her many files. No doubt Stedman had taken her to see it already, capitalizing on her ready-made interest.

"Yes, they did features on it in several papers and magazines." Helena paused a moment, then, "Our working together got sticky at the end, although we've remained friends—obviously, as I felt free to consult him when I was building our team here." She glanced in the rear-view mirror. "His wife, Olivia, moved in with me for a time. That was a few years ago."

Paul felt a constriction in his chest. Olivia living with a

woman? Then he realized he was reading into her words the insinuation in Peg's letter. No doubt some innocent gesture—Helena helping a fellow academic leave her cheating husband—had caused Stedman to dream up his sick accusation. This made everything clear.

With some relief, Paul confessed, "He was never a favorite of mine. I was surprised at the recommendation."

Helena didn't seem bothered. "I daresay he thinks no better of you. But I've found that people are far more helpful computers than the real thing. They sort, reject, select on a far more sophisticated level, taking into account not only the factors you request but a dozen or more variables that fit the spirit of what you're looking for but could never be translated for a computer. Those intangible factors by which we all catalogue people but would be at a loss to put into words. The half dozen snap judgments we make all the time but never verbalize to ourselves about how a person will react in a given situation."

"That doesn't sound like Stedman's strong point."

"It's mine. The people I asked were, in a sense, blind samples. I gauged their offhand suggestions, gathering a wealth of information they didn't even know they were supplying."

"Sometime you will have to tell me how we came to be your choices." Paul lowered his voice slightly, hoping to talk under the conversation in the back seat. Nakae was telling the women some tale about an early priest who spoke Náhuatl to the Indians, Spanish to the army, and Latin in church.

"Anytime you like," Helena promised, slipping her hand across the seat. "Although we can't take all the credit for our good fortune."

Paul, pleased at her tone, calmed down, let his mind wan-

der. It was good to see the sights. Along the highway, cattle
and sheep grazed. Beyond them, in green fields, grew sweet
potato trees and those they called the silk-cotton. Here and
there he saw patches of ash covered in vines, and everywhere
clusters of beehives.

He imagined his roommate as the many-languaged padre
Nakae was discussing. It amused him, half lidding his eyes,
to picture Father Takamori, the missionary priest from
Kyushu, wearing (in Paul's mind) what looked like a samu-
rai robe with a black scarf at the neck, and a flat black hat.
Father Nakae Takamori, his grinning face indomitably
pursuing souls, one of them being the Indian Pablo Sin-
clairez, worshiper at the temple of El Tepozteco. He saw
himself chanting at the foot of the pyramid, saw Father
Takamori gleefully shove the image of the old god off the
cliff, finally, in a frenzy, pound it to bits in the valley below.
He saw the other Indians rise up with him and drive the missionary back to Portuguese-speaking Japan, that Catholic
stronghold, leaving the vast paradise of pagan Mexico to its
ancient ways and Náhuatl tongue.

Paul laughed aloud, and Helena, puzzled, joined in.

Typically, Jean and Nakae had not dressed up. Helena
wore a yellow gauzy dress with lace at the neck; he was in
his (eternal) spare suit; Esperanza wore a very North
American black dress with a flat gold necklace that looked
very old; Nakae was in his cotton pants and Guatemalan
shirt, and Jean in the woven skirt, embroidered blouse, and
fringed shawl of the oldest Indian woman.

Descending into Cuernavaca, they circled a *glorieta*
with a huge statue of the Virgin in a sort of Roman arch,
and then, following Esperanza's instructions, turned and
twisted around the wide, lovely residential streets lined by

flowering trees whose golden cups nestled in what looked like magnolia leaves, banana plants, mimosa, palm, and, everywhere on every wall, masses of purple and orange bougainvillea. The walls themselves, stuccoed adobe, were painted pink, yellow, lime, and bright blue, and every house was roofed in red clay tiles that echoed the red clay pots and red-brick driveways safe behind locked black iron grilles.

Around a corner in a very old district, whose thick trees shut out the sun, and whose brick streets slowed the movement of the car, they came to a stop before Number Five.

"That wall," Esperanza said, pointing to one across the street that was a faded dusty rose, "is three hundred years old."

"What do I do now?" Helena asked her.

"You must honk. They will come."

Helena did, and then a young girl ran out to unbar and swing open the heavy gate. Paul could see that each vertical rod of iron widened into a carefully welded scorpion, whose pointed tail made a sharp spike on top to discourage intruders.

The group was escorted through the front garden by an older woman who took them to the door where Segundo Gómez waited, in European silk shirt and pants, his mustache waxed, to welcome his guests.

"My house is your house," he said to the women, giving each of them a kiss. Nakae he brushed aside, as if a gardener were attempting to enter the house, but Paul he welcomed with the typical ritual of handshake, two-armed embrace, and back clap. "My house is your house," he repeated.

"Thank you for having us," Paul said.

"It is nothing. Come in, come in."

Only Esperanza walked quickly into the room. The rest

of them stood transfixed at the door. The combination of
the vast space, marble floor, and walls of art had the impact
of a museum. Between them and a large atrium in the back,
complete with flowers, cockatoos and parrots, two low white
couches cut the room (which must have been forty feet
square) in half. On one of them a stunning woman reclined.
When they were almost to her, she rose, a very tiny woman
with a great bun of hair and high heels, and held out her hand
to the men to be kissed.

"I am Isabel," she said, "wife of Segundo Gómez Pani-
agua." She laughed, a deep rumble, as if it were a joke to
identify herself in this way. Her greeting of Paul and
Nakae was the reverse of her husband's. She glanced at
Paul only briefly, then put her arm through Nakae's and
drew him close to her. "Your father was at Sumiya, isn't
that so?"

She spoke English, as Dr. Gómez had. Esperanza had
explained to them that this would be a courtesy to the guests.

"He was the bonzai master." Nakae beamed.

"And was he *really* Barbara Hutton's lover? Do tell me
the true story."

Nakae demurred. "He admired her."

"And she? Did she admire him?" Isabel Gómez ran a red
fingernail down the front of Nakae's shirt, stopping at his
waist. "Tell me."

"She found no fault with his work."

"I love scandal."

She greeted the women, making a little face at Jean's
costume, giving Esperanza the long embrace reserved for
family, then addressing herself to Helena. "You are in
charge of all of them, Doctor? Tell me everything. Segundo
tells me nothing. 'We are having North Americans,' he says,

as if that is all I am entitled to know. If it weren't for Jaramillo—" She called out to the painter, who answered from somewhere out of sight, to the left.

Following the sound of the voice, Paul saw that up a few steps was another, low-ceilinged room, perhaps twenty feet square, which held a table large enough to seat two dozen, and, past it, another atrium filled with flowering vines and exotic birds of paradise.

"And have you your father's interests?" Isabel Gómez asked Nakae, drawing him down beside her on the white couch.

"Perhaps our visitors would like a tour of your art," Segundo suggested to his wife.

"You are right." She rose again, aware of the dramatic effect of her white dress and vivid coloring. She pointed to the wall on their right hung with six large canvases, the highest two above their heads. "Here, see, the rounded women in their rebozos, these are Zúñiga. He is easy to recognize. He is also very high-priced today. His best ones are his pregnant women. See, here."

She moved them back toward the indoor garden. "This is by a North American woman, Woodard. She does the giant dresses, as James Dine does the bathrobes. This one is called *Christening Dress.*" She led them slowly around the vast room. "You will be interested. This is also by a North American woman. It was a gift to me. It is our armadillo." She pointed to a small bronze sculpture beside a vase of amaryllis.

"But I have kept the best until the last." She led them up the three steps into the dining room. "Here are my Jaramillos."

On facing walls, Paul saw two large canvases, perhaps eight feet high. One was a chicken coop, with a dozen iridescent black roosters and white hens staring out, as if from a cage; through the bars, around their feathers, and even between their stringy feet, the mountains and, faintly, far away, the pyramid could be seen. The other was a similar painting, this one with a single pair of roosters of the same iridescent black. It depicted a cockfight in the center of the square in Tepoztlán. Again the roosters were in the foreground, larger than a grown man, and behind them, tiny, the church. Looking closely, you could see that they were perhaps not fighting cocks, but Aztec dancers with bells on their ankles and feathered headdresses. Paul did not understand how this was implied—they were clearly birds—yet something in their stance, with the old square beneath their feet, in the arrangement of their ruffled feathers and the tilt of their combs, let you know that they were also festival dancers.

Paul was amazed, and ashamed of himself for his amazement. Rosa's chiding comments about "painting chickens" had biased him.

"Jaramillo will one day be Mexico's foremost painter," Isabel declared, "when Zúñiga is long forgotten. He is our Picasso."

At that moment, as if waiting to make his entrance, Tomás, in a bright pink shirt, came bearing a tray of drinks.

"Little scorpions for the women," he said, passing generous salt-edged margaritas, first to Jean and Helena, then to Esperanza, and finally, with a small bow, to Isabel Gómez.

She explained to them that Mexico's worst variety of scorpion was the *margaritatus*.

"For the visitors—" He handed Nakae a very tall chilled glass. "Your apple, yes?" And, to Paul, a similar slender frosted glass. "Peñafiel on ice."

"What for us?" Segundo seemed amused rather than

jealous that the young man had taken over the duties of the host. "I wait to see what you have for us."

"We will drink like men." He handed Segundo a small glass of clear aguardiente and raised another to his own lips.

"Come," Isabel said to the painter. "I'm hearing about the great love affair of Barbara Hutton."

"Isabel covets Sumiya," Tomás told Nakae. "She envies a woman who can have an entire house dismantled and brought across the ocean for her pleasure."

"It is now a restaurant," Nakae said.

"That is the greed of the new owners. Peacocks, stone fish, and high prices. We are speaking of another time."

When they were all seated and sipping, Segundo Gómez addressed Helena. "Have you been successful in your work, Doctor?"

"Everyone has been most helpful." She glanced at Jean as if for corroboration. "My friend has been studying the production of corn; Mr. Takamori, the raising of chickens; I, the family structure; and Mr. Sinclair, our attorney, has been guaranteeing that our project does not get us into trouble with the government. As you know, taxation is a constant fear in our country. It is not as it is here, where money passes hands but little sticks that can be proved."

"You are less fortunate."

"We are, and must be careful."

Isabel tapped her fingernail against her glass to show that it was empty. When Tomás stood, she said, "No, no, Jaramillo. Let Lupe do it now. You have proved yourself." She rang a tiny bell tucked behind a vase of yellow flowers on the end table. Then, with a wink at the painter, she said to Paul, "I hear you made a most unfruitful climb up the mountain?"

"It was. But our guide got us down alive." He motioned toward Tomás.

"I did not want to get myself in trouble by losing a visitor in the gorge." The young painter laughed.

Nakae, disappointed to have lost the attention of their hostess, gave his explanation. "The mayor did not come because of the mass. He had the key."

"He was there," Jaramillo said. "The mayor was there. He brought the drum, remember?"

Paul tried to picture again the stumbling, drunken man going slap, slap on the stretched leather.

"He said the mayor had sent him." Nakae looked agitated.

"Everyone knew," Jaramillo said. "Everyone knew it was the mayor."

Paul felt himself grow angry. Was that possible?

Tomás addressed Segundo. "You have made the climb in the past, have you not?"

"Every young man does so."

"You recall that along the way there is much joking and telling of tales."

The handsome doctor nodded and touched his mustache. "One must rest. It is a treacherous climb."

"And drinking."

"One must fortify oneself against the height."

"As we climb, we go through the stages of celebration, isn't that so?"

"Certainly."

"We toast our friendships."

Segundo lifted his glass of 150-proof rum in salute.

"We remember old grudges."

"But of course."

"We give in and weep. Some of us fight."

"Men need to vent themselves."

"Finally we sing and dance."

"Until the cock crows."

"This is how it goes with us. Everyone drinking at the same pace until we are all together in the same state of drunkenness. Until our singing comes out as a single note."

"That is true."

"But on the night of the climb two men went with us who did not participate in our ritual. Naturally the group had to wait until these men left to continue their festivities."

Isabel burst out in her deep rumbling laugh. "Jaramillo told me the next day. The two of you did not drink a drop!" She touched Nakae's shoulder with a red fingernail. "Surely your father was not a sober man?"

The painter spoke as if still talking only to Segundo. "No man has ever before made the climb without a bottle."

The doctor raised his glass, as if to toast such a tale.

Nakae grinned wildly, but Paul could see that behind his glasses his eyes were wet and that he was struggling for control. "It was an experiment, I see. We were part of the ladies' experiment, Sinclair."

Was it possible that he and Nakae had been chosen because of their abstention? Certainly Todd Stedman would have recalled such a fact: he and the Grunts drank like swine.

Paul didn't believe it. The women couldn't have known. They wouldn't have planned such humiliation. He tried to meet Helena's eyes, expecting to read a denial, but she glanced away.

The ghastly night of the climb returned to him in all its sickening wet and cold, its fear and its crushing sense of having been tricked. He felt himself stiffen, grow still, the cold roll of anger returning. He didn't believe it.

"Is that true?" he asked.

But Jean cut his question off. Her voice sharp, she addressed the painter: "And where is your Rosa tonight, Tomás?"

Isabel clapped her hands for Lupe. "Come. We must go to the table. The squash-flower soup will get cold." As they rose, she said, "You must not put horns on Jaramillo. He will one day be Mexico's foremost painter. The foolish Rosa was not invited. We have a dinner for eight. That is what you are used to in North America, is it not? We do not invite the chicken keeper also. He is a coarse man. Isn't that so, Esperanza?"

Small fresh blossoms held name cards. Helena and Jean were placed on either side of Segundo at one end; Nakae and Paul to the right and left of Isabel, at the other. Tomás and Esperanza, treated as family, sat opposite one another in the middle.

As the wine was being poured for the rest of them, and, by prearrangement, little cups of tea for Paul and Nakae, their hostess entertained them.

"I will tell you stories about horns." She touched two nails to an eyebrow. "Tomás Jaramillo Peña, our Jaramillo, is descended from Cortez and his most beautiful black slave. Yes, it is so. While other men broke their backs in the silver mines and pawned their sons, his fathers came from conquerors."

"An invention," Tomás protested.

"And I am descended from Isabella, *the* Isabella, and a local man whom Ferdinand had murdered for his audacity. This is not widely known. Her infant was packed off, out of the palace. I know this; I have the royal blood."

"What would your German father say to such a story?" Segundo chided her.

"Takamori," she continued, "our romantic Japanese, is the son of the heiress and the bonzai master. It is in his face."

"I don't think that is possible," said Nakae, beaming nervously.

"And Esperanza—" Isabel leaned across Nakae to the other woman. "May I tell your story?"

The quiet woman in black said, "I am a guest at your table."

"Esperanza is from an old cacique family who were burned off their land by Zapatistas. Her grandmother was seized by Zapata himself—it is so—even as the land was confiscated and her grandfather driven away. Poor Esperanza. No man would marry her, as she was from the old landed people. What man could offer her a home? She was ready to dress saints when the loud Avelino Álvarez Aguilar came along, a man not too proud to become 'a daughter-in-law,' eager enough to marry a woman with many lands."

The doctor glanced down the table at Esperanza. To his wife, he said, "Enough. Your tales are the fantasies of an idle woman."

"I am not idle." Isabel tapped her empty wineglass for a refill.

"Your imagination runs away with you. Our visitors must be allowed to enjoy their food."

"It is delicious, all of it." Helena took a generous bite of the fiery chicken dish before them, hot and tasting of lime and jalapeño.

Across from her, Jean was silent, watching the girl and old woman slip in and out, exchanging plates. Dressed as she was, she looked more a servant than they did.

With the carne asada and tiny stuffed, mild peppers,

Segundo Gómez introduced serious talk. "Do you know, Doctor"—he addressed Helena—"that our drug policy here is that anything can be sold over the counter? Tourists can buy our Kaopectate with Aureomycin; farmers can buy enough DDT to fog the countryside. Inside us and out, our bugs grow fat and contemptuous of our poisons. We are ripe for an epidemic to wipe out half our country."

"If it weren't for the drought, we couldn't survive." Isabel laughed her low rumble.

"That's true. The first year we get enough rain may be fatal." Segundo threw up his hands, while Lupe and the older woman brought them almond flan and little powdered cookies.

By the time they got in the car, Paul felt slightly nauseated. He attributed it to the revelation concerning the climb, coming right on top of Peg's letter about Stedman. The cumulative total felt, perhaps, too much like returning to school days, when he had often been the butt of jokes concerning his sobriety. His face felt at once hot and clammy cold. Damn them all, he thought, attempting to keep a rein on himself—and their mothers.

"We've time for a brief look at the market," Helena announced, explaining that there was still daylight left, that if they hurried, they would not have to travel the winding road and sharp curves by the dark of the moon.

"The market is important," she said as Esperanza directed her along the tortuous old streets toward the center of town. "Women take the bus from Tepoztlán to buy for their booths at the Sábado Market. They come to shop for their families, for festivals, for weddings. Husbands think any woman who takes the bus to Cuernavaca is meeting a lover. I want to see where the buses arrive."

"It is Sunday," Esperanza reminded her.

"I know there will not be many. But we might, another time, need to come, to see for ourselves."

They passed a huge jai alai stadium that looked like a mammoth bird aviary with its high screened dome, and wound down wide streets lined in orange trees with whitewashed trunks. Esperanza pointed out a government hospital and told them that all those with government jobs, forty percent of the population, received free medical treatment.

Helena turned her head toward the back seat. "Nakae, would you like to see Sumiya, as long as we're here?"

"No. It is a restaurant now. Anyone can go. They have sushi and martinis. It is not like in my father's day. Even the bonzai gardens are not the same; they are a factory. No one cares today." His tone was distant.

"Paul? You're being very quiet. What did you think of our exotic Isabel?"

"I got us there. You're the one who knows if our dinner provided what you want."

Helena smiled. "You are both sulking."

Jean, from the back, said, "We were outwitted by the doctor's wife. She arranged for Tomás to tell his tale."

"Was it true, then?" Paul raised his voice.

"Later. This is no time for all that." Helena shook her head slightly.

He did not know if that meant the matter was not to be discussed further in front of Esperanza or if it meant Helena wanted to wait until the two of them were alone. A part of him devoutly wanted to believe the latter. He grasped at the hope that it was some experiment involving the climb which had caused her to hold her distance from him. After all, it was only fair that she not let him get involved with her as long as there had to be a secret between them. Perhaps this had cleared the air. He felt a flicker of relief, but it was overruled by his churning stomach. "The food was very rich," he said thickly, although at the time it had seemed no different from the food at the inn.

Helena laughed. "That's why you're cross. You've got indigestion."

"I am a little queasy," Paul confessed, feeling, in fact, ten times that at best.

"Nakae?" she inquired.

"I am fine," the other man answered stiffly.

"The ice cubes. I told them no ice cubes."

Jean said, "But surely the water at that house is safe."

"Paul?"

"I'm all right." He tried to get himself under control. It might be in part the sudden descent to the lower altitude of the valley. Plus he had been angry when he sat down to eat; always a mistake.

"Say the word and I'll stop."

"Nothing like that." Paul forced a laugh. There wasn't a degree of nausea in the world overwhelming enough to make him vomit on a public street. At least the negative factors in his Virginia upbringing were positive ones in situations like this.

"Here we are," Helena announced, her mind back on work.

She pulled the Datsun into an almost full lot directly off the principal street, and they walked, the five of them, as if they were still in the car, he and Helena in the lead, the others behind. They turned when Helena turned, slowed when she slowed, until they reached what looked like a series of airplane hangars opening one into the other, the ceilings far above, the stalls jammed with more food than Paul had ever seen assembled in one place in his life.

Each seller, surrounded by half a dozen competitors displaying identical produce, tried to outdo the others in artistry. There were radish rosettes, tomato pyramids, ornamental onion bouquets. On open shelves were arranged head-high mounds of mole poblano, sculptured into forms; trussed doves; fresh fish arranged into fans; strips of uncooked beef tied together like leaves on a branch; banana stalks enough to feed a thousand; papayas strung like lights; raw, skinned rabbits, dangling by their feet, their necks dressed with ruffles; clusters of pancreas, brains, livers, hearts, and even whole baby goats, made into intricate sculptures, like the insides of an abattoir created by Salvador Dali.

There were the usual powders for impotence, black urine, sweating, spitting blood. All hawked against a backdrop of heavily political murals, Rivera style, showing the workers processing food.

The mobbed aisles were suffocating; the stench was overwhelming.

Paul dragged after the group, trying to rally as they came out the back of the last building and Helena called, "There they are, the buses."

"I'll show you where the one from Tepoztlán arrives," Esperanza said. "Then we must go."

"There is still another hour of daylight."

"Paul is not well."

Helena turned to him. "Just five minutes, I promise." She followed Esperanza across a side street to a concrete lot where buses were arriving and leaving in all directions.

Paul watched people queuing up to get on, carrying mesh bags which dripped innards and rotting fruit, and buzzed with flies. Turning away, he stared straight into the eyes of a tethered bull, who glowered back at him, horns out.

Suddenly Paul doubled over, a knife twisting in his stomach. As he threw up, in plain sight of several hundred people on the streets of Cuernavaca, he thought: It is not possible she did that to me. And, in his misery, even he was not certain which woman he had in mind.

20 EVIL SPIRITS

WITH THE upheaval of vomiting a second time, he soiled himself, but it was too risky to stop on the high, winding mountain road with no streetlamps and the moon dark. There were few cars; but all the drivers, Helena swore, were drunk, and they would be hit and plunge down the mountainside, so they crawled home, with Paul's head on the dashboard and him sunk as deep in shame as he imagined possible for a grown man.

He remembered getting in the shower to clean off when he got home and then spending the night afraid to sleep for fear of soiling his bed and himself again, dozing lightly, dizzy and unsteady with the sudden loss of water, running back and forth from their small bathroom to the bed. In the back of his mind surprised that Nakae did not call any of the women in. He heard, from time to time, voices outside, whispers, but then the slatted door would be dragged closed again.

By Tuesday he realized that Nakae had permanently disposed of his trousers, the ones he'd had on in the car, and had unpacked him some clean underwear, cords, and a fresh shirt. As he lay in bed, able to keep the first liquid down since

Sunday, two things were uppermost in his mind. One was a fervent prayer of thanksgiving that they had indoor, working plumbing. The second, that Nakae had nursed him like a comrade on the battlefield. Surmising, correctly, that the embarrassment would be compounded if he'd had to deal with Helena or Esperanza about it. Paul was touched; there was no one in the States who would have done that for him. He wondered, were the situation reversed, if he would have done the same for Takamori. And decided, ashamed on another level, that he would not. That he would have stayed at the inn, thinking to spare the other man humiliation, until the coast was clear.

Tuesday afternoon Esperanza was allowed in to apply the old remedies. She rubbed Paul with salt and yarrow leaves to cleanse him of bad water. She fed him with mole and made him taste a special loaf of bread she had baked in the form of a doll, its face colored red.

Paul did not object. He had consumed two full bottles of Kaopectate with Aureomycin and could well believe that, as Segundo Gómez had said, the bugs inside him thrived on it.

Late that afternoon Nakae himself came in sick, shaking all over.

"Tepoztlán is above the malaria belt," Paul told him feebly, trying to offer reassurance. He registered that Nakae was no longer smiling and wished to help him, but he still had trouble with the bed pitching like a ship whenever he lifted his head.

"I have done the forbidden, Sinclair."

Paul made a noise of sympathy. What could be forbidden in this village?

"I destroyed an ant hill. The one that was high as a table, by the chicken pens." Nakae crawled into bed and covered everything but his head. He had to stop a moment to quiet the chattering of his teeth. "They eat the corn crops, but the people do not stop them. They get in the chicken feed, but they do nothing."

Carefully, Paul propped his head on his arm so he could see his roommate.

"Today when I am out there, Avelino is spreading mango leaves on the hill. The ants are crawling over them, heading like an army to the coops. These are large ants, flesh-eating. I do not think they will stop at the grain, but see that they will head for the pullets, who are caged and helpless.

" 'Stop them,' I say to Avelino, but he shakes his head. 'What will be will be,' he tells me. Suddenly something in me explodes. The chickens have become important to me. I want to show that it is not necessary to lose a third to a half of them. I have kept them dry. I have kept the grain from rotting. I have swept up their droppings so that they don't get diseases from the parasites. Now he is telling me that the ants, which I am seeing with my own eyes marching straight for the chickens, are to be left alone.

"I fetch a large bucket of water from the feeder—shoving the chickens out from under my feet, growing ill with the smell of them, terrified of the feathers, I confess it—and I take this bucket outside to pour in the cone of the hill. 'You have to get the queen,' I tell Avelino, the cowering son of a mother. 'You must not,' he screams. 'You must not.' But I have a stick in my hand, and taking care that I am jumping up and down so that they do not climb up my shoes, I dig into the hill to the bottom where the queen lives. I rake the hill with my stick, and then I pour the water on the queen.

"When I look up, Avelino is crossing himself and crawling to the gate, which he unlocks. Then he commences to run on foot down the highway, bumping into the dairy cows, calling out to the heavens. Leaving me to stop the ants as best I can and lock up after him."

Paul lifted his head. "What you did makes sense." The nausea came back, and he shut his eyes. "He is good for nothing."

Wednesday, when Paul awoke after his first good night's sleep, he was unsteady but settled. But Nakae neither spoke nor opened his eyes. Paul dressed and went for Esperanza.

"Evil spirits live in the ant hills," she said, using the local term, *los aires*. "That is the belief. Avelino has said that Nakae will die. He has told it all over the village. He had an uncle who destroyed an ant hill and died a horrible death. He is telling everyone."

"Is that possible?"

"Segundo Gómez tells me that a man can die of fright." She rubbed Nakae, pale as a piece of parchment, with a powder made of laurel, palm, fir, plum, and ash. She put it on his forehead, the palms of his hands, the soles of his feet. Then, as if to stop his last breath from leaving his body, she stretched him out on the bed in cruciform position and pushed the powder up his nose until he sneezed and sat up.

At noon Helena and Jean stopped by to invite the men to supper, promising rice, tea, and absolutely no ice cubes.

Throughout the day the street reported many irregularities. The woman who lived next to the house with the fine white pig had found two double-yolked eggs at breakfast. Her neighbor had heard a cock crow at midday. The wealthy woman who lived next door to Esperanza found a dead snake in her kitchen. The man who cleaned the small barrio church by the water fountain found a bat above the altar.

At dusk, as Nakae and Paul, shaky still, walked up the

cobbled street to the women's house, Avelino stuck his head out of his yard and hollered at them that he had heard a possum cry in the night and that Nakae had cast a spell upon the whole village.

In the women's living room Paul sank gratefully into the rope chair by the door. Their quarters were not as sparse as his and Nakae's, having a living room with a woven rug and local pots on a blue tile hearth. Jean, as promised, did not make them eat her rough-ground corn in any form and had even, somehow, rid the kitchen of its heavy, overpowering smell.

There was wheat bread, cheese (which Paul did not risk), rice, a bland pasta dish, and an orange cake for dessert. Nakae ate like a starving man, to calm his shakes. Paul was cautious.

"Are you cross with us?" Helena asked. She and Jean were in the painters' smocks and pants which he knew to be their off-duty clothes.

"It is not your fault I destroyed the ants," Nakae answered, morose.

"Tell him about the ant hill," Jean instructed Helena.

"I am most ashamed." Nakae grew red.

"No, it will be of use to us, that you have gone inside their customs."

"Avelino reports," Helena said, "that the queen was not destroyed."

"He did not tell me!"

"He wanted you to suffer."

"Son of a whore."

"See how Nakae knows the language," Jean said mildly from the small counter where she was cutting up banana for Paul.

"I didn't mean about your fright." Helena returned to

her earlier question. "I meant about the climb." She poured herself another glass of wine. "Paul?"

"Did you know," he asked, "that the other men would not accept us?"

"We thought, rather hoped, that would be the case."

"Because we didn't drink with them?"

"It was a good guess."

"Tell them all of it," Jean said, setting a dish before Paul. "Eat this," she told him. "Nothing beats papaya and banana. You'll be good as new."

"I told them," Helena answered.

"No, tell them all of it."

Paul found thinking quite difficult, as though his mind lived in his upset gut. "Surely if all you wanted were nondrinkers, you could have raided a Southern Baptist church and been done with it."

"We were looking for more."

Nakae had a second piece of orange cake. "Maybe Avelino is lying to you about the queen?"

"What more?" Paul asked.

"Strong fathers; virtually absent mothers. Someone unlike the men here. You cannot have a sample of a population evaluated by members of that sample. How did we know the previous studies of Mexican men in this village were not done by men like them: mother-centered, alcohol-dependent? Women like us go into the field to redo the studies done by men without considering that gender is not the only factor. I mean"—she looked at Jean, who sat listening as if to a pupil, running her fingers through her short hair—"look at us. We drink more than we should. And mothers—don't get us started on mothers. Both of us have been in therapy for years to unload our mothers off our backs."

Paul forced himself to take a light tone. "It must have been akin to hunting for one-eyed, left-handed hemophiliacs."

Helena smiled. "Something like that."

"How many of us did you find?" he asked. "To select from."

"Twenty. Remember, we also had to have someone with the language. About twenty. But we hadn't screened for certain totalitarian attitudes that had to be ruled out. Plus serious fruitcakes were eliminated."

Paul shook his head and took a gingerly bite of banana. "I feel like a guinea pig."

"The village is the guinea pig," Jean said firmly. "You are the maze we constructed."

Although she said "we," it was clear from both her tone and her manner that she meant "I." He was surprised at her air of authority and wondered if he had been misled by her habit of blending in with the women around the square. By the fact that she did the cooking and notetaking here in the house.

"May I inquire," Nakae asked testily, "who gave you *my* name?"

"The grants officer we worked with. Our theory was that we'd ask only men; we wanted men that other men had found sticklers for the rules."

Paul made a wan smile. His whole life altered because he'd turned a classmate in on a technicality.

"We were very lucky in both of you," Helena said.

"Was my nationality also requested?" Nakae asked Jean.

"Naturally." She did not appear bothered by the question. "It was my idea. I said, 'Let's have one of them Japanese.' "

"May I ask why?"

"For one thing, because less than one percent of Japan's population is Catholic—"

Helena interrupted. "Jean wanted to disqualify you after she learned your father had converted, but I told her it was like a vaccination."

"For another," Jean continued, "I thought you would be able to see better than the rest of us how very ancient mores are woven into the fabric of a modern culture. We were fortunate that you also had roots here in Mexico. Coming from Japan and having lived here give you two sets of eyes in a sense. The rest of us are going to be blind to much that you see. Any one of the rest of us could go home tomorrow, but if you left, we would be in danger—as has been the case in so many other studies—of recording only what we are able to recognize. Let me give an example. I have read that had an airplane landed in a cornfield two thousand years ago, no one would have seen it; it would have been invisible because no one could 'recognize" it. Do you follow me?"

"I am most flattered," Nakae said.

"You must take the offensive with Avelino. Make him afraid of you. Surely you know enough of their ways to do that."

Nakae brightened. "In Japan there is a fox who can turn himself into any shape. Villagers fear a stranger on a lonely road or an old woman asking for help with her firewood, for it may be the fox. When someone is found dead by the road, everyone knows it was the fox who tricked him."

"That's the idea."

"I will tell him I am a nagual—a man who can turn himself into an animal. He will be afraid of provoking me. He will fear everything on four feet."

Jean nodded and made swift notes as he expanded his plan.

Helena sat with Paul in the living room. Through the high, narrow window he saw the thinnest edge of a waxing moon.

"You're not cross with me, are you?" She smiled at him, her face catching the lamplight.

He shook his head. He felt very close to her. She had made it clear that she'd had no choice; she as well as he had been carrying out orders. The evening had put his mind to rest about one thing at least: who was in charge. Clearly this had been Jean Weaver's project from start to finish. Helena had doubtless been cast in her role as *una güera*, to walk about the streets and make of her blondness a magnet to draw the necessary people to her. And Paul in his suit, a North American who walked with such a woman, he, too, played his part.

And now—it seemed obvious how Jean had manipulated each of them—she had made a further contrast in the eyes of the village between the two men, in order to make Paul the outsider and, therefore, Nakae the insider. Even their illnesses differentiated them. Paul, his bowels opening like a faucet, his stomach refusing food, was a victim, the butt of a familiar joke, of a malady whose very name assigned it to the outsider. *Turista*: the complaint of the tourist. Whereas Nakae, falling victim to the nebulous *espanto*, the fear, a condition which implies belief on the part of both the sorcerer and the bewitched, was one of them. No tourist ever died of fright; no tourist ever became lame and trembling from an ant hill.

"Helena prefers harmony," Jean said, handing Paul a cup of steaming green tea. "That is her style. I say a sharp blade cuts better than a dull one."

"You get more flies with honey . . ."

"It must be late. We are not even arguing well."

"I want Paul content here, because I believe in a few months he will have made a place for himself. Gained certain confidences which the rest of us cannot. I had begun a campaign to get you to stay on, Paul, but given the mishap of this week, I've decided to soft-pedal that for a spell. I wish you'd not got sick this late, if you were going to. Usually that hits and is gone a bit sooner. . . .

"I'm going into the capital in the morning. Driving in before the work traffic hits, or rather, before the bulk of it—I understand there are three shifts for government jobs just as there are three shifts in the schools. At any rate, Segundo spends his Wednesday nights there so that he can put in a full day Thursday at the federal hospital. I have in mind to see him there, where he works and, perhaps, whom he meets." She stretched, looking as if she were imagining the doctor's rendezvous. "I'd hoped you could go with me. If you'd been well, we might have driven in tonight and missed the traffic altogether."

Paul felt a rush of hope at her words. Was she saying that constraint was no longer necessary between them? That they could stay the night together, away from the others, in the capital? He recalled the small, old hotel with the vine-hung windows where he'd spent a week with Peg. He wanted to go with Helena at once, cursing inwardly the knowledge that he was in no shape to survive the winding roads. "Can it wait a week?"

"Maybe we two will go again." She let her eyes rest on his face, promising. "It depends on what I find."

"I'd like to help." He looked at her.

"You already have. In many ways."

Jean put on her glasses and began to read over her notes.

It seemed a hint, and besides, Paul was deeply tired. He thought the sooner he was asleep, the better his chances were of keeping the supper down where it belonged. And, therefore, the sooner he would be fully well and able to go with Helena, at least to talk with her, alone, about all that had happened.

He took her hand, as if to say good-night. "We'll let you get some rest, if you have to start early in the morning." Her skin felt warm and firm.

Jean looked up. "Stop by the corn mill tomorrow, if you're out."

"I will. I'll be up and about." Paul let her know that he understood he had been requested to get back on the job.

"It has been a most illuminating evening," Nakae told the women, giving each of them a small bow. He looked his old self again, cured, confident.

In their room, after the light was out and Paul nearly asleep, Nakae whispered, "Are you awake, Sinclair?"

"Almost."

"I did not tell them that Esperanza also goes into the capital each Wednesday night. She goes, she says, to see her sick sister. Her old mother comes to watch the children and feed them supper. Her sister has been ill for a very long time."

Paul tried to connect this with Helena's trip. "But surely the women keep track of everyone?"

"I do not know."

Paul couldn't think.

"Keep it to yourself. In some way I will find out if there really is a sister."

"Everyone has a sister." His eyes wanted to close. He did not think that necessarily meant Esperanza was meeting Gómez. Maybe ten thousand people went into the city every night of the week. In a city of twenty-one million that was possible. He himself would go see anybody's sick sister before he'd stay a night in Avelino's company.

"Tomorrow we'll talk about it," he promised.

Paul slept, and then, toward morning, something woke him and he sat up. Nakae was not in his bed. The sky outside was palest lavender; it was barely dawn. He called out, and the answer came from the low doorway.

"I am here," Nakae whispered. "If you listen, you can hear animals running, many animals running in the dark."

Paul went to see what his roommate was watching. At first he could make nothing out, and then, there they were, running close to the ground, swiftly, barely visible: foxes, the tigerlike ocotochite, coyotes, deer, wild ponies, a pack of small black dogs.

"A fire? Is there a fire?"

They leaned out but smelled nothing. After perhaps half an hour they saw many women hurry by, rebozos over their heads, as many as thirty, crossing themselves furiously as they went.

"The devil is about," one of them called out. "The man in black, riding on a horse. We are going to church."

Paul dressed, very much wanting a cup of coffee but afraid to risk it still. The atmosphere was contagious, and he felt the slight crawl of fear on his arms. Something was amiss. He hoped that nothing had happened to Helena.

The woman who had previously reported the eggs with the double yolks ran into the street, her hands covering her face. "A hen has laid an egg without a shell!"

Then, as the sun rolled its flat light like a giant snake down the length of veintidós de febrero, bringing daylight, almost as swiftly a rumbling started at the top of the street and came toward them like a cat crawling under a carpet, buckling and then smoothing.

They heard a scream, and the woman with the pig ran into the street. "Mother of God," she cried, falling onto the stones on her knees.

"Get in a doorway," Nakae shouted to Paul. "It is a quake." The Californian, familiar with rolling earth, splayed himself like a cross in the doorway to the bathroom. Paul, too tall, too curious, stepped out into the street to watch as the coiling headed west to east down their cobblestones to the intersection of cinco de mayo, where people were screaming and running for the church.

The quake beat them there. The buckling ground reached the building, shook its four-centuries-old stone like a rabbit in a dog's mouth, and then passed on out toward the flat land and the chicken pens. Still heaving, a long crack slowly formed, like a moan, down the entire length of the sanctuary.

The women stopped in their tracks and crossed themselves before the Virgin with her moon and stars.

Coming up behind him, Nakae crowed, "It is heading for the ant hill!"

By nine o'clock the men of the village had agreed that the quake was El Tepozteco, venting his anger at the church that had kept his people away from his temple on the dark and rainy night of the climb.

Looking east, Paul fervently hoped that the god's revenge included liberating Avelino Álvarez's seventy thousand adolescent chickens.

FAN WAS passing the time for them while Mew was on the phone.

"I've been putting ears of corn out for the squirrels; I had half a bushel left, which I was never going to use. It was an experiment, mostly because they were getting fat as hens climbing up the pole and packing their tummies on birdseed. I put out a couple of ears—shucked, raw—and they didn't touch them. I thought I'd have to put out a sign. It's like Mrs. Ebberly's Burmese, Mousetrap, I sometimes leave a tidbit for him, a little raw chicken liver—which you know you're not supposed to eat now, because all the bad things they fatten them up with go to their livers—and Mousetrap sniffs, as if for a minute he thought it was going to be food, and then, because he eats only Friskies, trundles off to lie down by the birdbath and dream of pouncing."

"It's too early to put out birdseed. They should be eating the aphids off the roses."

"I know. It's the first year I've had the feeders up while the bath was still out. But Mew likes to see them all flocking around."

"You'll send them flying south two months ahead of time." Peggy laughed at the idea of all the birds in Charlottesville heading for Boca Raton in late September.

"Anyway, I was telling you— Then, one afternoon, I'd taken a bath and was toweling off, looking out the window, down on the yard, at the yellow rosebush, and there were a couple of squirrels wrestling over one of the ears of corn, and while I watched, one of them ran up the tree with it in her teeth, and a little bit later I saw it stuck up in the crotch of a branch, way up, and now it's gone. Into some hole. Yesterday I put out the rest. I'm going to keep my eye out for half a dozen cobs dropping on the snow, midwinter."

"The red maple?"

"The yellow. They live in there like a high rise. I think it's gone condo this year."

The two women sat on Fan's sun porch, a map of Mexico spread out on the nearby coffee table: the epicenter of the quake circled in red, and Mexico City, and then a small dot due south of Mexico City, slightly northeast of Cuernavaca, directly in the path between the resort of Zihuatanejo, near the worst of it, and the capital, where thousands were reported crushed beneath the giant buildings that sat on the old island marshland.

"If you're that close to the world's largest city . . ." Peggy fretted.

"Isn't Calcutta the largest?"

"Look it up."

"I can't believe you. Here Paul is lying under a heap of rubble somewhere and you're checking your reference books. You're like a perpetual fourth grader."

"That's what he said."

"I didn't mean that."

"I guess I reached Charles's age and got such a kick out of knowing how to learn things that I never got over it—"

"Peg, hon, I'm sorry."

"Don't be. Let's look in the *Almanac*."

"*Farmer's* is all I have."

"Never mind."

Mew came into the room and held out his hand for a cup of coffee. "No lines into the country, period. All I can get is that Acapulco and Guadalajara are okay. Americans clearly ask only about resorts. I got a recording from a news station."

"What is the largest city in the world?" Peggy asked him.

"Actual, not census?"

"Actual, not census."

"Shanghai."

"Do you know that?"

"Sure." He scratched his head, looking like a man who's been asked to deal with the outside world too early in the morning. The three of them had all seen the news on TV, and Fan had put the large pot on, knowing they'd both be on her doorstep in less than half an hour.

"How can people with families down there be getting information?" Peggy was grateful to him for his efforts.

"They can't."

"Did you try the consul?" Fan thought in terms of proper channels.

"What consul?"

"I don't know. Ours there or theirs here. You know. That's their business, isn't it?"

"I called the TV stations. That's *their* business."

Peggy put a piece of warm coffee cake on a napkin embroidered with a tiny hen and two chicks. She didn't worry about the butter dripping on the ironed cloth. Fan had put her favorite linens out to cheer them up.

Her friends were waiting for her to say something. Finally she did. "He'll be glad."

"Paul?"

"He's gone down there to help out. Now he'll have a chance. Can't you see him, ladling out food and bandages and extra bedding?" Peggy stared down at the spicy apple-cake. "In his shirt sleeves, the way they show Americans in Africa. His hair a mess. But that zeal in his eyes that they all get, as if to say, Here, at last, is something awful enough to be real."

"You've seen too many war movies," Mew said, tsking her.

"Actually, I was sort of picturing that hospital scene in *Gone with the Wind*. Remember? When they are lying around on pallets and groaning, and the main characters are sweaty and dusty but having a great time?"

"He does always play Melanie to your Scarlett, doesn't he?" Fan said.

"I'm glad," Mew chided, "it's not me clawing my way out of some building; the concern you girls show warms the heart." He handed his cup back for a refill.

"It's our way," Fan told him.

"I'm just mentioning that your way is on the chilly side."

"As opposed to your references to your patients in intensive care?"

"That's different."

"Sauce for the goose—"

"Have you heard from Baxter's papa?"

Peggy felt the color rise in her cheeks. "Todd? Not this morning."

"I can see the scenario: he goes down and rebuilds the

building that fell on his rival. A fine public gesture. Accepts no fee. Poses with the widow."

"You don't like him, do you?" she asked.

"Instinct." Mew drank his coffee.

"He's been such a help with Edward."

"Pink has been a help with my godson, but you're not going to bed with the old goat."

Fan scooted her chair close enough to Mew to flick his leg with her napkin. "And she's not going to bed with Todd Stedman. All you had to do was ask *me*."

Peggy smiled. "Fan will be the first to know."

"Paul will get word to you. That's your best bet. He'll know when he can get through." Mew got up, put on his vest and striped suit coat, and gave her a kiss on the cheek.

"No. I got mad and told him not to write me anymore. That I didn't want to hear from him."

"Well, well."

"It was the damn suits." Peggy made a face. "Silly of me, I know. But he asked me to send him a couple of middle-weight suits, and I simply saw red. I mean there are stores down there, and if he's going to leave home—I don't know, it's the way kids go off to college, stalking out the door and slamming it, and then mailing their laundry back for Mom to do."

"Did you send the suits?" Fan asked her.

"No." Peggy wiped her fingers on the chicken napkin. "Serves him right."

When the phone rang, Mew said, "I'm not here. I've left. I'm on my way. Ten minutes ago."

Fan waved him off and said to Peggy, "You want to get it? This hour of the morning, it's got to be—"

"I'd rather not. It'll be Spence."

From the door, Mew looked back, car keys already out.

"Spencer Cox, our right reverend rector, will not know that Mexico has had an earthquake until it appears in *The New Republic*."

"Peg, for you—" Fan held the phone around the corner.

"All right." She had to admit that her heart gave a lurch. Fan would have put Spence off, handled the matter herself. It must be Todd.

"Hello."

" 'Lo, Pig."

"Dad!"

"None other."

"How did you know to find me here?"

"Where else, if not at Fannie's? I figured you'd be in a sweat to know if your Don Quixote was up to his neck in the ruins, so I did a little checking around. Cuernavaca is still standing. So the surrounding area must be fine."

"That's so good of you. Mew called the news station, but they said they couldn't get through."

"I still have a few connections."

"So how are you?"

"Betts and I may be getting hitched."

"That's number five."

"It's not number five to me; it's Betts."

"Sorry."

"She's a great girl."

"Bring her around."

"One of these days. You doing okay?"

"I'm worried about Paul."

"A little danger will clear his head."

"The boys would like to see you."

"One of these days. Give them my love."

"And you—"

But he was off the phone. How kind. Who on earth could

he have called? Someone in the military no doubt. He still missed his war days, she knew that. The excitement of it was in his bones. Ned Ruggles with a new glamorous wife. They had all been glamorous. Well, she'd be happy to have Betts, too. They were always glamorous with exciting jobs, and with them her dad was his old self. You could almost see the medals imposed on the front of his open-necked shirts and spot the military snap to his step as he stode across the golf courses of Virginia in his bright blue pants. It must be the same, only worse, for athletes. What on earth could you do with yourself for the last fifty years of your life? Be a pro? Sell insurance? And she thought of Edward; Edward, so like his grandfather. Was it all going to be downhill after qualifying for the Open? If that was your peak at nineteen, what happened then?

How could Paul not see that? She knew he would be very angry or, rather, very hurt—how she hated it when Paul put on his "hurt" demeanor—that Edward was dropping out of school. Yet how happy her elder son was; even his voice on the phone had a lift, a spark she hadn't heard in years. He had promised her to pass, just pass, his courses for this semester, on the condition that she help explain to his dad that he was taking two full terms off, to play, to get on an overseas circuit, to really give the game everything he had. After that, he would make a decision about college.

She should stop worrying about what Paul was going to say; it was her responsibility now. And that was a relief. Although sooner or later she supposed she would have to talk to him about it, before the boys went down to visit, if they did.

Fan came in from seeing Mew out, having given Peggy some privacy on the phone.

"It was Dad."

"He didn't say so. I thought it didn't sound like Todd. That old rascal, he could have told me."

"He called you Fannie."

"Did he? That sweetie. Had he seen the news, I presume?"

"He'd called a source." Peggy showed Fan on the map what her dad had said.

"That's a relief."

"Assuming he's right."

"Of course he is."

Peggy fretted. "Do you think Charles will hear at school?"

"I'll call and tell his teacher at old B-M that things are okay."

"Would you mind?"

"Unless you want to talk to him?"

"If they call him to the phone, he'll think it's something awful."

"True. Sit tight, then."

Peggy took off her shoes and tucked her feet up. She studied her cup without really seeing it.

Fan came back. "I unplugged the phone."

"Is that a good idea?"

"Just a half hour."

"You're right."

"So tell me, how are you really doing?" Fan was wearing an old favorite gray jumper, originally corduroy but now more the texture of challis, a flowered blouse, and espadrilles. She had tied her short hair back with a bow.

"I've such mixed feelings."

"About Paul?"

"I suppose. About what's happening to us. To me."

"You never really loved anyone else, did you?"

"No."

"This guy is just whistling 'Dixie' coming around, isn't he?"

"Not exactly." Peggy, who had never lied to her friend, did not want to start now. "I had planned to see him in Washington this weekend."

"Are you serious? Peg? But you're not now, surely."

"No." She had decided at once, seeing the news, that she would have to cancel her plans. Now nothing seemed clear. "You remember," she said to Fan, "I used to say back in school that I didn't want someone like my dad, who had to have the sound of applause all the time? I adore my dad—who wouldn't? and they all do; he can charm the flowers right off the wall. Edward is like him. Give either of them an opponent and an audience, and every nerve in his body comes alive. But what that means, if you happen to be the one loving him, is that you're always part of that audience." Peggy looked at her friend. "Or you're the trophy."

Fan let her talk.

"Paul was different. He used to say he ran against time, like a runner, instead of against the other racers. It made him very special. One in a million. The idea that Todd once took someone he wanted and that he got back at him—I don't know. It has raised all sorts of doubts in my mind. That maybe Paul didn't compete because he didn't want to lose again. That maybe he picked me because he knew he wouldn't have to worry. Then I start to thinking that Todd is filling my head with another image of Paul when, after all, I was there myself, I should know. Then it all comes back, my thinking nobody could be as close as we were, and then all of a sudden his leaving that note and disappearing. I haven't gotten over that, Fan."

"What if he comes back?"

"I don't want him to."

Fan filled their cups and lit a filter cigarette. "You don't mean that."

"Maybe I do." Peggy stared down at the map and then at her cup. It was impossible to sort it out. If he was really in danger, then that was all that mattered. If not, then she would not be pulled back into her early feeling about him. She had dreamed about Paul lately, that was the funny thing. She'd done it each night after her phone calls with Todd. Each time she had seen him so clearly and heard him speak words he'd actually said to her at other times (these must be stored in the mind like film clips, available for the unconscious to use when it wished), and each time he was telling her that he'd lost something he had to find. The last time she'd waked up shaken. It was the shock of seeing him so clearly, so close, talking to her in that earnest way. "What, Paul?" she'd asked, but then he had frowned and drifted off.

This morning when it happened, she'd not gone back to sleep at all. It felt as if he knew her plans with Todd and were trying to reach her, to present his side.

"I can't figure it out, Fan," she said.

"Maybe there's nothing to figure. Give it time. It looks like this was a narrow miss. Maybe it was enough of a scare that he'll be back on the first plane out."

"Out of where? Not Mexico City."

Fan picked up the map and put it down. "I don't know."

Peggy moved to the window. "I don't see any ears of corn."

"Look up high, in the forked branches."

Peggy didn't look. "At first I missed Paul dreadfully. I couldn't remember a time when he wasn't there. We grew up together. We met when we were children, and then we grew up."

"You were luckier the first time around than some of us."

"Sorry. Here I am—when you've been through—"

"I haven't been through anything. I stumbled over a few things, but that's over and done with. It builds character. I have more character than a dog has fleas. Sometimes Mew says to me, 'Relax, it doesn't take all that much character to get along with me.'"

Peggy laughed. "He has a bit himself."

"Having someone die, that's tougher. You can't have it out, and you can't be glad."

"You two are a good pair."

"That's what we say."

"Don't you sometimes wish you lived together? Don't you miss that?"

"Cohabiting with my once-husband was like stepping in an ant bed. I'm not going to take that risk again."

"Even with Mew?"

"Especially with Mew. We've patented happiness, and its name is separate abodes."

Peggy hadn't understood how this could be true. How you could love someone and not want him there every night, so that you rolled over and there he was. How you could do without feeling the touch of his shoulder, curling up spoon-fashion against him as he slept, slipping back into bed, after wandering around, to the warmth of him and the steadiness of his sleep. That first night after Paul left had been lonesome beyond belief. She'd rolled the covers up and made a cocoon for herself on the chaise and slept until her alarm went off. Then the next night she'd piled all the pillows on Paul's side of the bed and slept with her back to them, so that the bed didn't feel empty.

It seemed inconceivable to her that it hadn't been the same for Paul; how was it possible that he was sleeping alone by choice? Now she saw it differently. If she had found someone else so soon, then certainly he had already done so. She had been right, earlier, to suppose that he had someone else.

"Fan, what do you think, really? I know you and Mew have talked about it. Is there another woman? I mean, surely there has to be."

"We have. We've talked about it. But Mew says no. He says that Paul—now don't take offense—that Paul can't cross the street without the safety patrol to show him the way. You know what I mean."

"That's the type you hear about who doesn't know what hit him. Some woman at a convention. Some client. Some widow who won't take no. Can you see Paul dealing with that? Can you see him confiding to me that he can't handle it?"

"Trice would know."

"I'd never ask her."

"Why not? Maybe she's down there dying to tell."

"No, she's part of Paul's world, and I'm not going to intrude on it. Paul sent a message to Charles through Trice, and she's been sweet to him—they're up to something—and that made him feel a lot better. I'm not going to make her violate a confidence. Charles would think it was about him." She slipped back into her shoes. "Oh, Fan, I couldn't bear it for Charles if anything happened to Paul. I think he puts up with me only because I got him Paul for a father."

"Spence will want to come pray over you."

"Mew is a dreadful cat, isn't he, about Spence?"

"Professional jealousy. They tend the same flock."

"Maybe I'll walk down and talk to him. Will you be here awhile? Or do you have to get on to the shop?"

"You mean the phone? I'll transfer the calls down there. We've just got our Christmas wrap, and we're going to have such a mob the police will be out."

"Oh, show me."

"Peg, you can't mean that. Now?"

"It's just what I need."

"You're sure? I just happen to have a sample here. Let me put the phone back on the hook." Fan went into her workroom off the kitchen and returned with a large sheet of wrapping paper.

Peggy looked at the three bright yellow chickens, each wearing a gold crown and carrying, under one wing, a red-wrapped gift against a blue background. The trio repeated in diagonal rows, with "THREE WISE HENS" in gold block letters beneath them.

Fan had done so much with Fowler's Fancies since her mother retired. Peggy remembered it from college days as a place quiet as a library on a homecoming weekend. A whisper sort of place that very old ladies in gray crepe de Chine frequented to get door prizes, or when the downtown jeweler's didn't have a place setting listed, or, if the recipient was only a niece by marriage, a hasty wedding present. Fan's mother was a plain woman who had no liking for the giving or receiving of gifts that "just sat there," and her feeling colored the shop. Fan had made of it a wonderful, year-round fair.

"I didn't see how anything could top the one last Christmas, dragging that tree."

"I think that each year. And then, when it comes to me, I get so excited I could pop."

"I still like the hen on camelback, remember? Bringing the baby bottle."

"That was years ago. I have them all, in a scrapbook in the attic."

"Maybe you should do a retrospective."

Fan returned the paper to the workroom. "Are you sure I should let you go off alone?"

"I'm fine."

"Come with me. You can help me wrap."

"I need to sort it out."

Outside, they stood a minute before Fan got in her car. "It's glorious weather, isn't it? September and April should last six months each."

Peggy felt crushed at having to cancel her trip. Todd had sent lilies every day. He had been there for her call on Tuesday; had called her on Wednesday. They were easy with one another on the phone, yet at the same time always fencing, sparring. It felt good. She had grown to like the evenings by herself and to anticipate the one o'clock conversations. She was ready to take it a step further.

But now, of course, she couldn't leave, not this weekend. It wasn't that Paul couldn't locate her if he were in trouble—Fan could handle that. It was the boys. Charles, and Edward when she located him, would be worried. They already felt shut off from news of their father; his letter had been so unsatisfactory, almost incomprehensible. She couldn't let them see that if Paul was in danger, she was nonetheless ready to take a shuttle to see this man she had only recently met.

She and Charles would walk down to Pink's and give him her dad's news: that things didn't look too bad. They could have the old man to dinner, perhaps, all of them hanging around the house, available if Paul got a line out to reassure them.

Or, she thought, angry with him afresh—and all the more so because her sudden fright over the disaster had reminded her how mixed her feelings still were—they could all be there when he *didn't* call. When he made it clear to his wife and sons and father that even now, when they were all worried about him, he didn't care enough to get in touch.

A T F I R S T I was so set on following them I didn't understand what was happening. All I could think about, never
mind how absurd it sounds, was that with the ground buckling as if we were on some animal's back, I was never going
to be able to keep him in sight."

They were in Helena and Jean's living room. Helena,
dusty still, scared but with the frantic elation of fear, was
talking nonstop, her words pouring out as Jean sat listening,
her notebook in her lap, and Paul and Nakae sipped flat
Manzanita.

"At first it rocked the cars, buses ahead of us even worse,
from side to side, exactly as if a bunch of kids were pushing
us back and forth, only more frightening. A lot of people
got out, screaming and waving their arms in the air. It was
like a carnival ride, except that it didn't stop, but I kept on
driving, because Segundo kept on driving also. He got to
a part of the city I didn't know, with shabby older buildings.
I parked and got out behind him. With all the shouting and
confusion he didn't notice me, and I didn't bother to be careful. I mean, police and bystanders were shouting that the
buildings were falling, for us to get away, to leave, while

people ran by us carrying their belongings wrapped in blankets. Everyone was fleeing, as if a tidal wave were headed in their direction. They seemed, all of them, to know which way it was coming—"

"Here, too," Nakae interspersed, "the animals and birds all went in the same direction."

"Anyway, just as he got to the corner, with me behind him, and about three hundred people rushing past us the other way, the hotel and the two buildings on either side of it, all about four stories high, began to crumble. Then one whole side of the one that Segundo had run up to fell away and crashed into the street.

"He was looking up, shouting, 'The door, get in the door,' and I stared up in time to see Esperanza crawl to a doorway, pull herself up, and stand in the frame, like a spider in a web, and then, while the two of us watched, the floor vanished. Next, the doorframe dropped to the second story and then the first, and Esperanza spilled out into a heap of rubble. She ran across the street into Segundo's arms as the rest of the building, with people screaming inside and on the street, collapsed. You've seen a crane throw that demolition ball against some old building and the whole thing fly apart, with a gust of mortar and brick dust and plaster cracking, and then there it is, lying on the ground? Well, it looked like that.

"I gave up all pretense of not being there, because Segundo was weeping, great tears rolling off his mustache, holding her against his chest, sobbing that she was his life, his heaven, his heart—it was a wonder to me he didn't crush her in his fright and relief. I think she must have broken or at least sprained her ankles, but that is nothing, was nothing at the moment. I never saw anybody as wild as he was. Esperanza seemed very calm. Probably she was in shock. 'You should not have come here,' she told him. 'You should have gone home.' Then she remembered that he was due at the hospital. 'There will be no hospital,' he shouted. 'We will have to explain,' she told him, pointing to me. He looked at me, but it didn't register. Then, not bothered by my presence, still holding her, he asked, 'Did you come in your car?' When I nodded, he said, 'Follow me out of here.'

"Driving back was a nightmare. Water mains had cracked. At every corner there was a mob of people we almost had to drive over to get out. We could hear screams coming from all directions."

Jean had a street map of the capital on which she had drawn circles with colored pens. "You must have been here, the Colonia Morelos. That is an old section."

Helena bent down, squinted, nodded. "I suppose."

"What about the water?"

"I told you, the mains burst. At least there was water in the streets."

"Most of the twenty-one million residents have no water. It is delivered by truck."

"I don't know then." Helena did not want to talk about the specifics of the city. She had been frightened, and moved by the lovers. "Walking in the street felt like walking on bubble gum."

Jean shaded in three large districts in red. "Here, too, the Colonia Juárez and Colonia Roma must have been severely damaged. The whole city is built on that fill. The foundations are not made to withstand shocks, especially the government buildings. Segundo was right about the hospital; the contractors cheat on kickbacks, so all the shoddy buildings will have gone—schools, hospitals, offices, tenements."

"No one would go inside." Helena couldn't stop. "Everyone was in the street. They were afraid they would get trapped or crushed. The streets were buckled so that we had to drive on the sidewalks or turn and head the other way. It was a nightmare, trying to get out. The sky was almost white with dust, as if there had been an industrial fire. In a few places walls had fallen on cars, and in one, on a school bus. Some people were naked—it was early, you know—scrambling for clothes, wrapping themselves in blankets or shawls.

"By the time we got out of town you could hear the sirens, and people were leaning over, trying to find out from their car radios what was going on."

Jean drew some arrows on her map. "It must have hit only the first shift," she said. "That was better than later, if it had to happen." To the men, she explained, "They come in shifts, workers and schoolchildren both. With twenty-one million and only one subway it is the only way to move that many people in and out. They come at seven, eight, and nine, and leave at four, five, and six. This must have hit—?"

"Roughly seven-thirty."

"Then maybe the second shift was on its way." Jean did some figuring. "What are they doing, I wonder, about typhoid? At seven thousand feet it takes twenty minutes to boil water long enough to kill the bacteria. Or more. It boils at such low temperatures because the air is rarer. With that many people—" She ran her fingers through her hair. "Typhus, salmonella, typhoid, hepatitis, cholera. Dysentery as a matter of course."

Paul felt queasy as she named over the possibilities that could disrupt the body. His sympathy poured out to the city full of people. What would it be like to be sick as a dog, with no control over the spasms at either end of your digestive tract, humiliated, shamed, running to get out of the way of falling plaster? Tentatively sipping his tepid apple juice, he felt a lurch inside.

"Where are they now?" he asked Helena, taking advantage of Jean's silent computation.

"Who? Segundo and Esperanza? He took her home; to his home, I think, because they turned off toward Cuernavaca. At least I assume so. I did not want to call. Perhaps Isabel will not care. They seemed no longer to worry about all that. I guess I should've looked in on Esperanza's children, seen if her mother was frantic out of her mind with worry, but I haven't. For one thing I'm still in shock; for another, I'm afraid I'll run into Avelino and he'll have a fit. It seems odd, doesn't it, that we haven't heard from him?" She looked at Jean and then Nakae.

Nakae stared at the floor. "I have learned that he and Rosa were at the chicken coops when it hit. That many chickens got away. But I did not go to see."

"You should have, Nakae," Jean scolded.

"He is still angry at me about the ant hill."

She brushed that aside. "The radio said this morning that all soft drinks were bringing five hundred pesos or more. That people were afraid to drink even the coffee, in case the water had not been boiled. They will be coming out of the capital, pouring out. Refugees. We must make sure we have what we need, before every family here suddenly has half a dozen or more 'relatives' appear." She put the map away. "The mill will be busy. I am going to the market before everyone floods in for the weekend. You find out where the lovers are," she instructed, and left the room.

In a few minutes she was back in her rough skirt and embroidered blouse, sandals on and a basket under her arm: back in disguise. "You—" She looked at the men, first one and then the other, no longer keeping up the pretense that she was not the one giving orders. "For God's sake, locate our principals. Nakae, you've let that fool put a hex on you. Get ahold of yourself, can't you? The fowl can spread disease, which we don't need any more of. Paul—" She looked at him and shook her head. "Take a slug of Kaopectate and get into your suit, can you? We've got to give the illusion of business as usual. There is going to be a mass panic in the capital, and it will spread out into the villages around here like ripples on a pond. Half of Tepoztlán has been in the church since it struck, huddling on those benches even after the ceiling and bell tower cracked. You'd think they'd stay away, but it only made them pack in the faster. Father Domingo has no doubt lost his voice by this time assuring them that God isn't mad at them for their peccadillos. If every one of them was bedding where she shouldn't be, there is going to be a lot of rosary fingering."

She gathered up a sack of corn to be ground. "Helena, open the office, can't you?"

Helena, exhausted and with a taped wrist, looked at her blankly. "If you had seen them together. The tears running off his mustache. And her in that doorway, riding it like a kite, down three floors as the building fell around her."

Jean sighed and opened the door. "We will meet here for supper."

Helena stretched out her legs. She looked dazed still. It had taken her half a day to go in and come back. The car had arrived in one piece, but she was still shaken.

She lowered her voice almost to a whisper. "You could hear the people shouting and crying. I could hear them behind me as I left. I expected some of them would try to take the car or hitch a ride, but no one seemed to see those of us in vehicles. They were too frantic, too fright-

237

ened. I never saw people out of control that way. Everywhere you looked. I don't know what I expected. That the streets would buckle and their homes fall down and they would be like Red Cross workers in documentaries? How stupid we are about each other." She looked at Paul and blinked back tears.

He wished they were alone. "Perhaps you should have a nap," he suggested.

"No, Jean will be craning her neck until she sees me coming down the street. She's right; we are being unprofessional. I am." She shook herself, as if to dislodge the terrible images of the disaster.

Nakae rose with great reluctance. "I cannot go out to the chicken pens," he declared.

Helena did not seem to care. "Jean's not making you go out there. Just ask around. Esperanza has friends on the street. They will know if she is home. Where Avelino is. Nakae?"

"I will find them if they are here." At the door he looked at his friend. "Are you coming, Sinclair?"

"I'll be along in a little bit."

Dispirited, Nakae left alone. Paul half expected him to send a sly wink over his shoulder, but his roommate's mind was on his unwelcome task.

Paul dragged the heavy door shut and turned to Helena. "What can I do?"

She stood close to him. "Rub my shoulders," she whispered.

He slowly stroked her back and arms; then he took off her yellow jacket and began to massage her tense shoulders and the nape of her neck. When he felt her relax, he put his arms around her and pulled her to him. "Come lie down," he said. "You've had a shock."

"If you had seen them—" She pressed her face against him. He continued to run his hands down her back and then her hips, still holding her close to him. She did not move away; it was as if it had taken this danger to break through her resolve.

"If you had seen them together—" She lifted her face to his, looking in his eyes. "Segundo was crying, and all the while clinging like a child."

"It must have been terrible." He soothed her.

She closed her eyes. "She was almost killed."

"You could have been hurt." He felt her tremble. "You've had a bad shock." Paul cupped her breasts with his hands and bent to kiss her. "Come lie down." He parted her lips.

"Sinclair, Sinclair!" Nakae hollered from outside, banging open the door. "She is screaming. You must come."

"What?"

"Esperanza?" Helena stepped back, dazed. "Is he after her?" She shook herself. "Paul, you must go." She pushed him away. "You must help her."

Furious, he followed the babbling Nakae down the cobbled street. Then he, too, heard a woman's screams. He listened, to orient himself, and there it was again: a shriek of pain, coming from the direction of the chicken farmer's house. He ran, twisted his ankle on the rocks, got up, and hurried into the fancy courtyard, past the glittering metal scorpions.

Avelino was bellowing, loud enough to wake the dead, "Whore, whore."

They found Rosa in the kitchen with her forearms pressed against her face to protect it, him beating on her with his fists, trying, without much luck because of his clumsy bulk and the fact that he was reeling drunk, to kick her as well.

Nakae hung back while Paul pulled the madman away and flung him out into the courtyard. "Get control of yourself," he said. "Leave her alone."

"Whore," Avelino shouted, his voice slurred. He slid down to the ground. "Mother-squeezing whore—"

Rosa followed him out, one eye swollen, her mouth bloody. "Does he think we can eat the canvases? What does he think I screw his fat belly for if not to feed myself? A sow would be ashamed to screw him." She turned and flipped up her skirt at Avelino, who tried to rise up and get at her again.

"We were in the chicken shed"—she wiped her face with the bottom of her skirt, cleaning herself up as she talked— "that pigsty of a shed, when suddenly the floor flew up in my face and we heard a sound like twenty thunders." Frustrated, she dropped her skirt. "He went outside without his pants, hollering about his chickens." She giggled and pointed her finger at Avelino. "They were a sight. Flapping around like hens whose necks had been wrung. They didn't know how to fly, all of them crowding, stepping over each other, on each other's heads, to get out this hole where the ground had sunk down below the wire. He had no pants on and was hollering at them, thinking they'd flap back to him." She laughed and stuck out her tongue.

Avelino struggled to his feet in a rage. "I am losing money every day of my life. They are dying. Every day hundreds of them are dying and stinking up the place, and I can't get them out without getting myself pecked to death. And she is after me for some of my money. I have no money. I am losing money every day. Now this, now the coop has a crack, a hole." He whirled, shaking his head to clear it, and focused his rage on Nakae. "It is you. You brought it upon us. You tried to kill the queen, and now the spirits are killing my chickens. I should kill you. You should be dead for messing with the ant hill. It is your fault. They sent the sickness, and now they have sent the rumbling ground." Before Paul or Rosa could stop him, Avelino had lunged at Nakae, knocked him down, his glasses off, and was trying to pound him into the flagstones of the fine courtyard.

Paul pulled Avelino off his friend and gave him a shake. He told Rosa to go home and clean up.

She put her fingers to her head and wiggled them at Avelino. "Where is your wife? Your horns are growing by the hour." And then she was gone, barefoot, out into the street.

Paul dragged Avelino inside, took off his shoes and got him to lie down on a heavy wood bed, carved and old, quite an heirloom. He would like to have smothered him with a pillow but resisted the urge. The children would be gone to school, but where was the servant? And the old mother? Perhaps they did not risk coming into the house when only Avelino was there. He could not blame them.

Outside, Paul told Nakae, "Clean up and go to the square. I'll be down soon. You've located enough of them for one day."

He gave his friend a clap on the shoulder for his troubles, hoping it contained no hostile edge. He didn't want to add to Nakae's troubles. He couldn't blame him for running for help, given his terror of the chicken farmer and his assumption that it was Esperanza in trouble. No doubt the Japanese had wanted to fall through the ground at the sound of the screams or, more likely, run in the opposite direction. But he hadn't; he'd done the right thing. If at the worst possible moment. Paul turned his irritation from his roommate to the chicken farmer. It was as if Avelino had by some crafty sixth sense picked that time to interrupt Paul with Helena—a perverse talent that he didn't for a moment doubt the fat, greasy man possessed.

He glanced up the street, longing to get back to her, but knowing if he returned without a full report on Rosa, he'd be sent out again.

Grudgingly—because Rosa had a talent for complicating the simplest situations—he hurried around the corner of the painter's house and knocked on the other side. He would pop in, make sure she was fine, and be on his way.

"Come in," Rosa called.

When Paul entered, he saw Isabel Gómez sitting on the side of a large bed, in white slacks and bright orange blouse. "The murals," she was saying to Tomás, "the murals will be destroyed. You must be the one to save them."

Rosa busied herself as if everything were normal. She produced some sticky, sweet fruit juice for Paul. "Pay him for his time," she said over the shoulder of her torn blouse to Isabel. "I got nothing from the chicken sticker."

Tomás scowled at his wife. He looked uncomfortable, clothed only in a pair of drawstring pants. Paul wondered if he and Isabel had been making love and surmised that they had, for she was smoking a fresh cigarette and her blouse was half unbuttoned.

"The Luis Nishisawa mural is in the hospital. They will be digging people out all night, tearing at the walls. We must rescue it. Jaramillo will be seen in the ruins, peeling *Air Is Life* from the walls." She paced around the small room. "Rosa, don't sulk. Get him to come with me. You can see it is important to his career. There will be photographers from around the world. They must all have pictures. They will run the picture of digging out the baby. They will run the picture of the man whose wife is trapped but still alive ten feet down. They will run the baby again. They will run the weeping man again. Then the world will want to see something else. Art. They will want to see that the capital is a city as fine as Rome or Paris. They will want to see the art. When the bombs came in the war, falling on Europe, there was much outcry about the Louvre. Was it all right? About the Sistine in Italy. Was it all right? Were the treasures saved? They know no one here but Rivera. They think we are primitives, political painters. But we will show them Jaramillo, digging in the ruins with his bare hands, carefully applying the *strappo* adhesive, rescuing one of the finest murals in the world, offering it, perhaps, to a museum in North America for restoration." She sat beside the painter on the bed. "Jaramillo, get up and come with me."

"It is dangerous."

"There is the relief on the ceiling at the hospital, designed by Beltrán. We can save it as well. Aluminum. It will not have cracked. We will cut it into sections. There will be cameras—listen to me—from every capital in the world. Today, tomorrow, Saturday, there will be cameras. Then they will find something else. They will grow tired of the baby and the bereaved husband, and they will find something else."

"Mérida's murals in Colonia Júarez will be gone. The rest are too dangerous. Please, Isabel, let me be. I don't want to go. I have not painted in a week. Rosa is on me like ants. I can't get anything done. Now go."

"Jaramillo. Tomás." She turned to Rosa. "Can't you reason with him?"

"Pay him," Rosa said. "We have to eat."

Isabel waved her hand as if this were nothing. "You tell him," she said to Paul. "It will make his career."

"He is right; it is dangerous in the city."

"Segundo got in and out." She stood and flung her cigarette out the door into the yard. "He was not afraid to go in to see her. How is it that you are such a coward? Segundo is afraid of nothing. For love he would hold up the buildings with his bare hands."

Tomás stretched back on the bed. His feet were dusty. "I want to paint."

"My husband is a brave man."

"So go find him."

"She is there. I must give them time. It was a shock. She will have to recover. Decide whether to have her 'sister' be killed or to locate her somewhere else. He will have to recover, too; it was a shock. He was a ghost when he brought her home. A shattered man. He will need time to get himself back. This afternoon I will see if he is at his office here. Then I will go home. But you, Jaramillo, you could be on the front page of every newspaper in the entire world. If you were not such a coward."

"I don't even like Luis Nishisawa. He is a hack."

"He is very fine."

"Nor Beltrán. He is an imitator." He yawned. "If all their works are destroyed, then there will be a place for mine. Perhaps the Ministry of Communications has toppled as well, and with it the smears of José Chávez."

Isabel closed her eyes wearily. "You have my sympathies, Rosa," she said. "He is a lazy man."

"Pay him," Rosa murmured, slipping her ripped blouse over her head and pulling on her Guadalajara T-shirt. "He doesn't do it with you for nothing." She leaned over and flicked her hands down the older woman's breasts. "Not an old sow." And then she took her sweet drink and went out into the courtyard.

Hastily, Paul followed, not wanting to be left alone with Isabel and Tomás.

Rosa padded across the dusty courtyard and leaned against him. He put an arm around her, saying, truthfully, "I'm sorry the bastard beat you up."

She, thinking maybe this time he was going to become cooperative, pushed against him, nestling her face on his shirt. He could feel it damp, and wondered if her mouth was bleeding again.

Just then he saw Helena hurry down the street, not stopping or even turning her head when she passed the entrance to his house. He called out, but she did not hear.

Cross, he shoved Rosa away. "I have to go."

"Maybe I'll bathe at your place. Is Nakae there?"

"Leave him alone. Avelino has done enough to him already."

"I will see."

Paul, hoping that Nakae had already made it to the square, kicked the side of the adobe house in frustration.

At that moment Tomás came out with Isabel. He had put on a fancy Oaxacan wedding shirt and brushed his black hair so that it had no part, in the style of romantic Mexican heroes. He looked, Paul had to admit, young and handsome and ready for his performance. It made Paul think, as the sight of Tomás frequently did, of Edward.

"It is expensive to save them," Tomás was saying.

"A picture. With a picture in the newspapers you can sell every painting."

"It is dangerous."

"The worst is over."

"I want to paint."

"Later, Tomás. It is time to think of the future of Jaramillo."

"You only want the roosters on your wall to increase in

245

value." His voice was sullen, but he turned up the street with her, headed, Paul guessed, for the inn's parking lot and her car.

"Perhaps that is so." She slipped an arm about his waist. "I look out for what is mine."

Paul felt a rising jealousy at the sound of the possessive. Everyone had someone; everyone but him. "Mine." He repeated the word aloud. "Mine. Where the hell is *mine*?"

23 A CONVERT

He and Nakae joined the women for supper, which was, as in his first days there, mostly corn-based tamales and tortillas, the strong smell of freshly ground corn meal filling the small house.

Paul was not in his suit, but in a cotton shirt and a clean pair of cords, which Esperanza had got washed for him while he was sick. (He could not help it; every time he thought of Peg, no matter whether he was angry with her, put out because he had received no inquiry concerning his safety, or even, as tonight, missing her, all that fled before the fact that she could not send him a spare suit when he asked her to. That she could not do even that: a simple, not expensive favor. If the shoe had been on the other foot, if Peg had run off, fascinated by one of her projects—and lately something in him stirred wistfully at the memory of her excitement, her energy—saving that damn gorilla's kitten, say, and she'd written back for clothes, warmer clothes than she'd anticipated or cooler ones, he would certainly have packed up a box of her things and sent them out by the next mail. Wouldn't he? Would he?)

He had waited all day for some sign from Helena that

he had not totally imagined their earlier time together. He'd gone down to the square, but been intercepted by Jean, who'd sent him to check on Segundo Gómez, to see if he was in his office. By the time he got loose from that wild-goose chase and arrived at Helena's Estudio Antropología, her waiting room was swelled with women, all wringing their hands about the quake. She had smiled at him and waved, just as she might have done on any other day.

Now, tonight, she was being overtly affectionate with Jean, patting Jean's waist when she stopped to serve the plates, letting Jean stroke her hair while the coffee boiled. Once, no, twice, during the meal she reached over to touch Jean's hand. He didn't know if this was to make him feel a fool or simply to placate the sharp-eyed project leader, but it hardly mattered.

Irrationally, he knew, not only irrationally but absurdly, he blamed Helena's change of heart on Todd Stedman, who, after all, had got him into this mess to begin with. First it had been Olivia snatched from him, then Peg, his wife, his lawfully wedded wife no less, and now, somehow, even here a desirable woman had been literally jerked from his arms by—it seemed, it felt, and no amount of reasoning would make it go away—Todd and his insinuations. As if the shifty sophomore's power were such that his very naming of the relationship between the two women had made it so.

But if Paul was in the pits, no one noticed, because Nakae was on the verge of hysteria. In the shower, he told them, he had seen welts on his legs and then, putting on his trousers, had been struck by a severe pain, and now—he got up from the table to demonstrate—he was limping. He was going to be a cripple; he was going to die. The chicken farmer had put a curse on him.

"Avelino is all bluff," Jean said, making a few notes and then pushing her glasses on top of her head. "Don't let him get to you. He's mad because you kept him from slapping the painter's wife around. Forget it."

"He is coming after me."

"More likely," Helena said mildly, "he'll be coming back after Rosa. Really, Jean, we should check on her. Invite her to spend the night." She glanced toward the bedroom in the back, still wearing the same yellow jacket that Paul had earlier removed.

Jean made a dismissing gesture. "She can take care of herself, that one."

They ate sliced fruit and drank a last cup of bitter coffee. Tired, testy, everyone fell silent. It was as if they had all at once run out of common words as well as common ground.

At that precise moment the great worm under the street, the cat under the carpet, returned. This time they could feel the floor rock from side to side as if they were on a lazy nag.

By the time they rushed out into the street, under a dark sky lit only by a risen half-moon above the church, the quake, moving this time across courtyards south to north, had passed the town.

"Another!" cried one of the half dozen women gathered together.

"The devil is about!" screamed the woman whose hen had laid the egg without a shell.

The woman with the white pig pointed to the north. "Listen—"

They did, and far away they could hear the crashing sound of stones tumbling down the mountainside.

"This time it will destroy the old god's altar."

Jean let out a weary sigh and slipped her arm through Helena's. "What next?"

Then, running up the street, blazing torches in hand, the stink of burning gasoline rising into the air, came a handful of raging villagers, men, led by Avelino Álvarez.

"He has brought this down on us," the fat chicken plucker shouted, running toward Nakae, with a torch in one hand, his eyes red as its flame. "Get him."

Nakae moaned and looked wildly about.

Jean stayed him with her hand and nodded at Helena, who stepped forward, the blond woman with the forgiving smile on her face, to calm them down. "Takamori has not caused this," she said. "Be on your way. If you must blame someone, blame the earth." She stamped her foot on the street to make clear her meaning. "It has an aching back tonight. It is old."

But her words went unheeded, as the men lunged for Nakae.

Frantic, eyes bulging, he fled down the street, one leg stiff and half dragging after him, straight down the cobblestones of veintidós de febrero to cinco de mayo and then across the center of the square to the courtyard of the church—and behind him came the men in pursuit, and then Paul and Jean and Helena, and the other women who had gathered in the street, and even three yellow dogs, roused from their slumbers, who brought up the rear.

"Save me, save me, Father," Nakae shrieked, and out from the church came an amazed Father Domingo, aged, arthritic, like most of the area priests in those days of dwindling recruitment, a local from the village.

"Come in, my son, come in." Father Domingo crossed himself and looked up at the Virgin over the door in delight, as if to say that here, at the end of his life, was the reason he had been herding this tiresome bunch of half-hearted parishioners for half a century. With one arm around Nakae, drawing him into the dim, stone-floored sanctuary, the old man with the bent back shouted out at Avelino and his posse. "Shame on you, Avelino Álvarez Aguilar. I'll see you in confession."

That was only a threat, as everyone knew that oxen could not pull men to confession and that forced to confess or leave the church, none of them would be members.

The crowd murmured, waiting a bit to see if the Japanese came back out, and, when he didn't, started to disperse.

Avelino and his friends took out their bottles, cursing roundly as they poured themselves generous drinks.

Then a woman's voice whispered loudly, "Watch out for toloache."

Another picked it up. "Be careful when you drink your coffee in the morning, foolish Avelino."

Then all the local women laughed and made the sign of horns against their foreheads.

"He is not man enough to keep his own wife home," the woman with the hog called out.

Jean said, "They know he has beat up Rosa."

"Tomorrow," the woman with the preposterous hen murmured, "she will be pulling him through the streets like a burro."

At that Avelino sent up a howl to the skies that mingled with the sound of the distant rockslide.

The women's revenge, Paul thought, disheartened. This is where I came in.

24 FIVE HUNDRED SCORPIONS

Heavy stones lay all about the base of the pyramid, huge fragments of the towering buttes behind it, but not one pebble lay on top of the altar itself.

Paul could not verify this, for the largest stone of all had fallen directly on top of the trap door that led up from Tepoztlán. Word reached the villagers slowly that the second quake had closed their valley off from visitations by El Tepozteco forever. Men from Ixcatepec and Santiago, villages whose streams also drained into the Río Atenco, had gone up the back trails to see for themselves. It was true, they sent word, the old god had been banished by the church for cracking the sanctuary and silencing the bell.

Paul listened carefully around the café and the square for rumors that blame had been placed on Takamori, but this did not prove to be true. No one from the area believed that an outsider could influence a god, no matter what he had done. Even the incident with the ant hill was brushed aside. Those who sickened and died from *los aires*, their limbs withered, were men who had known better since boyhood, men who got what was coming to them for other matters. Anyone knew the way to fight ants: you chopped the yamatl leaves, the milky juice of which could flay the skin off a man's hands, and heaped the foliage over the bed. That was the way you did it.

But the stone shutting the valley off, this was a matter of much concern. That, coupled with the fact that suddenly, on the afternoon of the twenty-first day of September, the rain did not come. The clouds built up, as always, lingering above the repaired chicken pens with their reduced populations, and above the jagged rocks, which now stuck up above the old god's altar like gigantic chipped teeth. The wind blew from the north and east. But nothing happened. The clouds hung there until sundown and then faded into the sudden nightfall.

Everyone said it to her neighbor: El Tepozteco has only one punishment; he takes away the rain. The dry season had begun—three weeks early. There would be no last rainy days to sweeten the ripe corn; there would be no last splashes into the underground springs.

Many believers rushed to take effigies of their name saints into the midday sun, to remind them what the land was like without water. Women, preparing for three extra weeks without rain—weeks that would fall upon them in April, when the earth was parched and packed, the trees bare, the windstorms bearing stinging dust—began to carry and store what water they could.

For a week they coaxed the men, saying they should cut the corn soon, while it was meaty and juicy, and they did. It was the eve of the Feast Day of San Miguel, and Father Domingo carried a cross out into the fields and blessed them, to keep away the high winds. But as soon as he left, the villagers took down the cross and moved to another part of the harvest. They knew that the increased winds were blown by El Tepozteco, and they did not wish to anger him further. They were made especially nervous because

Domingo, the priest, was a namesake of that other early father who had hurled the idol down from the mountain— which was not a good omen, not on a day when the clouds had again built up, hovered all afternoon, and then blown away to another valley.

They picked the fresh corn and roasted some, putting the ears on sharp sticks and holding them over the open flames. Paul ate an ear, burning the tips of his fingers, wishing for butter and salt, then remembering that because no salt occurred naturally in the valley, the villagers had learned to use little of it, especially because the corn was rich and did not need it for flavor.

He stood watching as many, many families he had not seen before chopped and drank and ate together. And, because they were all engaged in the same activity, it seemed a larger crowd than even at the Sábado Market. Here was a real community, and again, as he had before, when watching the harvesting of the yellow plums or the women piling their blankets with peppers around the edges of the square, he felt them to be part of a single body. The body of a large, essentially benign animal who slumbers and wakes and is playful, but snaps when provoked.

He tried to think of a proper name for it, the animal that these people composed, but today he could not find a fitting image. His mind was dry as the fields.

Later the rich who had fled from the upheavals in the capital came to town with friends, foreign journalists, artists, gamblers, and they bought generously of the fresh corn, delighted with the unexpected, early harvest.

Cows, decorated with banana leaves and the sweet heart-shaped yolosuchil flowers, were led through town in a processional. In the empty lots men shot homemade fireworks into the air.

That night, on veintidós de febrero, the smell of roast pig let everyone know that the woman next door to the woman whose hen had laid the double-yolked eggs had given in and slaughtered the great white hog, to have a feast of celebration before the hordes of homeless from the city and the long dry months killed it for her. Those who came and tasted hoped that the fragrant smell of mesquite and amaquapite would propitiate the vexed god and gain them one last week of rain.

Nakae, converted in earnest, spent most of his time with the aged Domingo and looked his old grinning self once again, safe where he could not be reached by Avelino and his band. He began to keep Paul awake far into the night, talking of the importance of his father's conversion in his life, of the example his father had set, of the new life his father had begun once he turned his back on his old ways. He wore an image of the Virgin on a leather thong around his neck and fingered it whenever he talked to Paul about the narrow escape he had had the night of the second tremble.

"I feel great shame that in my own country, in my own district, when the brothers came across the ocean to convert my ancestors, we devised great torments for them, taking them to the hot springs and scalding them until they recanted or died; tying stones about their necks and flinging them into the sea; burning them. In my sleep at night I can hear their screams. The burden of it is on me. Can you understand this, Sinclair?"

"At that time," Paul responded, lying on his back in the close room, "the Inquisition was going on in Spain."

"But those were heretics. Those were not believers who were put to death. These, in my country, were true believers. Jesuits who gave their lives to spread the word."

Paul didn't answer.

"I can hear them, and sometimes, at night, when I wake, I can see their faces, in torment but making no sound, and their faith is a marvel to me. For twenty-five years I resisted that which I longed for, because I did not want to follow my father. I was not able to accept that he was preparing the way for me."

"You're overreacting to Avelino. You don't have to put on sackcloth and ashes."

"I am going to be a priest, my friend. There is a great need for them in these small villages. The number has fallen away; many in the church are still angry at the action of the government in the revolution, stripping the church of its power, forbidding the wearing of robes. I will restore it. I will be like Father Hidalgo; I will ride my burro across the mountains, spreading the message."

"You hate to ride."

"It will be humbling for me."

"Wasn't Hidalgo a revolutionary?"

"First he was a priest."

Paul turned his back and pulled up the covers.

"I think I have never told you, Sinclair, that the man who really converted my father was the one we call the Japanese Messiah, who lived perhaps four hundred years ago. This happened in the remote, barren, distant, painfully poor corner of Japan from which my father's ancestors came. There, in those days, the peasants who could not pay their taxes were dressed in straw coats that had been rubbed with lamp oil, bound, and set on fire late at night, to make 'fireworks' displays, as examples to the other villagers. This man I speak of, that my father had heard of from his father, was called Amakusa Shirō. He led these poor farmers in a rebellion which resulted in the slaughter of thousands and even stricter laws than they had suffered under before.

"What attracted my father to this man's story was that after these facts Shirō did not commit ritual seppuku, as he should have according to the practices of our country, because he was a secret convert to the new religion brought to his part of the world by the missionaries. My father let his mind imagine the fierce inward battle that Amakusa Shirō must have endured, torn in two between the old way that commanded death before dishonor and the new religion that taught him his life was not his to take.

"Sinclair? Are you sleeping?"

Paul felt utterly and completely deserted.

The next day was Saturday. He sat up and immediately lay back down as the room began to swim and he broke out in a cold sweat. What now?

For the week since the stone had been rolled across the opening, nothing had gone right in the village: children had sickened, nursing mothers had lost their milk, the plums had started to rot on the trees, and everywhere hens ceased to lay eggs. Women put their buckets and pails of water in the sun to settle, or stirred roots in them to make it pure, as word had reached them of the number in the capital who had fallen ill from water turned bad by gas and fumes let loose by the rumbling beast under the ground.

Trucks from the city no longer delivered soft drinks— Peñafiel or the apple Manzanita—and no wonder. The price they could bring for a single bottle in the capital was more than they could get for an entire case in the mountains.

Paul began to shake and his teeth to chatter. He did not

know if it was the water in his coffee, the roasted ear of corn, or Nakae's nocturnal ramblings, but he knew he was sick again.

It can't be malaria, he thought; there are no mosquitoes this high. It must be cholera. Or salmonella. No, that has severe stomach pains.

Perhaps typhus.

But what did it matter?

Stumbling out of bed to go to the bathroom, he felt the stone floor icy beneath his feet. I have a fever, he decided. Clumsily, he slipped on his shoes, forgetting in his confusion to shake them out, and jammed the toe of his left foot into the raised tail of a scorpion. He yelled and flung the shoe at the wall, but the lovers on the other side were not home (were seldom at home anymore, either of them). Nakae, damn him, was at the church already.

No one heard him, and no one came.

After he had hobbled into the bathroom, he looked at his foot. Already it was swollen and red, as if half a dozen bumblebees had stung him at once. He tried to feel around for a stinger—out of reflex, back to being a boy—and then realized that scorpions put in poison. He fell back on the bed, trying to collect his wits, to wait for the room to stop spinning and the pain to go away. Out of the corner of his eye he saw a pair of them, red and black, wiggling and waving their tails, lying on the pillow next to his face. He threw the pillow across the room and shook out the bedclothes, inspected the ceiling—from which the pair must have fallen—and then, realizing he had been stung again, collapsed onto the hard, sheetless mattress as he tried to catch his breath, and everything went dark.

When he awoke, Nakae told him he had sent for Father Domingo to pray over him. Paul tried to sit up, to shout at his roommate to go away, to return to the way he had been before, to leave him alone.

"Send for Segundo," he hollered. "I need a doctor."

Segundo Gómez arrived, accompanied by Esperanza. She put a compress of maguey leaves sharp as needles around his head to keep the scorpions away, and another compress by his foot, which she bandaged.

"It is because the rain is gone," Segundo said, not bothering to take a look at Paul. "They come when the air is dry."

The doctor did not leave Esperanza's side, and as Paul swam in and out of consciousness, he saw Segundo caressing her hair or resting his cheek against her shoulder as she moved the poultices for Paul.

"I nearly lost her," he said. At that, great tears welled up in his eyes, and he had to wipe them away while Esperanza got Paul to drink a glass of something sweet and thick which she said would take the fever from him.

"Sleep," she told him. But before she left, she set a candle on the small table between the cots. Intended to keep the scorpions from him, it smelled to Paul, drowsy from the potion, something like the bay leaf candles used along the Virginia beaches to keep away mosquitoes.

When he awoke, Helena in a yellow dress and Jean in native garb were sitting on the side of Nakae's bed, talking. He kept his eyes closed in order to listen, although he found it hard not to shift his foot, which burned as if it were held to a flame.

"I think it's in the water," Jean said, her voice flat and tired.

"It will get worse without rain."

"Oh, I don't mean literally, germs. I mean whatever it is that happens to men in the tropics. I mean, look at them. Here's Paul flat on his back, whimpering like a baby. Nakae has become a nanny in a black robe. Segundo has completely quit seeing patients unless she is with him. And Avelino, he becomes more stupid by the day. Whenever he comes into town, every woman makes the sign of a rope around the neck, to torment him. Even Tomás has forgotten how to paint. He is like a monkey sitting on that rich collector's shoulder."

"It was the quake."

"A disaster only brings out into the open what is already there. It might have taken us longer to get the facts without it. That's all. Although I can already see the warm reception we're going to get with our findings."

"There are ways to say it that won't alarm."

"Tepoztlán Revisited: Men Bypassed?"

Helena laughed in a low voice. "Shhhh."

"I think he's awake. You can tell because his eyelids are fluttering. Aren't you, Paul?"

He opened his eyes and gave in and moved his miserable burning foot back and forth on the cool sheet. "More or less."

"You died last night, and we are the harpies sitting by your side in purgatory."

"My foot wouldn't be this sore if that were true."

"There is no pain in purgatory? What about hell?" Jean ran her fingers through her hair. She looked exhausted.

"Did you bring us down here to watch our collapse?" he asked, half serious.

"Of course not." Helena sounded upset.

Jean said, "You should never lie to sick people."

Helena bent down. "Can we get you anything? A soft

drink? I hear the inn has got some in. They'd have to, for the flux of visitors from the capital."

"Yes, I'm very thirsty." Paul shivered.

Helena touched his forehead. "You're hot as an oven."

Jean said, "Hell, let me see." She felt his head and the back of his neck and inside his wrist. "Oh, damn." She walked to the door, looked down at the basket on her arm, then flung it to the floor. "We can't send you home in this condition."

"Send me home?"

"Isn't that what they do to soldiers?"

"I don't have a home," he croaked. His chest felt tight, every breath an effort. He closed his eyes.

Helena leaned over him. "Should we call your wife?"

He opened his eyes. "I'm thirsty."

"I'll be right back with something."

Jean kicked her basket. "Don't, for God's sake, Paul, die on us."

"I feel too bad."

"Good. Keep it that way."

Alone, he realized he had not answered Helena's question. Not directly. Did he want them to send for Peg? Never. He wouldn't want them to tell her if they buried him here in a wooden box. (What did they do when wood was so scarce? You couldn't bury someone in a stone box. Maybe they put you out somewhere for the birds to find? Or lugged you to the first ravine along the pathway to the pyramid and dropped you in? He imagined himself, tied in a sheet, clattering all the way down to the deep hole at the bottom, splashing in and then sinking down into the caverns below the mountain, to float forever like a soul in limbo, homeless and unclaimed.)

His mouth felt cracked. His mind wandered back to his family. Had Charles got that check? Was Edward still angry at him? Perhaps Peg and Todd were clinging together now like Esperanza and Segundo—and he imagined the house in Charlottesville where he used to live falling apart in sheets, with Peg, the way she'd looked in college, red-gold hair, green cashmere sweater, that smile, holding onto the doorway of the upstairs bedroom, bracing her feet in the doorjamb, falling, falling down through flying bricks and crumbling walls to land at the bottom and race into the arms of the muscular football player. Imagined Stedman, the sophomore, in his letter sweater, holding her against his chest, tears running down his smooth, boyish cheeks, murmuring, "*Mi vida, mi cielo*."

Paul saw also, as he tried to lick his parched lips and failed, Tomás, in the courtyard of his house here, merge into an image of Edward being berated, dragged out into the street by Isabel, who had become Paul himself. Paul-Isabel was explaining to the boy the glory that would be his as a Rhodes scholar, the pictures in the paper, the fame that awaited him, and Edward-Tomás was protesting: "It is dangerous. It is expensive. I only want to play tennis." To which Paul-Isabel turned a deaf ear as he dragged him away, saying, "I look out for what is mine."

He was crying dry tears, the room swimming around him, when someone came and lifted his head and helped him swallow a glass full of chilled carbonated water, and then—in the dark behind his closed eyes—he was again on the rocky trail, in the pelting rain, watching other climbers dip handfuls of cold water from the swollen mountain stream. Cupping his own hands, Paul gave in at last and drank and drank until he was no longer thirsty.

25 A GENTLEMAN'S REVENGE

P<small>EGGY</small> let herself into Fan's, an hour early for Saturday lunch.

Fan was watching the hurricane on TV. "Our evangelist said he prayed that God was going to wash away Atlantic City and Fire Island, but keep him and his followers safe." She looked up and motioned to Peggy. "It appears as if he's right. Look at that." On the black-and-white screen, Peggy could see the camera scanning the boardwalk, gusts of wind blowing waves of water over the planks, gale force winds ripping at the façades of the fancy casinos. "They've evacuated the entire town."

Peggy helped herself to a cup of coffee. "I wonder what the person is sitting on to take those pictures."

Fan turned off the set. "You're early." She was barefoot, in a quilted robe with stitched chickens on the pockets. Mew was in his green golfing trousers, not on call.

"I got a letter from Paul."

"Paul? Is he all right? Why, that's wonderful. How could you just sit there and let me fall under disaster's spell?"

Peggy took the letter out of the battered envelope. "He

wrote it before the quake. Almost two weeks ago."

"It's a wonder it got here at all."

"When I saw his handwriting, I assumed he was writing to let us know he was all right. But then it was worse than not hearing. Here—" She passed them the letter.

Mew read aloud. " 'Tell that bastard to stay off my turf.' " He chuckled. "I see you waved your suitor in front of his face like a flag before a bull."

"No, actually my letter, the one he's answering, was weeks ago. That first day Todd and Baxter— Oh, aren't letters awful? Arguments about time past. It makes me want to cry with frustration. At that time I thought Todd, I only thought Todd was an old school friend of Paul's—"

Fan took the letter and read it twice. "Homesick boy, this is. That doesn't sound like our expatriate."

"He hit a snag in his plans, I'd say," Mew conjectured. "Even before the upheaval."

Fan said, "Maybe you should try again to call him."

Peggy shook her head. "I had Trice send two telegrams. I have no idea whether they got through."

"If she can't reach him, no one can."

"I tried a couple of days ago to call the little hotel in Mexico City where Paul and I stayed that time, just on an impulse, because the number was in my address book. As if the fact we'd stayed there would make the desk clerk available, and she would give me information. But I never even got an operator, of course. They are still referring you to that toll-free number in Washington."

"Everyone is too busy digging that baby out of the rubble."

"And the art. I saw in the paper, they're peeling off the frescoes."

"I didn't know you could do that."

Mew looked at the letter again. "Did you ask Charles about the check?"

"He's with Pink for the weekend."

"Sly fellow, my godson. He probably has an investment portfolio by now."

Peggy let Fan refill her cup. "If it had come yesterday, I could have called Trice to see if he'd made a return reservation before he left. 'I only signed on for a month,' he says. But surely if he planned to be home, I would have heard." She returned the letter to its envelope. "I had got used to the idea he wasn't coming back."

"I confess I had, too," Fan said.

Mew sipped his drink and watched the birds.

"I finally asked Trice if there was some other woman."

Fan clapped her hands. "You didn't tell me."

"It seemed such a petty thing to do. But after I had made up my mind about Todd, I guess I wanted some justification."

"What did she say? I can't believe you didn't tell."

"She almost died of embarrassment. She worships Paul and couldn't say a bad thing about him if she were on the rack. I think she thought at first I meant her, and she'd go to him in a minute if she could take Charles with her." Peggy made a small smile.

Mew got up and mixed himself a refill. He liked to splash the Snappy Tom on ice and then float a little vodka on top of that. It was the same theory as Irish coffee, he said. Less alcohol gave you a bigger punch. On his free Saturdays, he gave himself three before their lunch and then a big nap afterward.

He said, "A man isn't going to let his secretary know. He'd let his wife know before his secretary. She has to believe that only the depths of your innate decency keep you off her. If she thought there were some widow with diamonds in the picture, she'd lose your patients' fees, switch the x-rays, and notify the wrong next of kin."

Fan scooted her chair close to his and popped him with her napkin when he sat back down. "That's why you don't move in."

"I'm revealing all, this nice mild morning."

"Widows with diamonds, indeed."

"Grass widows can get by with garnets."

"I appreciate that, but I'm no longer grass. Now that he's under it."

Peggy turned the envelope over in her hands. The check didn't bother her; if Charles had it, it was safe. That boy, so like his father. She thought of him fondly.

So like his father: that was the way to look at Paul's letter. "What if it were Charles down there?"

Fan didn't understand. "You said he was with Pink."

Mew got the drift. "Wild horses couldn't drag an admission from him that he'd made a mistake."

"If he had written this—"

"Man to man?"

"Man to man."

"Straight from the shoulder?"

"Straight from the shoulder."

"He'd expect you on the next plane."

"Oh, Mew." Peggy tried to think it out. Charles was the key. She remembered the first time he had been allowed to walk home from school alone. He was an hour late. An hour later than her outside expectation, which had allowed for dawdling, for Charles's slow pace. She'd called Paul at the office, interrupted him with a client.

"Should I go after him?"

"How did you leave it with him?"

"That he would get home by himself. But surely he's lost . . ."

"Possibly. But let him work it out."

"What if something has happened to him?"

"The streets are crowded with kids and cars this time of day. If there was an accident, you'd have heard."

"School was out almost two hours ago."

"He's got to solve it. If you go for him, he won't try again."

"Sorry to get you out of a conference."

"He's okay, Peg."

Sure enough, Charles had appeared about fifteen minutes later, looking slightly the worse for wear. He swore he had not got lost, that he had spent a while trying to decide which was the fastest way to come home, when it turned out that the shortest way had one bad uphill climb.

She'd wanted to swoop him in her arms and plaster him with kisses, she was so relieved. But he was her second; with your first you learned to bite your lip or pace the floor but not to hover. Instead, she gave him two pieces of double fudge cake and herself a long, hot shower.

When she remembered that afternoon, it was as if Paul had answered her question already. If he had intended only a month all along, then he'd get himself back.

Reading over his words, that he missed her, that he was not planning to stay, she could not feel a relief in them, for all that had been left unsaid. It was not clear that Paul understood that he could not come back only to some of them. To Charles. Or to her. To Sturdivant, Postewaite. Or his dad. If he came back to any of them, it would have to be to all of them, and that meant Edward, too. You didn't get to leave some of your family, selectively discarding them like old ties that had grown too wide or too narrow for the styles. Either you were part of them all, or you weren't.

Paul was homesick—for his house and things as usual. But there was no apology in the letter. He'd left because he was disappointed in them; now he wanted to come back because he was disappointed with what he'd found down there. But it wasn't that easy. Things had changed here.

Peggy set her cup down. "I'll let him get back on his own."

Mew came over and sat by her on the couch, giving her shoulder a hug. They faced the louvered glass and the half dozen feeders that Fan had put out for his enjoyment. At his own house, he didn't bother; by the time he got home, he said, even the owls were asleep, and at the hour he got up, even the early birds were still brushing their beaks and shaking off the twigs from their nests. He liked to sit for hours on his free weekends, while Fan designed her papers or worked on her inventories, and watch them feed. Fan had given him bird books a few years back, but he didn't want their names. He had enough to remember. He just wanted to watch something that he didn't have to respond to in any way or learn a single fact about.

For this reason, he especially liked the birds that didn't migrate, his few lone companions, as he called them, who waited out the winter with him, those long months of short days and upper respiratory collapses.

"I'm still going to Washington," Peggy told him, knowing he didn't approve.

"It's your snakebite."

"I put him off last weekend, waiting to hear from Paul."

"Hon, don't ask my blessing."

"I'm not. Just advice."

"I've got grown kids in the West, making money hand

over fist. If they'd listened to me, they'd still be here riding their trikes."

Peggy gave him a pat. "Thanks. Anyway, my suitcase is packed."

Fan said, "First you have to eat my ham loaf and corn fritters."

"Sounds wonderful."

Mew held up his glass. "I'm entitled to another one of these first."

Fan motioned to Peggy. "Come talk to me while I dish it up. He likes his last one to take a spell."

Peggy gave him her cheek for a kiss and got up to go into the kitchen. In the doorway, she turned and put Paul's letter on the coffee table. She was not going to let him appear like a ghost and haunt this weekend.

She was tying on an apron, out of habit, and because Fan kept half a dozen on a hatrack by the breakfast table, when the phone rang.

"I'm not here," Mew hollered.

"They aren't calling you. This is Chuck Childress's weekend."

"He's been known to value a second opinion about the time I'm into a third Bloody Mary."

Fan handed the receiver to Peggy. "For you." Her face looked puzzled.

"Hi," Peggy said, not thinking, expecting it to be one of the boys.

"Mrs. Sinclair? This is Jean Weaver, the head of the project in Tepoztlán. Can you hear me? I'm calling from a public phone at the inn. It took me an hour to get through to you."

"Yes, I can hear you. Is Paul all right?"

"Not really. He's got a bad bug of some sort. I don't

know if it's more than that. At any rate, he has a high fever, and there isn't anywhere we can move him. The doctor here works at the hospital in Mexico City also, and even if we could transport him safely to the capital, that hospital is in shambles."

"Yes, I've seen pictures."

The other woman didn't say anything.

"Are you calling for permission to treat him there?" Peggy tried to get the straight of it.

"I'm calling, for God's sake, to ask you to come down here. I don't want to be responsible for him anymore. This whole thing has given me a raging case of the hives, a bad conscience, and I've had a fight with my colleague."

"Dr. Guttman."

"You're on your toes."

"Is this a toll call? Are you paying with coins?"

"No, it's on the cuff at the inn."

"La Posada."

Jean Weaver let out a sigh. "I should have called you the day he arrived."

"Tell me about Paul."

"He is probably all right. But if I hadn't called and he'd worsened—"

"Did you notice ulcers on his skin?"

"Ulcers? All I know is he was hot, really hot." She seemed to be thinking. "He was stung by a scorpion, plural. A bad place on his foot and one on his ear. In California most people don't find them any worse than a bee sting, but they have lethal varieties here. This is the first trouble we've had; they showed up when the rains stopped."

"Scorpions have little comblike things back by the genitals that perceive ground vibrations. They must have come with the quake."

"You know a lot." Jean Weaver sighed.

Peggy hesitated. "Paul may not want me to come."

"He's in no shape to decide. I am. I feel so damn guilty about the two of them. I tell myself not to, that it was part of the risk, but I can't help it."

"Paul and Mr. Takamori?"

"That's right."

"But how is this your fault?"

"It was my idea. To show that a mother-centered culture broke its men. The trouble was that it worked too well; your husband and Nakae, with traits so different from the locals, had no immunity whatsoever to the culture. I'd have done better to bring in Bible-thumping—"

"That's unethical." Peggy let her anger show. "It's as if you had brought two women into a group of isolated soldiers to prove that they would be raped."

"Don't think I haven't made similar comparisons myself."

"What happened to the Japanese?"

Jean drew in her breath. "He converted to Catholicism."

"I had no idea what was going on."

"We should have got waivers."

"Is it possible to fly into Mexico City?"

"Tourists are exiting in droves, and journalists are coming in. That's all I know. The airport is open. I called them just now. If you can get here, I can meet you."

"Don't get off the line," Peggy said. "Dr. Weaver?"

"I'm right here."

"Fan." Peggy turned from the phone. "Get me your *Sky Guide*."

Fan slipped the booklet of airline schedules from the cubbyhole desk by the breakfast table where she paid her bills.

"If I can get a reservation," Peggy said into the phone, "I'll be in between"—she squinted and put on her reading glasses—"nine and ten your time. There's a flight out of National at three-ten and one out of Dulles at six-ten, and they both arrive about nine-thirty. One must stop in Houston; it would be helpful if they told you. Shall I call you from the airport?"

"Leave word by six if you are not arriving. I'll walk back up here then and check. We're only an hour from the airport in the capital, but with all the confusion, I'll allow two. Let me give you the number."

"I have it." Before hanging up, Peggy asked, "I'm curious. How did you find me here?"

"I don't have any idea where 'here' is. Paul listed three numbers on the forms Helena had him fill out. This was the second."

Peggy smiled. "The third would be his dad's."

"It's a large, confusing airport. There's a café behind an art gallery."

"I'll be in a red jacket. With two bags." Peggy hesitated. "I believe Paul wanted an extra suit."

"I wouldn't worry about that at this point."

"Thank you for calling."

"Thank you for coming, Mrs. Sinclair."

"Peggy." It was clear the woman had not heard her given name from Paul.

Off the phone, she wrote down what Fan was to do. Get her into Mexico City tonight, from either airport. Get her out of Charlottesville in time to connect.

She went back to the sun porch, taking a fresh cup of coffee with her. She told Mew what Dr. Weaver had said. "What must I take for him?"

"Paregoric, for starts. They'll ask you if you have any drugs, but you can—"

"Yes, perfume bottles. Make-up jars. All right."

"Fever, you say?"

"High, she said."

"There are about as many diseases in the tropics as there are leaves on the trees—"

"She said he'd been stung by scorpions. I remember reading that they've found a microbe, a cousin of TB and leprosy, that occurs in Uganda, Nigeria, Malaya, New Guinea, Mexico, and parts of Australia, all the places that were once connected in a southern landmass. It's like the discontinuous distribution of plants. Anyway, when the bacteria started, there weren't any people, so we have no resistance to it. It's spread by something cold-blooded, they think. Do you think a scorpion is a possibility?"

"I'll ask the pharmacist. Better, I'll call Chuck Childress. He did a tour on tropical diseases. None of it may have stuck to his gray matter, but it won't hurt to ask. He'll enjoy being paged at the hospital anyway. Break the routine. Make him think he's on TV."

"The microbe causes ulcers."

"Treat it like a jellyfish sting then, more than likely. On the other hand, a scorpion's sting might resemble a snakebite. Hit the central nervous system; paralyze the lungs." Mew scratched his head. "I think what we have here is an early Bogey movie."

"Something for me to take, as well."

"Too bad you don't have a week's notice. It will have to be Lomotil."

"All right."

"Peg, hon, do you think this is a good idea? Your dashing off? Haven't they got doctors down there?"

"She wouldn't have called, I know, unless it was serious."

"It's risky, especially now."

Peggy shook her head. "I have to go. I'm still his wife."

From the kitchen they could hear Fan, making calls, then issuing reports. "You can get in, but you can't connect. Oh, damn, X-six, that means 'not on Saturday.' Now why would they fly into Dulles on Sunday and not on Saturday, I ask you? X-six on that one, too. All right. Maybe you can catch this. That means a wait. But if the night flight . . ."

Mew made notes on Fan's doodle paper, writing down the names of medicine, changing his mind, waiting for her to get finished on the phone.

Peggy made a list, too. What to take. Who to call.

After it was set, Mew dropped her off at home and gave her two hours to get packed, locate her passport, empty out bottles and make-up jars. He was on his way to the pharmacy. They would take her to the airport. Did she want to see Charles before she left? Was she going to talk to Edward?

Peggy washed her hair and packed two suits for herself and two for Paul. She packed walking shoes, a sweater for the mountains at night, a pair of pajamas for him and a pair for her, in case they were sharing close quarters with other members of the team. She packed a new toothbrush for him, one that hadn't been contaminated by the water down there, and eyedrops, because Mew wouldn't think of that and she remembered how your eyes stung from the fumes hanging over Mexico City and how you were afraid to wash them out.

Her real fear, which she hadn't voiced over the phone or even to Fan, was that the hurricane here, blowing off course up the coast, would make flying uncertain, might delay or even cancel her flight. But that was a risk she'd have to take.

She called Spence. "Pray for him," she said.

"Tomorrow, in intercession."

"For me, too."

"That I'll do at once. Be careful."

"I'm scared."

"As well you might be."

"Help Pink look after Charles."

Spence laughed. "He won't take too kindly to that notion."

"You might want to remind Pink that he needs to get Charles there early tomorrow."

"You let us tend ourselves."

"I'll have to."

Peggy could not bear to call Todd. She felt overcome with grief, although whether for him or for herself she wasn't sure.

Last weekend, when she'd canceled, he seemed to understand. But this was not the same. This was good-bye.

"Todd?" Her voice was steady.

"Peggy?" He sounded surprised. "Where are you?"

"Todd, I'm going to Mexico."

"You're what? Since when?"

"Paul is sick. Dr. Guttman's friend just called."

He made a noise of protest. "What can you do the two of them can't?"

"Take responsibility."

He raised his voice. "Did he ask her to call you?"

"I don't know."

"The coward. He got himself into that fix; let him get himself out."

"I don't know whether he did or whether he even wants me to come. But I'm going."

"When?"

"I'm taking a supper flight out of Dulles."

"Stay tonight. I'll put you on a plane in the morning. Nothing is flying out in this weather."

"Dr. Weaver is expecting me."

"I'll meet your shuttle. Drive you out there. We can talk."

"Don't, Todd."

"I'll go down with you. I know Guttman—all too well."

"I wouldn't do that to Paul."

"You can't tell me you're coming to Washington and then change your mind every time he gets a head cold. He left you, don't you remember? He left. He forfeited the right to have you bail him out of every mess."

"I have to go, now. Fan and Mew are taking me to the airport."

"Let me meet your flight. At least give me that."

"Don't you understand?" She could feel the tears on her face. "I'm giving you Edward."

There was a long silence, and then she heard the lift in his voice. "I'll be glad to look after him."

"Yes," she said. "I know." She wiped her cheeks with the back of her hand.

"Tell him, will you? Tell him his boy is in good hands."

"Good-bye." She cradled the phone. She knew her tears were not for Todd; he had won what he wanted, something of Paul's. They were for herself. It was she who had lost, to both of them.

Peggy stood still until her eyes were dry, then gathered up all the lilies in the house and laid them to rest on the compost heap.

26 THE BATTLE OF NOVGOROD

CHARLES tried to figure out what was going on. First his mom called, and then she came and cried on his old jacket and said it was good news and that Dad was really sick and hadn't told her, and she was going down there.

Even though she didn't know for sure that people could land in all the mess of hotels all lying around in pieces or even whether she could get out of the country with Virginia Beach and places like that all washed up. And the more she said what good news it was, the more she bawled.

Granddad pretended not to notice and patted her and said that Charles was already practically living with him, so that wasn't going to make any difference anyway. Nobody would even know she was gone. You'd think a thing like that would make her mad, but she liked it and sort of cheered up.

"Charles," she said to him when they were alone on Granddad's porch, with old Fan and Mew hollering at her from the car to come on, come on, "I got a letter from your daddy. Written before he got sick. He says that Miss Trice had a check for you?"

"I got it." He tried not to picture the neatly folded piece

of paper taped under the terrapin shell on his desk in case she could read his mind.

She looked toward the car and didn't know exactly what to say to him. Naturally, what she wanted to say was, How come you're carrying around six thousand dollars and I didn't know it? and, Don't you know kids don't get to have money and not show it to their moms? but she didn't. She just kissed him and said, "Well," and then she was gone.

She had on the red jacket that Dad liked a lot, that she didn't wear much because she said redheads couldn't wear red, but she looked great.

He decided his dad's being sick *was* good news, because Charles had been afraid his mom was getting messed up with that man who was hanging around, the one who'd shown up at Christ Episcopal like he belonged there. Charles thought he was a creep. He looked like the kind of guy Edward was going to grow up to be. You could tell he'd been the kind who was a big jock in school, and had all the teachers thinking he was Mr. Clean.

Charles was actually relieved that his mom hadn't come to take him home. His granddad had promised to take him around the campus that afternoon, and then Mrs. Ebberly was going to pick them up and take them to the Boar's Head for early dinner. She always got her hair turned into an orange frizz on Saturday, and dressed up to kill and put on all her pearls and was in a good mood, teasing Granddad like she was about to marry him. And his granddad, who wasn't about to get married at his age, went right along with it. "We're only two doors from the old folks," he'd tell her. "Mighty convenient." They were embarrassing sometimes, but he liked it when his granddad had a good time and wasn't carrying on about how everything had been better when he was young.

Charles didn't think being young won any prizes. You could have a check for six thousand dollars, for example, and not even have twenty-five cents to blow on junk food. You could live in a house with practically the oldest red brick in town and still not get the kind of bike you wanted for Christmas. Being young was not having anything to say about much of anything that happened to you. When he had kids, he was going to give them about one day a month when they could say and do what they wanted. Like making your parents have a different kind of car, or moving into another house, or dumping all your brother's dumb magazines out on the floor for everybody in the world to see, stuff like that. Making everybody tell you what was really go on.

What if his dad was going to die?

"I've called us a cab," his granddad said. "They won't let me drive anymore. Five more years, and they'll move me two doors down."

"Did you tell Mrs. Ebberly where to pick us up?"

"At the university cafeteria. I always like to have their strawberry shortcake, midafternoon. It makes a nice treat for an old man."

Charles didn't say anything. He knew the cafeteria that his granddad always talked about, where he ate lunch every day of the world back when he was a real professor, wasn't there anymore and hadn't been there since Charles started going to the campus. The first time he hadn't known all that, and they'd walked up and down the street with all the bookstores and hamburger places, and every block his granddad had said, "I know it was here. Right here." And then, finally, his granddad had recognized the kind of tile that was in this doorway and the way the entrance was cut at an angle to the building, and he'd walked right in and asked them where the cafeteria had gone. He told them he'd eaten lunch there every day of his life, and they told him not lately he hadn't, Pop. It was now a bar, with a new glass front and a bunch of plants hanging in the windows.

But his granddad always forgot. Charles tried not to worry that Mrs. Ebberly might not know where to look for them. She'd been picking up his granddad forever, and he guessed she knew better than anybody where to look for the old man with all the white hair, in the baggy jacket he wore no matter the weather, and if there was the least nip in the air, this long knit muffler, gray as a rat, that looked about a hundred years old. Granddad's wife had made it for him; that's how old it was. Almost as old as Dad.

Charles loved to walk around the university with his granddad. He thought it was the most beautiful school in the whole world, and he had no intention, since he knew he was going to have to go somewhere because in his family that was the way it was, of going anywhere else. He thought Edward was a dope, because he could have gone, or pretended he could have if only he'd had the grades. Privately, Charles thought that his brother was a dummy and had maybe made really bad scores and nobody was admitting it. Like maybe he was at the bottom of all the kids who took the tests that were supposed to tell how smart you were. Like maybe even with his granddad's being a Distinguished Emeritus, they wouldn't take Edward.

At least Charles hoped that's how it was.

He liked best the old (naturally) red-brick student rooms that all had their own doors and opened off a kind of low, covered walk that made you think people had been a lot shorter when the university got started. Like maybe not much taller than Charles was right now, because his granddad was stooped, and so the two of them were about the same size and there wasn't a lot of headroom for them. You could walk along and sometimes look into the rooms, at least in the professors' quarters that each had two big rooms off the walkway, and you could see mantels and big paintings and bookcases and polished tables, and get some idea from all the stuff what kind of professor that might be. And on the little student doors they had their names on brass plates. That was the part Charles liked. Some days he could hardly wait until he was big enough to live in one of these little rooms and have a nameplate engraved with CHARLES PINCKNEY SINCLAIR. He tried to stop long enough to count the letters in a couple of them—he had a long name that drove the teachers nuts—to see if there was enough room. Probably it would have to say CHARLES P., which he didn't like near as well. Maybe CHAS. PINK. SINCLAIR, because he knew they called his granddad Old Pink.

His granddad was puffing a little, so Charles slowed down. The old man took his hand, the way he did sometimes when he was out of breath or his big, heavy legs were bothering him. It embarrassed Charles. It looked queer. You didn't hold hands with a grown man. But his granddad took no notice, and he decided the creeps who were going to snicker could do it, because his granddad had trouble whenever they got to the end of one house and there was this step down.

They always took the same route, starting on the outside walk, stopping at a really dark part so his granddad could say, "That's where I lived as a student," and ending up near the rotunda so he could tell Charles, "That's where I lived as a housemaster. When your father was a little boy." Charles knew all that. He knew where his granddad's old office was and where he went now, two days a week, to poke around. He knew it must be hard not to be a real professor anymore. He guessed that they probably made a lot of jokes about Old Pink behind his back, and that made Charles angry. When he was there, he would take up a bunch of money, and then there would be a brass plate on every place that his granddad had lived. The way there was for Edgar Allan Poe. And even, maybe, a crosswalk, in memory of him and telling how important he was.

"I attended my first class in that building, Charles. Did I ever tell you that?"

They had got to the big red-brick science building that his granddad loved, which had sunk about ten feet into the ground and was so old you could look down to where they'd cleared a place around the ground-floor windows, which were down in a basement now. Charles liked it that they'd dug out all that ground to let the windows show.

Charles wiggled his hand free and leaned his head back as far as he could. Around the top, at every corner and sometimes in between, there was a big carved head, an elephant, a bear, a tiger, a walrus, things like that, and, in between, in great big letters, the names of famous men. Men who were famous back then.

"They considered these the greatest scientists of all time when this classroom building was erected in 1876," his granddad said. "I bet not a student on this campus now could tell you the contributions of more than a handful of them." His granddad began to read: "Lyell, Darwin, Linnaeus, Cuvier . . . Most of them are hardly mentioned anymore. Not in science classes, certainly. History maybe. That's where we all end up: history." He took a couple of heavy steps in the soft ground. "Aristotle, Pliny, Huxley. You see my point? Still, they were important in their time. Dana, Agassiz, Humboldt, Rogers, Hall, Owen. Or we thought they were, back when the earth itself was more of a mystery than it is now." His granddad was reciting from memory, and Charles always looked to see if any names were left off, but they never were.

His granddad steadied himself on Charles's arm. "My guess is the only ones they know these days are Gray, his *Anatomy,* and Audubon, although I doubt either of them is fully appreciated."

Charles hammered his fists together to hurry this part along.

"Even this old scholar couldn't tell you who St. Hilaire, Werner, or De Candolle are. Imagine names major enough to be carved in stone, forgotten by even an old goat like your grandfather. Oh, Oxymandias."

Charles liked that, and sometimes said the name to himself, although he didn't know what his grandfather was talking about. He waited a minute, and then prodded, "Say the other. You know, pygmies."

Pinckney Sinclair leaned back his head and recited upward in a loud, deep voice: " 'Pygmies are pygmies still, though percht on Alps/And pyramids are pyramids in vales.' "

Charles got a lump in his throat every time, though he didn't know exactly what it meant or what it had to do with the dead names. Sometimes at home, at night, he'd lie in bed and say it over to himself, hoping he'd grow into the words.

Now, he knew, would come the battle. He braced himself so that his granddad could lean against him like a post.

"Did you know, Charles, that your paternal grandfather is the world authority, some say—I say myself, for that matter—on the famous Battle of Novgorod? That one piece of the Crusades, between the Germans and the Russians (still a very Eastern people they were, in 1242), that one battle, Charles, set the stage for our world wars. You don't know a thing about them either, I daresay. World Wars One and Two: for your generation what could they possibly mean? You'll inherit Vietnam. Even Korea, I suspect, will fade to a commemorative postage stamp." Here his granddad wobbled slightly, then regained his balance. "You should read my work, boy, the better to understand the world you're inheriting.

"At any rate, Russia was as retreating, as all encompassing, as difficult to conquer or even to conceptualize as the Prussians were aggressive, boundaried, and precisely conceived. It came down to—it always comes down to—a difference in the racial, no, we don't say that word these days, the national, nor that neither, hmm, it all comes down to a difference in the mind-set of the two peoples. The Germans, we'll call them that because to all intents and purposes they were, fought for the righteous Fatherland and the Russians for Holy Mother Russia. Even today a study of Novgorod is a study of contrasting tactics." He peered closely at Charles. "Sometimes a single battle has more importance than the war in which it is waged.

"It has become fashionable to say that it is unfashionable nowadays to study the past, but the fact of the matter is that in my day, as now, we thought ourselves the possessors of far too much new wisdom to bother with old and useless history lessons."

He let Charles lead him to a railing, from which vantage he could look down at the sunken ground floor of the old building. "Imagine the two armies," he began, eyes shut, reconstructing it in his mind. "The Prussians, composed of the Livonian Brothers of the Sword and the Teutonic Knights in their armor, riding forth to take the Russian city and its surrounding lands. Ridiculing the Russians, who fought clumsily, hurling the stones of their catapults back into their own men; disgusted at the Russians, who lived like cavemen by Germanic standards. Did you know that when they found the abandoned czarist fort at Kokenhusen, the sanitary conditions were of such a nature, the excrement hardly covered, that the very quarters crawled with snakes and worms? Imagine, then, these fanatical, self-glorifying, and above all self-controlled Crusaders attacking again and again the Russians, who, as is their way, retreated into the snow, dressed in their warm furs, their bodies snug as the flesh of a bear inside its pelt, guided by Prince Nevsky. Retreated, seeming to falter, until they had lured the Germans in their heavy coats of mail, iron masks on every face and iron lances in every hand—even the horses, those that had not frozen, coated in metal—out onto the ice of Lake Peipus. Can you conceive the terror as the sounds of the cracking began and the seemingly solid ground gave way and the lot of them plunged into the icy water to die at once, unable even to drown properly?"

Charles nodded solemnly. He knew that battle as if he'd fought in it himself. Sometimes he imagined he could even hear the sound of the ice cracking and the horses whinnying.

His granddad gave him a light cuff on the shoulder, saying, "Well, now, how about that strawberry pie?"

"We better cross the street. It's time to meet Mrs. Ebberly."

"Is it now? She mustn't be kept waiting. You must never keep a woman waiting."

Charles knew that someday his granddad was going to get run over crossing the street, but this time, the way they always did, cars screeched to a stop and not one honked as they walked slowly out into the middle of the street and across to the other side. Charles didn't know why Mrs. Ebberly couldn't ever get them on this side, but he guessed it was because the cafeteria used to be on the other side, and Granddad was used to crossing over.

She wasn't much better of a driver than Granddad was a walker, but she had a big black Lincoln Continental, and so most people stayed out of her way, the same way they did his.

When she was late, Charles had to get his granddad off on talking about how in his day the students had all been gentlemen and had come to class in coat and tie, and now they looked like unemployed carpenters or worse. Besides being illiterate. And then he would show Charles the sign on a corner shop which read: THIS DOOR IS ALARMED FOR YOUR PROTECTION.

"Unthinkable. That they can post such a joke in deadly seriousness."

Today Mrs. Ebberly slid by them almost as soon as his granddad had stepped on the curb. Charles didn't know if she had some kind of radar, or if she went around and around the streets until they showed up. She had her orange frizz hair and a black dress cut way down in the front.

"Pink, you sit here," she commanded, opening the passenger door.

Charles climbed into the back, and she beamed him a big orange smile. "Did you boys have a good time?"

"Yes, ma'am."

"Is it dinnertime already?" His granddad seemed surprised but settled into the seat with a sigh, glad to be off his heavy legs.

"I made us reservations for five, to give you time to acquire an appetite." She always said that, although his granddad was just like Charles, always ready to eat.

"Mrs. Ebberly and I have been going to the Boar's Head for thirty-five years. Isn't that right?"

"Hush. Charles thinks I'm just a girl."

"She was a tot when I used to call on her." His granddad chuckled. "Had pigtails down her back and lace drawers with bows on them."

"Pink, shame on you."

Charles thought they were pretty sickening, but on the other hand he liked it that they didn't pay a lot of attention to him. They weren't like your parents, who were always checking to see if you were having a good time or asking you did you have friends or were you going to do something soon that they thought you should be doing.

Mrs. Ebberly wheeled around a lot of curves out in the country, and Charles held his breath on the close calls, but then they got to the big resort-type place where the Boar's Head was.

Mrs. Ebberly had told him once that the place Granddad always talked about had been an old mill and that about twenty years ago or more they'd numbered all the pieces and reassembled it on this posh site with lots of golf and tennis and all that kind of stuff. Every time he went there, she was poking him and showing him that this part, this wall or these beams or half this fireplace, was the real original mill, but since there was a hotel on one end and on the other a big glassed-in restaurant that looked out at a lot of ducks and a man-made lake, it didn't look to Charles like a place his granddad would like at all.

But it might be that it was like the cafeteria: Granddad was still here, only it was gone.

His granddad unfolded his napkin and looked around in appreciation. He told the waitress how many years he'd been coming here, how it was his favorite place. He talked about the apple cider he was going to have, and then how he supposed he'd have what he always did: the Smithfield ham, baked sweet potato, and a piece of their famous pecan pie.

As usual, when the food came, there was this slab of what the menu called Virginia Country Ham, which looked soggy with water and had a maraschino cherry on top. Plus a canned peach half and a frozen roll. But his granddad didn't seem to notice; he never stopped talking, cleaned his plate, and pronounced it a fine dinner.

Mrs. Ebberly talked a lot about the ducks and how many people came out here now, to Boar's Head, from all over the state, especially from Washington. She said it a couple of times, that it was a favorite with people from Washington. Charles thought for one awful minute that maybe his mom had made up the story about his dad, and was going to turn out to be here with that creep Baxter's dad. He wondered what he would do if he looked out the window and saw them go by, like the couple there now who were talking at the edge of the fake pond holding hands.

Ashamed of himself for thinking that, he ordered the brownie crumble ball, which was ice cream rolled in nuts with hot fudge sauce on top. He always got that, and it made the rest of the meal worth it. It was great, and Mrs. Ebberly, who was always on a diet and didn't order dessert, took one bite of his granddad's pecan pie and one bite of his crumble ball—just a nibble, because she could see that he liked it a lot, and he gave her credit for that.

She always paid for the meal. He didn't know if his granddad knew that or if, somewhere in his mind, he thought that he was paying for it, or maybe he'd told her to do it once, a long time back, had given her the money, maybe, and then just forgot that part of it. It embarrassed Charles, but Mrs. Ebberly didn't seem to mind. He guessed if she had the Lincoln Continental and the ten pounds of real pearls, then she could pay for the soggy ham with a maraschino cherry on top.

She was okay.

It seemed to him that Granddad should have married her a long time ago. He didn't understand grownups who could get married and didn't. Like Fan and Mew. Or Granddad and Mrs. Ebberly. It was like Edward having that drawer full of gross magazines and no girl friend. What was wrong with all of them anyway? When he got big, if he looked halfway decent by then, and wasn't a pudge anymore, he was going to have a couple of girlfriends all the time. And then he was going to find somebody he could get along with, somebody who thought the way he did, maybe somebody like Sue Trice or something, and get married and stay that way.

Charles had got into the habit of having a good time with his granddad on the weekends while his mom was off with Fan and Mew or, lately, Baxter's dad, but then going back home on Sunday night. With his mom asking him a dozen questions and trying not to be let down herself, about it being just the two of them rattling around the house. Making them something that he liked, grilled cheese sandwiches or popcorn or hot chocolate, things like that. Telling him that before he knew it they'd be building a fire and it would be marshmallow time.

He didn't have any idea what his granddad did when he wasn't there and Mrs. Ebberly wasn't there. With the about ten thousand books it was easy to guess, but secretly Charles always thought that after his granddad walked to the door and waved good-bye, he just sat in his study and thought about his battle until his head nodded on his chest and he fell asleep. He imagined the inside of his granddad's head like a large-screen movie, with the Battle of Novgorod playing over and over, the Russians in bearskins shooting stones at their own men, then the ice cracking, the Germans falling in the ice water, screaming and clanking, and then a few bubbles, the credits, and it all starting over again.

Whether that was so or not, Charles didn't learn, because with him there his granddad decided to have a personal conversation, now that he was acting guardian.

"Did you move your bowels today, boy?"

"Not yet." Charles felt his ears grow red. At first he was sure he'd heard wrong, except that as loud as his granddad talked he knew that wasn't possible.

"You should have a regular time. The body can be trained. Pavlov and his dog. Same time of day every day; it's one of the most useful habits a man can have. I myself have never taken a purgative in eighty-eight years."

Charles made a noise in his throat.

"My own grandfather passed this advice on to me. He said that his retreating to the privy each day at sunrise set his bowels like a clock. In addition, once a week, before arising in the morning, he rolled a lead ball around his abdomen, following the path of the ascending and descending colon." He peered over the top of his glasses. "Have you established a regular time of day?"

"Yes, sir," Charles lied, wishing he were about a zillion miles away, someplace like Novgorod, in a bearskin.

"That's good. The Sinclairs give attention to their health."

How come my dad's sick, then? Charles wanted to ask, but didn't. "I guess it's my bedtime," he said.

His granddad looked at his pocket watch, whose Roman numerals almost filled its face. "Getting late." He patted Charles. "You know your way?"

"Yes, sir."

"I'll stay up awhile. I'm old; my bones don't need to grow."

"Good night."

"Good night."

Charles liked the small upstairs room that had been his dad's when he was a kid. It was supposed to look the way it did then, but naturally it didn't. No kid's room was ever this clean, and besides, there were half a dozen pictures of his dad, starting as nearly a baby in a playsuit, and then bigger, in short pants, and then looking about Charles' age in a suit and tie. He looked like he never smiled and was a grind and told his dad that he had a lot of friends when he didn't really have any. The pictures made Charles feel better about himself. Maybe he wasn't such a squirrel after all, if his dad had looked like that.

He lay in bed and pulled the pillow over his face.

He wished his mom would bring his dad home soon. They could even deposit the check.

Peggy followed Jean Weaver around a corner, down a stone street. The rocks hurt her feet, and she felt suddenly drained and terrified: of the place, of the small dark woman who had experimented so callously with her recruits, and, most of all, of seeing Paul again. What if he turned his face away from her? What if she found him dressed, busy at work, incredulous that she had barged across half a continent in the middle of the night to disturb him?

Her plane had been late leaving, gaining altitude in gray sheets of rain, residue of the hurricane, and late arriving in Mexico City. She was later, still, going through customs, although the inspectors, lax at best, saw her expensive American luggage—jammed with clothes, perfume, make-up, jewelry cases—only in terms of tourist dollars. Dumping her purse out on the counter, they waved her through; she could have been carrying a kilo of drugs, and, more or less, was.

Peggy had left her bags at the inn. She'd hurried past plum trees and a reflecting pool, ducked under stone arches heavy with vines, anxious to get to Paul. While Jean waited, she'd made quick choices, selecting paregoric for immediate relief from both pain and loss of fluid, a canteen of tap water from home, nitroglycerin in case the scorpion stings had acted like snake venom, a small lightweight can of grapefruit juice, which Paul liked when he was sick. She had a thermometer stuck down in a pencil box, and she took that also. The room looked like a medieval cloister, but she didn't give it much attention except to be sure it had a bathroom in case she could bring the patient back with her.

Not the patient. *Paul.*

Listening to Jean talk to a man outside the room, thanking him for the earlier use of the phone, or explaining who Peggy was, she'd been afraid she wasn't going to be able to understand what anyone was saying. It was not like the time she'd come with Paul, the two of them. Then he'd had the language, plus everyone had met her few guidebook phrases more than halfway, wanting to please the tourist.

The dark street was lit only by the pale face of the moon, which hung high over the mountains. It would be a month tomorrow since she and Charles had left Flushing Meadow, wondering where Paul was. There must have been a full moon then, too.

Occasionally, she glimpsed the shadow of a woman standing silently in a yard as she and Jean went by. At an ornate wrought-iron gate, Jean stopped to speak quickly with a woman in black, who smiled at both of them. Then, from the courtyard behind her, a young girl in shorts led a muttering, stumbling man by a rope around his neck, like a cow, past them and down the street.

After they had walked on, Peggy whispered, startled, "Is that his wife?"

"No. That's a girl he beat up rather badly. His wife has fed him something in his coffee that makes men stupid. He's harmless enough these days."

Peggy shuddered. Arriving at midnight, following someone she did not know and had good reason not wholly to trust, had alerted her. She could feel her senses sharpening, as if she were a cat walking a fence in the dark.

"Here." Suddenly Jean took her arm and pulled her off the street. "Here we are."

They entered a small courtyard, also with a plum tree, where a Bantam hen dozed, its head tucked under its wing.

In the low doorway of a white adobe house, a large, yellow woman stood blocking their way. She gazed across the space between them, and Peggy knew at once that if Jean Weaver was the mind that had set the trap for the men, this impassive woman with the full red lips and begrudging eyes was the bait.

Something about her reminded Peggy of the *rafflesia*, a voracious plant in Sumatra, the prodigy of the vegetable world—its petals a yard across, its weight over fifteen pounds. In full bloom, a brilliant flecked yellow, orange, and gold, it gave off the odor of rotting flesh to lure those flies that carried its sticky, yellow pollen. Once pollinated, the male plant dissolved into slime, while the female grew into a huge half-moon full of ten thousand seeds.

"Dr. Guttman?" Peggy asked, for, of course, it was she.

"Helena."

"Then I am Peggy."

"Come in. I don't know how he is. Maybe you will." Reluctantly, the anthropologist moved aside to let the other women enter the white-walled room, so intimate in the glow of one low light.

Behind her, Peggy could see Paul, eyes closed, breathing in flat, shallow breaths. "Let me be alone with him," she requested, afraid they would not go.

"I confess I could use some sleep. He's given us quite a scare." Dr. Guttman did not move. "We are four houses up on the right. The last one before you turn for the inn."

"I'll be all right." Peggy held out her hand to Jean, by way of saying good-night. "Thank you for calling me."

"It's my fault he's in this mess."

"He could have got sick anywhere."

"Thanks." The project director rubbed her eyes. "It's been a terrible week."

Peggy approached the bed. She whispered, "Paul?"

She touched his face, which was dry and hot. She laid her cheek against his, as she had done with the boys when they were babies, not wanting to risk a thermometer's breaking. Closing her eyes to concentrate, she decided: 104 degrees.

"Paul?" She lifted his head very slowly with her arm and let a few drops of Charlottesville tap water fall on his cracked lips. "Paul?" He was clearly dehydrated, whatever else had made him ill. She held the bottle of paregoric to his mouth and then stuck her finger between his lips, as you did with a baby. "Paul?" She knelt with her head against him, holding him, her arm locked around him.

After a time she got him to take first several sips of water, then a swallow of paregoric. "I'm here," she told him, being careful of the raw, red swelling on the side of his face. "It's Peg." She got him to drink the tiny can of grapefruit juice, drop by drop, hoping it would cool him. Hoping, also, that it would stay down. When he began to shake, she took the cover off the other small bed to wrap around him.

Her feet stumbled over something, and she bent down to move Paul's boots, lifting them by their caked laces. Straightening up, she saw Dr. Guttman in the doorway, staring silently in. Quickly, Peggy dragged the door closed, leaning for one frightened moment with her back against it.

She took off her shoes and jacket and climbed into the narrow bed with Paul, lying close beside him, her arms around him. Being careful not to brush against his feet.

Unable to stop herself, she cried on his shirt; hoping she was not chilling him, she sobbed without making a sound.

At last, toward morning, when he began to sweat and she knew his fever had broken, he tried to speak. His voice was rasping and cracked, as if his throat were too dry to form words.

She bent her ear to his lips.

"You didn't send my suits," he said.

28 A CHANGE OF HEART

T HEY WAKED early, went to her room at the inn, and made love.

At first Peggy was reluctant to undress, to expose herself. It had been too long; too much remained unsaid between them. But Paul, still light-headed, sweating now, naked, had pleaded with her, begged her to get out of her clothes. It seemed wildly wrong, as if in the moment of their finally locking together, there would be heavy footsteps running in the stone halls, fists pounding on the door, hands pulling them apart, tearing him from her and her from him.

She had never made love angry before, never, not once. She found herself handling him roughly, pushing and pulling at the same time, opening her mouth to him and then closing her teeth. When he cried her name over and over, she felt herself responding with outrage, as if he were calling another woman's name at the very moment of entering her. How dare he? How dare he call her name, as if he knew her? As if he had ever touched her before?

His body seemed that of a stranger. Always long-muscled, thin, it was now nothing but skin and bones, the stretched frame of an ascetic monk. Someone walled-up, wild-eyed, scourged, ravenous, who had no idea how to love a woman and was doing so much as a stray hound, ribs sticking out, teeth bared, devours a stolen piece of meat. Holding it down with a front paw, eyes on the door, growling low in its throat.

Paul. Could this be Paul?

"Peg, Peg."

"Stop. Let me be."

"I thought I'd never see you again."

"I thought that's what you had in mind."

He groaned. She could feel his rib cage move in and out. "I was a fool."

She did not answer. He wanted pity; she still felt anger. He had run off: the bad boy with all his belongings tied in a bandanna, who wants to come home when it gets dark and the wind starts up and the owl is out. Who wants banana cake and hot cocoa and relieved hugs from all his kin.

He'd got this trip out of his system. He was ready to come back and expected that "back" to which he was ready to come to be the same as when he had left it. She had not asked for the separation but had got it anyway. Now, trying her own wings, she wasn't yet ready for a reconciliation.

She pulled the covers about her, unable to shake the idea that just outside the door hordes of intruders were waiting to break in on them.

Something echoed in her head, something she had said to Todd. "I was a consolation prize for you once, Paul. I don't relish being one again."

"What are you talking about?" He turned to stare at her. His face was flushed. "Never mind. Given the company you've been keeping, I can guess."

"I want to know what she looked like."

"Olivia?" He shut his eyes. "I can't remember."

"I don't believe you."

He sat up, pulling the blanket to his chest. "For twenty-five years I've had to measure myself against a war hero, always coming up the buffoon to you, the petty clerk."

"I wanted what you were."

"You never let me know it."

"Your running off was not my idea."

"You made it clear that Edward was following in the great Ned Ruggles's footsteps. While mine were clown shoes." He shivered, sweating, his face damp. "Tell me the truth, Peg. Did Stedman get in your bed? Did he? You have to tell me."

"No." She knew it was a weapon she had, the lie, the lie of fact, but she didn't have any desire to use it. Lies were for manipulating. There was nothing she wanted from Paul.

"Thank God."

Besides, the truth would cut him deeper, as it always did. "I have left Edward in his care. . . ."

Paul rolled over and buried his face in the pillow. His haunches were nothing but bone. She did not touch him.

"It was me." His voice was muffled. "Nipping at Edward's heels. I was envious, if you want the truth: of his tennis playing, of his love of the game. My dad spent sixty years of his life on the thin ice of Lake Peipus. I guess I envied that, too. I wanted a match, a battle, of my own."

"Theirs was only a game; yours was real." Peggy covered him with the spread. What Jean Weaver had said on the phone was true: Paul had been broken, in some way she did not understand. "Don't get chilled," she said.

She looked around the vast, old room, reconsidering. This time apart would fade away; these weeks, disappear. She and Paul would become like those people who remarry and nobody can remember why they got divorced in the first place. Who go right on celebrating their anniversaries as if nothing had happened.

If for one unexpected month she'd been tightroping without a net, taking chances she'd forgotten, thrilling to the risk, she owed that to Paul. She would never have done it on her own.

It was her fault as much as his. The two of them had made a pact, in the unspoken way that couples did: I will not let you fall; I'll be there to catch you. It will be safe.

Pulling a sheet around her, she went to the door. A tray with coffee and flowers had been left for them on the cold stones. No one was there.

"You were right," she said to Paul. "We did lose something along the way."

She crawled back into bed with him, wanting to make love again. "You're cold," she said. "Let me warm you."

"What a lovely place." Peggy held on to Paul's arm as they walked down the little street she'd seen only in the dark the night before. The village lay before them, half a bowl, sloping from two sides toward an old square.

Peggy had argued that you never let children go out the day after they've had a fever, but Paul had insisted. Exuberant, he claimed he was completely recovered. Indeed, from the moment he donned his familiar clothes from home, he seemed to become a wholly different person from the wasted man of the early-morning hours.

"We'll have breakfast outside at the café," he'd told her eagerly, wanting to show her everything.

She had put on her Top-Siders and a wraparound skirt, brown with a border of red and yellow hens at the hem.

"You must meet Esperanza." He pulled her along. "She

tended us when we were sick, Nakae and me. I owe her a
great debt."

The warm-eyed woman was delighted to see Paul up and
about. "It was not my medication," she said in English, smiling. "It was your wife."

Peggy thanked her.

"Segundo will want to meet you. He is gathering plums
with the children."

Peggy looked around for the man she had seen last night,
but instead, a refined, mustached gentleman appeared. The
two men in three-piece suits embraced warmly.

"This is Dr. Gómez." Paul made introductions. "My
wife, Peggy."

"You are very fortunate."

But the whole time the man talked to them in English, he
kept his eyes on the woman, mooning like a lovesick calf,
murmuring endearments to her in Spanish, his eyes filling
with tears.

Behind the couple, at the back of the lot, Peggy could see
a group of children playing with butterfly nets under a huge
plum tree.

Back on the street, Paul explained to Peggy, "They are
lovers. She was almost killed in a falling building in the
capital—he hasn't got over it yet. He lives with her openly
now, on the days he is in Tepoztlán. It is no longer a secret.
He calls her his second wife."

"But last night I saw a man being led out of their yard
with a rope around his neck."

Paul threw back his head and laughed. "Ha-ha. Avelino.
The chicken farmer got what he deserved. His mind is mush.
Did you see a girl with him? Rosa, the painter's wife? She
is taking all the profits from the chickens."

Peggy was confused. She watched a glistening black

rooster hop up on an old wall. It must be a Cornish. There were many here she did not recognize, hybrids. An ugly turkey hen flapped up beside it and chased it away.

Paul did not stop talking. It was as if he had bottled up his words for a month and had to get them all out at once. He told her about Rosa's husband's pictures, about the climb up the mountain in the pouring rain, how the corn mills had changed the women's lives, about the woman with the white hog and the woman with the amazing hen, and who lived in all the houses. What struck Peggy was that he knew more details about these villagers than he had learned in a lifetime in Charlottesville. He sounded, she thought (with a mix of pleasure and anger), just like a grown man talking about a gorilla named Koko and her kitten named Ball.

"How I missed you!" he said. "Enthusiasm seems cheap in the States, with information so easy to come by and various skills a matter of course. But in Tepoztlán, every day, and I mean this, Peg, every day I was here the uppermost thing on my mind was what Peg would have seen, what Peg would have got a kick out of." He stopped to hug her, right in the middle of the cobblestone street—oblivious to the children with buckets and the man in black, riding a horse.

At the bottom of the hill, they came to a long line of women waiting at the mill. Peggy, recognizing Jean, went over to shake her hand.

"See how well he is today," she said.

"Amazing." Jean looked relieved, but did not step out of line.

Peggy realized that she must not undo the work the woman had done to blend into the group. She looked about her. "Calla lilies, how beautiful." She stopped a weathered old woman a few feet away and asked how much. The woman named a price which seemed exorbitant. Then, recalculating, remembering the rate of exchange quoted at Dulles—fifty times what it had been when she and Paul were here before!—she said, "I'll take them all," and made a gesture with her arms around the whole bunch of flowers. The woman nodded and took the thousand pesos, delighted. Peggy touched each of the flawless white cornucopias. Imagine, a dozen lilies, each as perfect as if made of wax, *aethiopica*, white lily of the Nile, here in this Mexican village. For two dollars. How on earth did these people live?

Some of the women followed her, staring at her red hair, touching the tiny stitched feathers at her hem. She decided she would send Jean some of Fan's skirts and aprons to sell. Anything, she knew from her reading, brought in from outside an economy was worth ten times anything traded within it.

Paul took her into a little family eating place that faced out on the square. The smell of coffee was very strong, and every table had a basket of bread. Peggy realized she was famished. At their outside table, she spread her sweater on the ground and placed the lilies on it.

She looked about for Mr. Takamori, thinking that the other man would be easy to recognize here.

In the room as they dressed, she had asked Paul, "Will I get to meet your Japanese?"

"Didn't he come in last night?"

"No. At least I don't think so."

"He is most discreet." He'd hugged her to him. "You will like him." Then, "I wonder where he slept."

Not knowing how long Paul had been sick or what he remembered, she had kept her voice casual. "Jean Weaver told me he'd converted."

Paul had brushed that aside. "Nakae? Oh, he was hysterical. The chicken plucker—it's a long story. I'll tell you later."

Now a man rushed toward them through the café. He beamed at Paul. "Sinclair, you are up!" He seemed overjoyed to see Paul and to meet her. She was most grateful to the Californian and rose to shake his hand, by way of thanks.

She apologized for keeping him from his room last night. She suspected that Paul was right, that the man had come in, found her sleeping there, and slipped out at once.

"Not at all," he said. "You have made him well."

"I was burning for my wife," Paul told him.

Peggy blushed as the men laughed. She could not believe Paul saying such a thing. What a wonder!

Nakae sat with them, waiting until they all had coffee before beginning a story he was clearly bursting to tell. "Father Domingo," he related, "is not pleased with me."

"Why is that?" Paul asked.

"It's because of the saint's name."

Peggy realized that she was waiting for Paul to repeat, "Saint's name?" in his old style. Instead, she saw that he listened attentively to every word his friend spoke, even helping the story along now and then with a nod of his head or a jab in the air with a roll.

"It seems you must have a saint's name. Domingo explained this to me, suggesting several martyrs of various descriptions, so that I could select one whose woes would serve as a model for me. I told him if that was what was required, then I would take Amakusa Shirō's name. Nakae Amakusa Takamori. A fine name, one that I would be proud to bear. 'But he is not a saint,' Domingo told me. 'How is that possible?' I asked. 'He gave his life for the peasants who burned like your torches here,' I said. 'He was the first to explain to his people that seppuku was not required.' 'He is not a saint in the church,' Domingo insisted. He mentioned to me Michael, Timothy, and Paul. Did you know you had a saint's name, my friend? At that I told him, 'What foolishness. Any church that does not recognize St. Amakusa, the Japanese Messiah, is no church for me.' Besides"—and at this point he looked at Peggy and made a broad grin—"I told him I liked to talk to pretty women too much to become a priest."

Paul enjoyed the story. He reached a hand across the table for Peggy's, giving it a squeeze.

"Have you seen Avelino?" Nakae asked Paul, clearly elated.

"Helena told me."

"All the men are quaking. They will drink their coffee only in the cafés. Everywhere you hear them whispering. Every wife is now suspect."

"Do you think she really did that? Esperanza?"

"Who knows?"

And at that he and Paul both laughed and repeated in unison, "Who knows?" as if this were the only answer to all questions.

Peggy did not want to leave. Here in the sun on the square in the magical mountain village of Tepoztlán she could believe in this new Paul.

"Here's to my old enemy." Paul touched his coffee cup to Nakae's.

"Who is this old enemy? Not the chicken farmer?"

"A man who once kept me from marrying the wrong wife and then sent me off on this wild-goose chase, which got some sense into my head." He lifted his cup high, like a knight downing mead. "To Stedman the Cheat."

Nakae toasted. "A good enemy is better than a bad friend."

"A good friend is the best."

"It is so."

Looking away from the men to the green mountainside, Peggy's eye caught sight of something high on top which seemed to tremble in the bright, morning light. "It's moving," she said, pointing to the small pyramid.

Paul glanced up. "The shrine of the old god."

Nakae nodded. "Who can no longer return."

But the men had lost interest in the local folkways. Their month in Mexico was completed; their minds were back on work.

"I am overdue in the classroom," Nakae remembered.

Paul chided him. "That's the disadvantage of your job over mine." He hooked a thumb in his vest pocket. "My clients will not have noticed my absence. The Wainwright case will be exactly where I left it."

Peggy shivered. His words recalled stories her dad had told of battlefield conversions. She held his fingers tightly. "Let's stay, Paul."

"No, the women have finished with us." In good spirits, he waved across the stalls to where Dr. Guttman, large and yellow, stood watching them.

Peggy gathered up her flowers and wrapped her sweater around her. She hoped she could be as good a sport as Edward had been a month ago, when, having lost his match and every set, he threw his racket into the air, delighted to have won four games.

She flashed the old Ruggles smile.

How happy Charles would be to have his dad back.

SHELBY HEARON, the prize-winning author of twelve novels, including *Hug Dancing*, *Owning Jolene*, and *Painted Dresses*, has received the American Academy and Institute of Arts and Letters Literature Award, as well as Guggenheim and NEA Fellowships for fiction and an Ingram Merrill grant. Her short stories have appeared in magazines and anthologies and have won five PEN syndication awards.

A long-time resident of Texas, Hearon now lives in Westchester County, New York. A popular lecturer and teacher, she has served on the staffs of many universities and writer's workshops.